NATASHA KARIS

What The Heart Needs

For Liz
Chauffeur, godparent, loan shark, friend.
That camper van will be yours yet.

"An eye for an eye will only make the whole world blind."

— Mahatma Gandhi

Contents

IV   Part Four

Don't forget...

...to get your exclusive **FREE** story at the back of this book. Not yet though – it is a follow on read so you don't want to spoil this story!

Playlist

Gabrielle Aplin - Stay
Fleetwood Mac - Landslide
Paulo Nutini - Candy
Nick Cave and The Bad Seeds - Into My Arms
Ray LaMontagne - Jolene
Declan O'Rourke - Sarah (Last Night In A Dream)
Gabrielle Aplin - My Mistake
Michael Kiwanuka - Cold Little Heart
Freya Ridings - Lost Without You
Sara Bareilles - She Used To Be Mine
Fleetwood Mac - Sara
Birdy - People Help The People
Jess Glynn - Home
Gabrielle Aplin - The Power Of Love

Available to listen at:

https://youtube.com/playlist?
list=PLXUprm9AeVXcScKBHxQ2Tzg00-xaZ7BBq&
si=MAiF8Ul3EixUpoKc

I

Part One

Chapter One

The car clock flashes one a.m. The engine is off, the key in the ignition just in case.

It is quiet on the street. The air windless, no trees move by a breeze, no passers pass by either. The only noise comes from the buzz of electricity from a faulty street light five cars behind, which started to irritate two hours ago.

The car is parked down the road a little from the house, behind a few cars, away from the streetlight, just in case he comes out. It's possible even at this time of the morning -there are signs the house isn't sleeping. For a start, the light at one of the front windows is still lit. Also, more than one shadow passes over the sheer curtains, so he's not alone. There is no rush. Patience is a trait I'm known for. The time or wait doesn't bother me. I will wait for as long as it takes, knowing with each hour that passes, his perception will dull, his inhibitions will drop, his reactions will slow.

Good.

All I've done for the last few years is wait. The last year alone has built up to this moment, *these* moments and I'll take the calm, the quiet, the wait, because later there will be no time to think, no more time to plan. Fine by me. The planning has all been done, repeated until I'm sick of it. I've plotted this night out in every detail, accounted for every scenario. No surprises can spring up, nothing can go wrong.

Although.

A fraction still inside of me wrestles with the wrongness of sitting in a car as I watch a house, as I trespass in an unsuspecting neighbourhood, on an unsuspecting man. I haven't gone crazy, not completely anyway, there is still a part of me that knows I shouldn't be here. The good part, the moral section of my soul, the sliver that is left, whispers: *go to bed, get at least an hour of sleep.* As the hours wear on, the voice gets louder, shouting as I sit here now: *what about the people who love him?*

The other part, the vengeful compartment, the ever-expanding piece in my heart that forces me to drive to a house without any recollection of doing so until I arrive, believes with absolute certainty there is nowhere else for me to be. With a clarity I haven't felt in a very long time, the decision has been made. Tonight is the night. The time has come to allow the vindictive part to take command.

Even though it's a sticky summer night, with a dead heat causing a slick of filmy sweat to clam up all over my porous skin, I shiver with the declaration.

I'm here to kill him. And by dawn, I'll have followed through.

Chapter Two

This isn't some spur of the moment idea. There will be no plea for manslaughter. It is murder all the way, premeditated for months, growing stronger and more powerful as each day dragged on. It won't finish here, for he is only one on a list. Ryan will be the first name ticked off. The experiment.

He has to pay. To experience the same pain I carry, to want to curl up in a ball, to beg to die. Yet there he is, inside a house probably paid to live in courtesy of the state, free as a bird, partying. And it's like that each time I sit in the car, the lights on late into the night or further into early morning. I've watched the house so many times his waking hours have become mine too.

It starts with Ryan. It has to, since what happened started with him.

Again, my good side nags, trying to convince me to turn back, to stop before I do something that will change everything, that will alter the rest of my life, that will stop the natural process of God's plan. *Wouldn't it be better, Lorna, if you just forgave? Can't there be another way to find a reason for all this and move on?*

I laugh out loud at the notion.

Never will I forgive Ryan. I will never forgive any of them.

My eyelid scratches with each blink. In the mirror, I find a blister on the inside of the lid. I cannot ignore how wretched I look. A year ago, after the trial, my appearance fell down on my list of priorities. Before, being attractive meant something. Now I couldn't care less, now I no longer want to be seen as a woman. The person reflected appears as pale as a corpse who died of exsanguination, drained of every bit of blood, my red hair shocking in contrast against the light skin. The black circles under my eyes are quite alarming, dark enough to appear as holes. I slide my finger over the socket just to make sure flesh is still there. No wonder I have a blister; sleep hasn't been my friend. Each night I try, for I know my body will give up if I don't get some. Yet every night, after I toss and turn, I find myself in my car, drifting down streets, on the same roads, here and there, biding my time, plotting. The best lullaby. Most mornings I wake with a cricked neck, a dry mouth from an hour caught sleeping, which is usually enough time to get me by, to get me through the next day.

No amount of sleep is enough to rest my soul. Even if I slept all day for a year, it would still not be enough.

The gurgle from my stomach reminds me I didn't eat. Another reason I have a blister. Growing up, that was a sign, when I pushed my body too far the blisters broke through, grating on my lid. A warning to slow down, eat better, take it easy. What do I care? All taste left me two years ago. My tongue is a desert, gritting and drying food. What do I want with nutrients? I want my body to reflect my mind, rotting and pungent. You have to want to live to strive for health and for me, that want is long gone. All I want, is enough to sustain, to get by, to give enough energy for the actions I need to take, there is no want or wish or will for anything except to hurt. I run my fingers along cracked lips. Although thirsty, I won't risk buying water as I can't afford to miss him leave. I search for a leftover bottle but the car is a mess, full from weeks of discarded food containers I grabbed on the way or after. You can barely see the floor with all the coffee cups and wrappers. A disgrace, but who will see it, anyway? There are worse things in life than a mess.

When the front door opens, my hands clench the steering wheel. Any resolve to do the right thing goes out the window when I see Ryan's foot. Just his foot is enough to send me into a frenzy. My first instinct is to put my own on the accelerator, so it's just as well the engine is off. I didn't want the sound to alert anyone. Also, I wanted the silence; there is no inclination anymore for the radio. My thoughts alone are enough to fill a thousand ears.

When I see him, when he steps out from the doorway, it is enough to make me suck in a sharp breath. Ryan always does that to me. Still handsome. Still affecting. The memories slap me as hard as a whack to the face. I flip the nostalgic feeling, turning it to want to hurt him instantly. How I want him to suffer. How I want to take my shaking hands and slam them into his face and use my thumbs to gorge his eyes out.

Three people spill out of the house, two of them laughing, all of them appearing drunk or under the influence of something. The two girls wear skirts short enough to show underwear as one bends down to pick up her dropped cigarette. Pink cloth, even though I'm at least ten feet in distance. It disgusts me, yet I can't turn away from the image. They are about Sara's age. They aren't recognisable. Ryan helps the pink underwear girl stand upright as she tries to find her footing. The girl runs her hand along the collar of his shirt but the way he ducks his head and shifts his feet says he's embarrassed at the gesture, as if she's crossed a line rather than continued on from something that has already happened. Fury flashes through me. My body slicks again, and the car becomes unbearably hot, I need to open a window but I don't want them to hear. Whatever happens, I can't alert Ryan.

It doesn't matter if he gave her the brush off or if he has no interest in either girl; staying celibate won't affect his outcome. If anything, it makes it worse that he could be just wasting time, wasting air and space. I don't care if he is with the pink knickered girl, or if he's been with the two of them at the same time. His life, the way he exists, is a complete mockery to Sara.

'Walk out on the road,' I whisper.

He seems drunk enough to have lost some of his reflexes. If he steps out onto the road, that will be my cue to turn the key and rev up and plough down. Never mind what happens to the two girls. At this moment, I don't care if they step out or get in the way. They are not my concern and anyway, nobody minded my little girl.

He doesn't step out. Instead, he and the girls shuffle on the pavement, passing back and forth a cigarette until a taxi pulls up and the girls clamber in. Ryan, hands in his pockets, nods goodbye, then watches the car drive off until the taxi has disappeared out of sight. Once gone, he still doesn't return indoors, seeming in no rush to leave the spot where he stands. He looks up and down the road and stares in the car's direction. My car. I tense, curse for parking too near. My hand goes to the ignition, to the key, willing him again to walk towards me.

If you step out on the road, I will follow through with my plan.

He looks away. Sparks up another cigarette. As he smokes, he lifts his head, stares at the sky. For the first time tonight, this week, probably this year, I look up. It is completely clear, a blanket coloured with the blackest of black, with pinpricks of holes shining through, burning, full of stars. On a different night, I would gasp at its beauty. He bends his neck back far enough it almost touches his spine. Unbalanced, he stumbles, then lands on his back on the grass. Instead of scrambling to stand, he commits to the act, rests his head on the lawn, unmoving. For what feels like hours, he lies there staring at the sky, smoking.

Could I do it now?

If I leave the car and tread softly, he won't even notice. I could hurt him before he has a clue what is happening. But then it will happen out in the open. And it will be too quick. Don't I want him to see me doing it? Don't I want him to die slowly? Or what if he notices me and runs? For him to suffer, I have to follow the plan.

I take my hand away from the ignition.

Sara loved cars. As a five-year-old, whenever it was just the two of us going to the shops or anywhere, she begged to sit up the front, asking non-stop until I relented. Years later I can hear her gleeful chuckle as I strap her in, her little legs dangling high in the seat from the booster, her red curls splayed out in all directions and her squeal with the excitement at being allowed. Even then, I would have to gulp back my emotion when the love for her would hit me and the worry that something awful could happen to her would twist my insides. Back then, I did that a lot, taking mental snapshots of our life together, wanting to remember every moment of that moment, trying to impregnate her smile, her freckles, her laugh into my long-term memory, knowing someday they would fade and change and evolve in adulthood. Thinking that was the worst of it, that it would be growing up that would take her away.

Fresh revulsion floods my bloodstream. I want to hurt. I want to rip, pummel, snarl, kick. To lash out, tear, scratch, dig. It needs to be physical, an outlet, to release some of what I hold inside.

I grab the door lever, and once clicked, push the door ajar.

Chapter Three

Whether from the noise or just coincidence, as I open the door, Ryan stirs. I freeze. Wiping at his eyes; not to prevent sleep or as a gesture of waking, but swiping under, taking away tears. Not sleeping, then.

For a second, I welcome the cool air that wafts in from the gap, then pull the door closed, stopping before it makes complete contact, before the click. Not changing my mind, for his tears won't change what I will do. There will be no sympathy, no matter how many tears he sheds. He *should* cry. He *should* be haunted for what's left of the rest of his short life.

He sits up, staring across the road, his profile sideways, staring at nothing for a long time. I admit, he looks lost. Distraught, even. But it doesn't change anything, for it can't bring Sara home. No amount of regret can, I know. I tried.

I'm cold now. The shiver has turned from shock that it's happening, to fact, and in a second, the night has lost its warmth. I wonder how he can stay out on the grass in just a t-shirt and jeans, staying stock still, staring into oblivion, alive and wasting, alive like my daughter should be. I grip the steering wheel and with all my strength shake it, wishing it was his throat, wishing I could make sound and scream, roar, spill my guts and pain out, leaving it on the floor, leaving it anywhere other than keeping it inside me because it is killing me, it is making me insane, ruining me.

My eyes sting with how unfair life is. Even if he cannot see, I will not cry in his company. How unfair that this living, breathing, waster of a boy can sit on the grass when my daughter should be the one who survived.

If she had to die, then he can't live.

It's early morning by the time he stands. He gets up unsteadily, walking with head bent almost to his chest, trudging the floor, dragging his heels. All the signs are there. Ryan is ready for his leaba, to tuck himself in and let oblivion overtake, unaware that this is the moment I've been waiting for to strike.

Chapter Four

Sara had this way of tucking into me when she slept, fitting her body into my body, reminiscent of her time inside while I was pregnant. She would slip into my bed at some stage in the night, where I would welcome her, opening out my arms, opening the space for her, even though Tim would grumble later about having no room, not caring what he would say because holding her was one of the greatest pleasures of my life. Love doesn't get much better than that.

That mop of hair would get everywhere, in my eyes, in my mouth. The bed invasion carried out in silence, where I would just inhale and smile, knowing there would come a day when she wouldn't want to climb into our bed anymore.

The images I never want replace the good ones. Of Sara lying on a slab. Her skin unreal looking, wax like, bloodless and blue.

Her skin held no warmth, cold and tacky like refrigerated chicken. Her eyes were closed. All I would have given to see what was underneath the lids, to look once more at those eyes that took in every situation within seconds. Their energy, their interest eradicated, turned off forever, unseeing for eternity.

They had already washed the blood away, but the bruising and open wounds couldn't dissolve with water. They tried to steer me from seeing her, telling me they already confirmed her identity from my DNA, from the picture of the birthmark on her ankle there was no need to confirm any further but I insisted, threatening to scream until they let me. Knowing it was the only way I would believe it, knowing I had to see what was done. Even though they covered her as best they could, it didn't hide the round welts along the collarbone, or the angry raised blisters from cigarette burns. My baby, but not my baby. The girl lying prone was different to the Sara I knew. With her broken, wrongly curved nose, her eyelashes gone, patches of raw skin where clumps of that vivacious red hair had been torn away. In other parts, little black stubs replaced the hair; coarse little fibres that took a minute to understand, took more than a minute, took me lying in bed later that night to figure out they were singed, blackened from being lit.

My Sara, but not my Sara. Although there was no denial, I knew her corpse completely, intricately, instinctively. All I wanted in that moment and every moment after, was to get on that table, to lie beside and hug her, breathe into her chest, give her my air, to make her breathe again, to pump her heart and make her somehow live. To find some way, any way.

Back in the car, I pelt the steering wheel, then claw at my own hand, digging my fingernails into the fleshy part between the thumb and forefinger, wanting to see blood, needing to feel pain, needing to inflict it on something, anything, someone, anyone.

'I'm sorry, Sara, I should have protected you, should have found a way.'

There, I cry until the snot moves into my mouth. The images never relent, no matter what I'm doing. All I can see is her on the slab. At the back of every other sight, day and night, with eyes open or closed, her image haunts me. How can I think of any other memory when that takes over everything? The only way to wipe it is to replace it with something else. To see someone else hurt, or as broken. Redemption is the only way to get some relief. Before I left the morgue, I swore whoever did it would suffer. As the details of her death worsened, my plan strengthened. Until there was only one way it would end. I will do what is needed, then join her.

The plan brought some comfort. It got me through leaving her alone in the morgue; it got me through the funeral.

Before I even knew who hurt her, the knowledge I would hurt them helped me wake in the morning. Once there were more details, I drew the list. For there is more than one person who led to the demise of Sara. Once arrested, belief in punishment got me through the trial. After, was a different story. After, I fell apart. Now, every wait is over, there is nothing left to hold out for. I've waited long enough.

I rip the keys from the ignition and this time when I open the door, I get out, grabbing the bag from the passenger seat. With my head down, I stride to the house, making sure not to pass by the window, keeping to the edge of the bush, planning to slip under like all the other times I worked up the courage but faltered at the last moment. This time I won't. This time I am ready. In my hand lies a skeleton key, already checked once when he was out to make sure it worked. That time, I didn't dare step inside. This time I will.

I stop. The front door is ajar. Is it a lucky break or did Ryan spot me and is waiting inside? Or was he too out of it to notice it didn't close? The hesitation lasts less than a second.

Singed black hair burnt into scalp.

I'm not scared. To be scared, you have to value your life; you have to want to live and I don't care anymore for that. If Ryan is waiting for me, if his plan is to hurt me, then I will make sure he finishes the job, and when he does, it is loud and public enough for him to serve time. If I'm dead by the end of the day, it will be an extra win.

I push the door open and step inside.

Chapter Five

The beat from a low sounding tune thumps from some room in the distance. Edging in, I peek around the door. No one hides behind. I close it, turning the latch so it shuts with a soft click, making sure an exit won't be easy for either of us. Then I creep, not wanting to alarm, not wanting to alert him to what is coming.

Blue light flashes intermittently from the end of the corridor, giving me some vision. It flickers like a strobe light. I stand in a foot scuffed hallway with four closed, paint chipped, once white doors. Two on each side. With a doorless archway at the end of the corridor. Light leaks from the gap in the door of the first room to my right, the one shadows moved in earlier. Outside the door, I cannot hear anything. If I open it when he's in another room, he may hear. Following the music is my best bet. I stop for a minute to rummage in my bag until I find what I'm after, until I hold the taser in my hand. The far end of the hallway leads out into one wide area. I edge along the wall, slowly, one step at a time, careful to not instigate any creaks, checking every available space as I go. Before stepping out to the unknown, I inhale, gathering my courage. Suck it in. Move.

The bareness of the room is a surprise. There are no cupboards or tables, no books or everyday clutter, just empty floors, bare walls, abundant space. A large, grey, battered couch stands out in the middle of the room, its back to the entrance, positioned opposite a flickering

TV: the source of the light and music. The room is dark, but there is definitely a shadow on the couch with a form big enough to be Ryan lying across. Other than two empty beanbags on the floor, it is the only place to sit. I move closer, my heart now racing. Closer. Holding out the taser like a gun, with my finger on the trigger, ready. There is no shake in my hand. I will not hesitate.

As I lean over the couch, there is a definite mound. A shape of someone on their side, covered completely. I edge my hand to a corner of the fabric, trying to shallow my breath. I snap the material back. A jacket comes away in my hands, leaving only a flat seat with a cushion I mistook for a head. Other than the jacket, which is draped over the length of the seat, there is a magazine covered with wrappers and some tinfoil. Discarded, crumpled up beer cans surround the floor. The nerves on my neck prickle. Where is he? Did he mean to make it look like he was lying there?

At the back of the room, there is a door, ajar. I try to keep my breath low as I tiptoe over, not wanting to pronounce where I stand too soon. The blood has rushed to my head, pulsing loud in my ear. Before entering, I listen, waiting for noise. Nothing. I turn the corner with the taser to my side, in case a hand tries to grab from behind the door.

Four cheap cabinets, with doors hanging off their hinges, a sink and a fridge. There is a cobwebbed space where the cooker must have once been. When I press down on the back door handle, it doesn't move. The key dangles at the jiggle. Not outside then.

He must have gone to bed. The only doors left are the four I've already passed. Ryan doesn't live with anyone, confirmed by my many times staking out the house, so I don't have to worry about another lodger. What I haven't checked before is inside, so this is unfamiliar territory.

No pictures hang on the walls. No mementos anywhere. Except for the rubbish on the couch and the flashing TV, there are no signs of life at all.

CHAPTER FIVE

At the first door, I turn the handle without hesitation, figuring it is better to handle this situation like ripping off a plaster; quick, so the pain only lasts a second. Only an unoccupied, disappointing bathroom with a crack in the sink and corner ceiling mould greets me. Before opening, instinct told me it wasn't the room, but I check behind the half hanging shower curtain just in case.

The next door I am more wary of. This one has a window out front. If it is his bedroom, he might have seen me or heard the door opening and could be waiting. Still, I enter. The room *is* a bedroom. The light is off. In the dark, I hold out the taser, my hand shakes, flicks from side to side with involuntary violent jerks. To stop from dropping it, I grip it with the other hand. I move to the bed. There is sound. Like the intake of breath, followed by a whoosh like an unsuspecting sleeping releasing air without fear. Should I wake him? Will I hurt just enough to alert, or should I go back to the kitchen for a knife to make him bleed? Would it hurt more to shock with the taser, or is it easier to just slash and slash?

Stick to the plan, Lorna. You didn't come for easy or quick. You came to make him suffer.

Resolve reinstated, I lean towards the bed, my hand hovers over the cover. My fingers curl around the edge, for I want him to wake with reassurance first, to open his eyes with a smile, thinking one of the girls came back, or picturing his mum tucking him in at night when he was a child. Then I want him to see the taser, I want to see his realisation that I have come for him and that nothing is going to be OK.

I yank the duvet away hard.

Flat mattress. Just a duvet bunched together. My breath comes out as if it's struggling in the cold; patchy and staggered, I struggle to suck enough in. Did he position both the jacket and duvet as a trick? What made the sound? I move to the other side of the bed, check in case he is lying on the floor hiding. On the ground is a square. The torch on

17

my phones illuminates a fish tank. Several fish float on the surface, bloated and colourless, their eyes opaque, some scales hang like phelm from their bodies. The water is brown. A pump spits and gasps; the noise source. I take a breath to try to still my racing chest while moving away. It stinks.

Calm Lorna, there's only two doors left.

Standing in front of the opposite door, I place a hand on the handle, ready to twist, but something stops me. A noise, like a gurgle, sounds far away. Ungripping, I move, having heard that sound before, my ears pinpointed exactly to where it comes from, I run to the other room and enter.

Ryan is there. Prone, on a love seat, eyes fluttering. Throat gurgling, choking. His lips are blue. There is white foam coming from his mouth. A needle sticks out of his arm and flaps away while his body jerks violently. One shoe has come loose from his foot, his sock has a hole on the big toe. The shoe lies face up, one red stripe pretending to be a logo that it isn't. There is foil and a spoon resting on a newspaper on the seat.

Chapter Six

At first, there is only relief. There is no need to do anything. I can just slip out, walk away, leave him to die on an ugly love seat. Or, I can stay and watch. Even if any neighbours see me leave, there will be no denying a druggie just overdosed; all I have to say is that I panicked. Brown vomit streams onto his shoulder. The only part of his eye visible is the sclera. My stomach turns with the sight.

He got to do it before me. He found a way out by doing the job himself.

There is no satisfaction in that.

'Not like this.'

I'll be damned if he gets away with dying this easily. The gurgling stops and the carer in me kicks in.

'Ryan. Can you hear me?'

No response.

I grind my knuckles on his chest, at his sternum, working quickly, my wrist flicking up and down. No response.

With the other hand, I rub my knuckles along those blue lips, knowing his life is leaving him. I put my ear to his lips. There is no breath. I scoop vomit from his mouth and make sure there is nothing else inside, obstructing.

Opening his eyes with my thumb and forefinger in the opposite of a pinch, shows the pupil is all there, a full orb of bright blue with only a pinprick of black iris. Definite overdose. A quick scan around the room gives me an idea of what he's taken. No cocaine evident. Other than the foil and needle, an upturned bottle of tablets lie on a coffee table. Ibuprofen, so at least it looks like we are dealing with only depressants.

In my backpack, I find what I'm looking for.

Catching Ryan by the jaw, I tilt his head back, then stuff the naloxone up his nose and give it a firm push. The spray makes contact. Carefully, I remove the needle from his arm.

I wait, knowing if there is any fentanyl in that overdose, he will need another spray. I put my ear to his mouth again and hear a faint breath. Shallow, still in trouble, but there, so no need for CPR. I push him on his side.

After about two minutes Ryan moans, tries to sit up, splays out his hands, gasps for a breath. I soothe him down. The one spray will do for now, as I don't want him waking.

The plan was to use the naloxone later. It doesn't matter, for there are other ways to prolong a death.

How long must it have taken for Sara to die?

I push away the thought, for I have work to do. The naloxone will do the trick, Ryan's brain will stay intact. The drug will stop the drugs he took, will stop them from killing him. But the near empty bottle of pills worries me, for he could stay unconscious for hours, meaning by the time he wakes it will be daylight and that could mean callers. I sit on a battered stool and think.

Should I leave him and come back another time? No. I can't be sure he will make it if I leave him alone. The effects of the naloxone could wear off and he might overdose again and then all this will be for nothing. Did he purposely overdose? The pills imply he did. If so, if he wakes up, what will stop him from finishing the job? Also, I can't guarantee he won't remember I've been here, ruining the possibility of ever being able to sneak up on him again. If that happens, I can still make sure he dies, but shooting him on the street or hiring someone won't bring the same closure. The satisfaction is in watching him suffer.

I run through different options.

Ryan is thin. The drugs have ravaged him, wasting those once idolised muscles. If I want to move him, with my training on how to lift a body, I easily can. My house is isolated. With no callers. I can keep him there day and night and no one will know.

Just like that, I make my decision. I walk back through the house, this time looking for something to help. In the bedroom, I rip the only sheet off. Then I remember seeing what I need during one of my stakeouts. I open the back door and there it is. Who knew when one of them robbed a shopping trolley and dumped it in the back, it would be so handy?

I clamber through the weeds, ignoring their itchy scrapes along my calves. The garden is more like dumping ground than anything else. An old car stripped of its parts, a mannequin drawn on, with the words, *screw me,* written across her breasts, stares at me, watches with eyes blacked out from permanent marker. I quicken my pace. A box full of emptied, discarded wallets swollen from the rain, lies abandoned on the ground. Another box is spilling out with needles, some crusted over with dried blood. How many veins did that shit poison? Some bile rises, burns along my oesophagus for I've seen enough. I grab the trolley and push it into the house.

Back in the room, I lay the sheet next to Ryan and start the mummi-fication process, wrapping him tightly, making sure if he does wake, he cannot move. It's easy to grab hold of him then. Catching the sheet by his legs and the neck, I tuck my hip under his waist and lift. He is heavier than I thought and I drop him back on the seat. I pull the single mattress off the bed from the opposite room and lay it on the floor, then roll Ryan onto it. He moans on contact. Wedging the trolley between the arm and the side against a metal box acting as a coffee table, I lean one knee on the seat, then grab both ends of the mattress in the middle and fold them into each other. After that, I slide one hand underneath, estimating where his neck is, then use my knee to hoist the end of the mattress. Once steady, I tuck my other arm underneath, cupping his thighs. Once that is done, it's just a case of lifting, then landing him on the metal rim. It's easier said than done. Ryan nearly topples out the other side, but I catch him in time. His body starts to slip into the trolley, the mattress threatening to swallow him. Holding the edges, I pull the sides flat, straightening, although I don't care about his comfort, or if he'll feel it later. I do it to make it easier for me to put him in my car; if he's wedged, it will be more difficult to get him out. Something green on the couch catches my eye. Tucked in between the cushions, right next to where I found Ryan, is a peep of something, just a corner. I pull it out from the gap. It's a picture. A dog-eared Sara stares out at me, a beautiful girl in a green dress.

Ryan was looking at my daughter before he overdosed.

Chapter Seven

It was meant to be a happy day. With her purse wadded with cash, Sara could spend all the contents on the dress of her dreams.

Instead, after less than two hours, the door slammed. On greeting, she collapsed into my arms. Within seconds, my shoulder soddened, the damp material of my blouse stuck against my breast, cooling the prickles of panic, reminding me to keep calm, to just be there for her. It was as if she had used all her strength to hold it together until she saw me.

'Whatever it is, we'll sort it,' I said, kissing her hair.

She didn't speak for some time, her sobs prevented catching breath. I waited.

'All the girls found one straightaway. All of theirs were perfect. I just looked like death. It's my stupid hair, I'm changing it to black.'

She cried out like an animal in pain, then tucked her head to my chest. 'My stupid hair, shaving it would be better.'

I brushed that hated red hair away from her face.

'Crying won't help. Do you know how many times I cried over mine?' I moved away from the hug so she could see me. 'No matter how many times you dye it, the colour will fight to come through. Blonde, brown, black, pink, the red will come through within a week. It will be a losing battle. It will be exhausting. Trust me, I learnt the hard way.'

Her chest hitches, but I've caught her attention.

'You used to colour it?'

'Every colour in the shop.'

I picked up a strand of her hair and held it out in front of us.

'And then you were born and I could never hate the colour again. Only then did I notice the different highlights, the fine strands of gold that appeared as if someone embroidered them.'

I pulled out a strand from the back, then displayed it between my fingers. Her face stayed on my chest, but she gave it the side eye.

'Dark at the nape, the hair almost crimson, hidden underneath the layers of different reds. Natural highlights they can't copy in a salon. Your hair allowed me to see the beauty of my own. If you dye it, you hide who you are and you should never do that. It makes us stand out.'

'I don't want to stand out,' she said, muffled into my chest.

'It doesn't matter if you don't want to, you can't not. You're special.'

She lifted her head to look at me, her eyes still dripping with tears. 'I don't feel special.'

I cupped her jaw.

'I know. What you feel is different, and that feels like the worst thing you can be at your age. As you get older, different doesn't feel as bad, until one day you realise it's your differences that make you special.'

I stroked that rich red, the deep auburn strands that ran the length of her back. 'You just haven't found the right colour dress.'

'Every dress in the shop *was* beautiful. They were just disgusting on me.'

I thought about how hard I used to find the right colours to go with my red hair and pale skin. I pictured my own Debs and had an idea. Holding her hand, I dragged her to my bedroom and burrowed in the keepsake boxes at the top of the wardrobe, until I found the one I was searching for.

'This is only to get an idea of what could suit you OK? I don't expect you to like it.'

I pulled out my Deb's dress, a green velvet full length number. Even though it was years later and had been plain, with no embellishments like what was around these days, I broke out in a smile, remembering how it had made me feel, how once on, the luscious fabric had spoken for itself. It had transformed my figure and my confidence. I felt like a movie star in the dress. Sara stroked the material. Not an instant refusal, a good sign.

'Try it on,' I said.

She winced. 'Mum, it's not my style.'

'Just to get an idea of the colour.'

She grabbed the dress and sloped off to the bathroom, bringing forth a pang of sadness that she wouldn't undress in front of me anymore. Over the last few years, everything to do with her body had become secretive and guarded and shut off.

A few minutes later, the door opened, too slow for my liking, me sitting on the bed, trying to act calm, ready to soothe, my fingers digging in to the back of my thighs with the nerves that this was a bad idea, that it would only upset her more, gearing up to placate and then she stood in front of me, a vision, like a pre-Raphaelite work of art, emerging from the bathroom like Botticelli's Venus risen from the sea or in the green robe, with those full lips, Rossetti's Astarte Syriaca came to mind.

She approached the mirror. Her breath caught. It worked like a lever, releasing my tears.

'See? Do you see what I see? You look beautiful.'

She smoothed her hands over the soft material along her hips, working her fingers to the top of her thighs, then back again.

'It's a little big.'

'We could get it taken in. Have it fit like it's bespoke.'

She turned to the side, then twisted to see the back. 'It's too plain.'

'We could add to it. Beading. Lace. Whatever you want.'

'My eyes look different,' she said, leaning closer to the mirror, staring at her reflection. And she was right. The green material made the green inside her pop, like two massive emerald orbs glowing in the light. The dress had done exactly the same for me. I walked over to her, stroked her hair.

'Do you feel special now?' I whispered in her ear.

She hugged me in answer.

Back in the present day, I pick up the picture, stroke my daughter's face, then look at the body in the trolley.

He still loves her. At least he still thinks about her.

I hope she haunts him every day.

I know now what I will do.

Chapter Eight

It's easy to roll the trolley from the house. Covering him with a duvet just in case anyone looks out their window in the pre-dawn light, I'm confident they'll see nothing but that. Even if they do, I don't care.

Getting him into the car isn't easy. Thankfully, the Skoda Octavia has an extra big boot, bought for dogs that are now long dead. The hard part is lifting Ryan out. Between the metal rim and the weight of him, I can't reach all the way under to pick him up. If I bend the edges towards each other, he will fall into the trolley and the walls are too deep to get him out without waking him or tipping him over. A groan makes me hurry. I climb into the boot, then drag the edge of the mattress as far as it will go until it rests on the floor of the boot. With a strength I never knew, I lean over Ryan and tip the trolley, not caring when it scrapes some of the paint from my car. Free from the metal, I yank the mattress. Ryan rolls the other way, in danger of tipping out. I catch the edge, then rotate him back to the middle. Only now, I am stuck between the car seats and Ryan. As I step over him, my eyes never leave his closed ones. My breath hitches. All he has to do is grab me and I'll fall.

Once back on pavement, I remove the top cover of the boot so he will have plenty of air circulating while still giving me a view of whether he wakes, then close the boot door. The click commits me to what I will do next.

The car drive passes in a blur, for all I care about is getting home. I drive within the speed limits, scared if a guard stops me with a druggie in the boot, not to mention the bag of weapons by my side.

A twenty-minute drive away, it is only as the roads change from rows of houses to increasing green, that my nerves settle a fraction. By the time I reach the one long, winding road, my breath is calm, my heart beat regular again. In the summer, Sara would stick her head out the window on this road. The shadows from the trees above would make her face look like a patchwork quilt. After my protests, she would sit with her back against the seat but leave her hand out, gliding it along with the wind, weaving it up and down.

On this drive, there is no open window. This time my concentration is solely on what is happening in the boot of my car. My brain won't go further, to what I will do once we arrive at my house, or what the hell I am doing bringing him there. Out of all the scenarios I previously ran through, this wasn't part of the plan.

From the mirror, I can't see his full profile, only the shape, a huddled mound. On the long road, a moan sounds from the back, low and painful. I pull the car to the side of the ditch and run to the boot. He is still unconscious but his colour has returned slightly. With no time to dawdle, I check his airways. Clear. Then check his pulse. Satisfied, I get back in the car. There are never any guards around here, so I pick up speed, hoping to distract my good side from trying to talk me out of what I am about to do.

Don't you care if he dies? The pills might still kill him. If you turn the car back around and drop him at the hospital, you won't be in any trouble. They will think you tried to save him.

My foot presses harder on the accelerator.

'Shut up,' I say. 'There is no going back.'

Chapter Nine

The gravel grates against the wheels on the long driveway. For the millionth time, I curse the lack of tarmac we never got round to doing. After a few years, I gave up asking Tim to tackle it. After Tim, I could never muster the energy I first felt when we moved in. Back then, lush, landscaped fields on both sides of the drive attracted me to the house. Now they can swallow me whole. Weeds hang high. They lean over as if reaching out their spindly vines to grab at you. The grass is the length of my leg, stopping at the middle of my thigh.

I like it this way. A foreboding sight when coupled with the house, the disarray sends away visitors or cold callers. With its magnolia paint blackened from rain and mould; its wood faded from the proud mahogany it once was, whitened in patches by the sun; the wooden slats on the porch buckled and covered in bird shit. Beautiful once, a welcoming house. My heart lifted each time I pulled into the drive.

Home.

Now it's just a place to pass out in. A place to meet oblivion while holding a bottle. A place to plot my next move.

Getting him out of the car is easier. In the house, I have equipment and don't have to worry about onlookers. Leaving him in the boot, I run inside and roll out the gurney, bought another time for a different reason. After manoeuvring it past the uneven slats of the porch, I finally reach the boot. He doesn't stir. Some addicts wake immediately on receiving naloxone. Their body rushes instantly into withdrawal, causing them to want a fix straight away even when their system is still fighting the overdose. Ryan definitely took pills as well; this is something I will have to deal with inside, for his unconsciousness and pallor are a concern. For now, though, he is still breathing and his heart is still pumping, so getting him in will be the first hurdle. Standing on one side of the boot, I line the gurney in front, leaving no gap between the two, and push the lever for the brake down. After going to the trouble of bringing him here, all I'd need is for him to break his neck. Moving to the outside of the gurney, I pull the mattress over the lip of the boot, then catch Ryan's legs, dragging his lifeless limbs over the mattress and onto the gurney, so his lower body lies on top. Then, I cup his head and lift the rest of him over the door of the boot, careful not to bump, to prevent him from waking. Careful too not to send him over the other side of the gurney onto the floor. He is thin but still, I wouldn't lift him to that height. Once unloaded, he moans, rocks his head but doesn't open his eyes. I strap him in tight, then push the gurney, safe knowing there will be no witnesses here, that no one will see. Or, if he does scream, no one will hear.

The den is a windowless, objectless room with the least chance of escape, so I roll the gurney in there, then set to work. At the medical closet in my office, I pull out an IV drip and check my supply of naloxone, as once the drug wears off, he might overdose again. Mixing activated charcoal with water, I return to the room, then cup his head and pour the black slurry down his throat, massaging it down his oesophagus. Inserting a tube would create a risk; charcoal in the lungs would be hard to explain to the guards. Ryan swallows, and I breathe a little. It has been under an hour, so whatever pills he has taken, the charcoal should absorb. He may vomit, or I may have to keep topping it up every couple of hours, but for now, once his vitals stay the same, I can grab a duvet and settle in the recliner to monitor him for the next few hours.

Although his breathing is regular, his heart might still arrest, or his brain might become starved of oxygen. If left unchecked, he could choke on his own vomit. It would be easy enough to take a defibrillator or ventilator from one patient I care for, but I can't risk someone seeing me, or worse, leaving Ryan to escape or die. I can achieve the same effect as both machines by hand, as long as I keep watch and act quick.

Anyway, what if he dies? I am only saving his life to prolong his death, only wanting him to live in order to suffer more.

His signs are stable, his chest moves up and down, his mouth partly open, quivers on the intake. Ryan is almost childlike on the gurney; his ravished body takes up only a third of the small space. Any stranger would feel sorry for him.

Not me, not me, not me.

I know what lies ahead. When he wakes and realises I won't let him go. When withdrawal kicks in, he will thrash and tear and lash out.

Like Sara did.

Chapter Ten

Sara tore my skin. Screamed, swore, spat. Told me she hated me on repeat. She pleaded and begged when I wouldn't relent. The pleas hurt the worst, they dug into my being, twisted into my soul.

Greasy-haired, with a constant slick of sweat. Her skin had smelled sour, the condensed mix of toxins permeating, decaying strong enough to make me reel back. There were marks on her face where she had picked at her flesh, trying to dig out the addiction. She had vomited until her throat had swollen and made her voice hoarse. Still, she called for me. Still, she begged. Her voice was more like a bark.

'How can you be this cruel?'

'I'm dying.'

'My insides are burning. It's eating me alive!'

'Why won't you help me?'

I couldn't stay in the room and watch her.

The groans and pleas carried even when I hid at the furthest part of the house. It was non-stop. My baby, always my baby no matter how big she grew. That bark, calling me every few seconds, made little nips in my heart, cut tiny incisions in the grooves of my veins.

'Please.'

'Help me.'

'I'm in hell. This is hell on earth.'

'Why are you torturing me?'

'*Mum... mum... mum!*'

The name was both an accusation and a prayer. Repeated on a loop, each time it inflicted pain similar to a knife stabbing, deepening the cut.

Until I couldn't stand it any longer. Half delirious, I got into my car and drove, not stopping until I ended up where I'd found her. Handing over the bag, she grabbed it with greedy disillusion. How I hated myself for loving my daughter enough to hurt her. For not being strong enough to make sure I carried it through. I failed.

That time.

Another flash. Buying the gurney, getting the room ready, clearing everything out, buying all that was needed in the event of an overdose, preparing for the what ifs, lying awake, wondering where she was, what was happening, driving around at night trying to find her and then the day came, the day of my nightmares before I knew what a nightmare call really was. Then bringing her home from the hospital, feeding Sara, clinging on to her as she went through withdrawal, letting her hit, spit, scream and then finally, mercilessly, some calm, followed by the tears, then the talking, until one day, months later, what felt like centuries later, a glimpse of my daughter came back.

Sara wasn't a saint. I won't idolise her or reduce her to a 2D character with a shiny surface, the flaws wiped clean. Sara was the most stubborn person I've ever met. Trying to teach a kid like that, trying to navigate them through life was a challenge some of the time, I won't lie. But after, when she calmed down, she'd come to me, slip into my arms, whisper sorry, nuzzle into my chest and I would breathe her in. It was always worth it. Through all the trouble, I still believed I would watch her grow. Once she got over her addiction, I relaxed a little, for we had survived the worst. From then on we were on the home stretch, we would sail along. How wrong I was.

Getting Ryan clean wasn't in my plan. Presented with the overdose,

I can change my expectations. Forcing him clean will be the ultimate way to make him suffer. I want his skin to crawl, to experience hell on earth, as Sara described. It is only right for him to experience what it's like to imagine his insides are eating him alive, to feel the gnaw at his bones.

Then, once he is better, I will still carry out the original plan. Let him feel what it's like to claw back hope from nothing, only to have it taken away.

Ryan flinches, groans, pulls at the strap.

Showtime.

Chapter Eleven

There are many firsts in a life. A toddler's first walk, a baby's first word, a teenager's first kiss, first grope, first love. A first I never thought I'd see though, is my dead daughter's ex-boyfriend lying on a gurney, while I wait to kill him.

Or the first time he opens his eyes and realises what I am doing.

When I pictured it, I saw his eyes widen, saw him claw at the shackles, scream at me. Instead, Ryan doesn't say a word. Doesn't struggle or plead. Just nods in recognition, accepting his fate. Then closes his eyes again.

Once the threat of any overdose is over, after the hours have moved to a day, I leave him thrash and sweat on his own. I keep him locked in but he doesn't put up any fight. Or more specifically, he doesn't fight me. His body fights *him* though, vomiting and convulsing, sneezing and sweating. I can hear the groans from every room in the house, and when I walk in, he is bent over, holding his abdomen. For a long time, I deliberate on whether to give him a laxative. In the end, I relent. Bowel obstruction or perforation can be a side effect of an overdose. I won't clean up his diarrhoea, so leave him two buckets, one labelled vomit, the other left up to his imagination.

There will be no other softening. No methadone or other medication to smooth the passage. I want him to feel every sensation. Uncomfortable is good. As I sit in the kitchen, as I suck on a cigarette, my eyes fixate on a list, my list stuck on the wall, comforted by the sounds of him retching or sobbing while I pour another drink.

Bide your time until the drugs leave his system. Wait until his senses clear, until he can look you in the eye and see he went through hell for nothing, that the only reason you did it was to torture him.

In the morning, I open the curtains and let the light in, not that I care about the importance of a sleep schedule, I just want to see him easily. With an addict, I know what not to do: never carry sharp objects, never leave your hair down, never, ever, turn your back on them. All my lessons, all my mistakes came to me the hard way.

As I check his vital signs, Ryan grabs me by the wrist. His fingers fit all the way around. The act doesn't startle; it is his strength that surprises me. I try to pull away. His hold doesn't budge, his athletic muscle still memorised in those wasted away arms. If he wants to, he can hurt me. My eyes widen, not from fear, rather from the memory of Sara in the same room, remembering her desperation, how she would have done anything to get away. Ryan doesn't fight me, though. Instead, he tugs on my wrist. Cracked lips, splits at the joins of the mouth. His words come out in croaks.

'Please, Ginger.' He tugs again. 'Kill me.'

That name. I haven't been called Ginger for a long time. A name started by my daughter. A name only called by her friends.

His wrist has a band of woven red and black frayed string wrapped around. My cheeks flush at a memory. It is gone as quick as it came, leaving only anger in its wake. I lean into him, whisper into his ear.

'No quick death for you.'

His hand drops, then flops away. I leave the room, locking the door behind me.

.

Chapter Twelve

Sara's death was slow. Nobody said those actual words, no doctor or pathologist or guard informed me about how long it took her to die. I knew from the depth and colour of the bruises that they had time to turn yellow, had time to try to heal, to expand and grow. The cigarette burns and singed hair told multitudes, yet still not enough. Her lying dead image tortured me, my brain turning over the many things that must have caused each injury, making me crazy, hoping what I imagined was far worse than the truth. When the family liaison officer visited, she gave a detailed layout, but it felt smoothed over. The trial confirmed my guesses. From the reported level of internal bleeding. By how far the ruptures had travelled by the time Sara took her last breath. From the vast number of injuries and the estimated time it would take to inflict them, a picture grew of Sara being tortured, violated, abused. When she couldn't take anymore, she gave up her life; her heart finally relented. Stopped.

The truth was way worse than my imagination.

Chapter Thirteen

Sara was always making things. Her hands always busy. Whether sketching or on her phone, or twisting her hair or tweaking something, it was a running joke that she never sat still. Around the time she met Ryan, she had taken up bracelet making, getting more intricate with her designs. Beaded ones for women. Delicate, with little charms, made from stretchy elastic cord. The ones for men she kept simple: embossed leather with names punched in, or woven cotton cord strung together.

In the kitchen, I sit and stew. Sara made the bracelet Ryan wears. The colours have faded but are still recognisable as the same colours she always used, in the same style she always designed. Has Ryan kept his bracelet on the whole time? Through addiction, through years of wear, has the string stayed on his wrist?

When he grabbed me, I felt the strength in him, in the way his two fingers and thumb gripped hard enough it threatened to cut off my circulation. He could have easily overpowered me, but he didn't. Ryan chose to let me go.

Chapter Fourteen

The next time I enter, Ryan hunches in the corner on the floor, shivering. The place smells of shed skin, of pus, the metallic scent of blood, the putrid gas of detoxing excrement, the stench of degeneration. Backing out, I take some gasps of fresh air, then return with extra blankets and a mattress already covered in a sheet. Not for comfort, I want to say; it is only because his withdrawal is ramping. Now that he can remove his straps, I need the gurney out of there in case he uses it as a weapon to hit me with or to smash the window. There are no other objects in the room.

Withdrawal is a slippery, ugly, deceitful thing. Just when you think you are over the worst, when you think there is no more you can take, hell reigns down. Seeing Ryan go through it makes me think of Sara and agree. It sure looks like hell on earth. He gets every symptom in the book. The body aches, the burning diarrhoea, the fragility of the flicking, unreliable heart with tachycardia, the height of fever, the constant running nose, the sneezing, the goose flesh formed into points on his skin, trying to get away. The sweating. Unbearable nausea that makes him wretch violently enough to bend in two. Green bile on tissues. Worse still is when the vomiting stops, the abdominal cramps force him to lie in the foetal position. The jittery nervousness, the restlessness, the hyperventilating panic attacks, the mania, the trembling. Not to mention the craving, the gnawing, the want, with no chance to sleep, the brain incapable of switching off. Although uncomfortable, none of the symptoms are life threatening. Despite all those symptoms, not once does Ryan shout. Doesn't beg. Stays quiet, silently suffering.

The first few days I leave paper bowls with soft food inside, like pureed fruit or vegetables. Bland food like mashed potato or pasta. He doesn't get hot food or cutlery. Even a plastic spoon can gorge an eye out when delirious. Before I enter the room, I turn the lock as loud as I can.

If he lashes out, I'm well equipped, making sure he notices the taser. To give him credit, I have yet to use it, but an addict is an addict and I won't drop my guard for a second. When I kneel beside him, I'm not scared. Wary, but not afraid.

The last bowl of food I gave him ended up on the floor because of his shakes. I do something I never thought I would. Whether from seeing the bracelet, I don't know, but I place a bowl of broth beside us. Dip the spoon in and gesture I will feed him. He opens his mouth wide enough for me to spoon liquid in.

There is an intimacy in feeding someone, a submissiveness by the person eating, a giving over of control, of allowing another to help, accepting dependence. Ryan never looks at me, keeps his eyes closed, or down, avoiding eye contact. It is the right thing to do, for I don't want him to see or look at me. It has been a very long time since I was this close.

The eyes are the same. Same curl to the eyelashes, same colour. Everything else about him differs from the young man I first knew. Sunken cheeks make me wonder has he lost many teeth. Unkempt coarse stubble covers his jaw, growing into a beard more every day. By showing that respect, by not meeting my eyes, I find myself soften enough to remember what he was like before.

Chapter Fifteen

The first time Sara set eyes on Ryan, I was looking at him too. We were at the game, the entire school was, an unspoken requirement in our small town when any match was on. The air buzzed with the swarm of people. Excitement mingled with the smell of chips, burgers and cigarette smoke. Jerry Luttrell bumped me on the shoulder.

'Should be a good night, Lorna. Finn tells me we have a secret weapon after transferring. Good enough to become pro.'

'What, this late in the term? How did they allow him on the team?'

Jerry shrugged. 'Haven't a clue. From the sounds of it, Finn made sure it would happen.'

The rumour must have spread through the field because instead of the usual shouting and roaring when the team appeared, a hush ran through our side of the pitch, everyone wanting a glimpse of the new kid. What I saw, was a muscular boy who knew everyone's eyes were on him, who accepted it but wasn't comfortable, his head bowed, his eyes flicking up to the crowd every so often, his hand raised as he did, introducing himself, showing respect. After that, he'd won us over, even before he played. When I turned to Sara to comment, I saw a girl transformed. She stared at him. Not in a goofy way, or as some love-sick girl, or a fan. Sara stared as if she recognised who he was, as if he had finally showed up.

It was the first time I witnessed the woman in her, glimpsed the hint of the adult inside and I smiled, remembering that sweet feeling of a first crush, not giving the moment the significance it needed, not knowing how my life had just changed forever too. Sara knew, though. There was a lot my daughter understood before me.

After that, I watched a whole field fall in love with Ryan Howe. Towards the end of the match, it was obvious who was leading our team to glory. One lad from the opposition performed a dirty tackle, going in low while Ryan was running, propelling him up in the air and landing hard on top of him, elbowing him on his nose. The crowd silenced, waiting to see if the injury was serious. Before trainers, or team players or opponents reacted; without looking at me or anyone else; without explanation or a word, Sara glided between the crowd, levitated it seemed, making a beeline for the pitch. I didn't stop her; I didn't have time and even if I did, I wouldn't have. Shocked by her courage and new found purpose, I wondered what she would do next, because in those teenage years Sara hadn't shown an interest in anything.

When she reached Ryan, she knelt on the grass, then handed him a tissue to mop up the blood. What Sara said was lost to me, her back to the crowd. What I had was a full view of Ryan seeing her for the first time. She held her hand out to help him up to sitting. He smiled at her, surprised at the gesture. His lips moved, spoke something indecipherable. He dipped his head while doing so, as if shy. Sara placed a hand on his. The crowd whooped, then roared, startling them both into action. Finn, the trainer, ran to Ryan with medical supplies, shooing Sara away. Getting to her feet, she walked backwards, even then reluctant to leave. Ryan's eyes never left her. The interaction must have only been five seconds long, but it was the delay in movement after, as Sara made her way back to me, that it turned from a sweet moment to something deeper. It was only as I watched Ryan watch her return, when she finally turned and I saw her face, saw the mutual utter enthrallment, that I knew life would never be the same for any of us.

Back in the present, I spill broth on Ryan.

What if I could go back in time and stop it all? There's no doubt that meeting Ryan cemented the stone that would become Sara's funeral slab. If only we hadn't gone to the game. If only I listened to her protestations and stayed at home that day like she begged. Would she have still had another moment with him at school? Would the attraction between them have been as instant somewhere else? Probably. I have never felt or witnessed such a pull between two people.

I stand suddenly, needing to get out, needing to get away. Ryan, his mouth still open, waiting for the next spoon, doesn't speak. Picking the near full bowl up, I leave. Locking the door, I lean my back against it as I heave and gasp. Once my breath settles, I run to the kitchen, throwing the bowl in the sink, halving the ceramic as it lands, not caring, or caring too much, wanting to damage something and better that it be the bowl than something irreversible.

Let him starve, I think.

Chapter Sixteen

Five hours later, when I enter again, Ryan rocks in the corner. Sweat pours in rivulets from his hair. His top is drenched, his hair slick, his boxers full of tiny holes, either moth bitten or burnt away from the many flecks of hash that escaped while he smoked. A scar cuts across one side of his right leg. *The* scar. His leg looks swollen; the blood pooling from lack of movement from being sedentary. He needs to elevate it, get the blood flowing, otherwise he risks infection.

In my hands, I hold a t-shirt, underpants and shorts, taken from the remnants of what was once Tim's closet. I hold my breath for as long as I can. The stench of stale sweat, putrid breath, like dirt or iron mixes with a sweet odour, pure chemical, of the drugs leaving his pores. All of it makes me nauseous. The sheet has a few circles of various yellows and browns. Loosening the corner furthest away, I shake the sheet free. Ryan lifts his head. He smiles.

'Sara.'

His face lights up with the hallucination.

This is as far as I go. Backing out of the room, I hold the clothes in front of me like a weapon; the sheet discarded. For a moment I contemplate throwing them on the floor but think better of letting him dress himself, in case he uses them to do damage.

After pulling the door shut, I lock it, then rest my back against the wood.

He thought I was her.

It sickens me. That he can look that happy. That he can see a woman who I can no longer see or touch or talk to because of him. If I thought it would bring her back, even in hallucination, I would take any drug.

Pain clutches at my chest. I am so tired of carrying it around.

If you hurt him now, he won't even feel it.

I know I'm right. If he's seeing Sara, he won't even know who I am, let alone what I'm doing. No, it has to be in his senses.

Bide your time Lorna, revenge is a dish best served cold.

Later, there is banging. A sound like feet scurrying on the wall. Clawing. All noises that suggest he is trying to climb. When they get loud enough to worry he is trying to do damage, I enter again. Ryan has scratched at his arms and face, creating long red welts running down his cheeks. Raised skin crisscross his arms. When I enter, his eyes are lost to his own nightmare, gone inside, gone far away from the room. He is docile, but I stay wary, for he might be trying to give me a false sense of confidence so he can make a dash for freedom. I close the door behind me as far as it will go, then edge to the side of the room to gather up the buckets. Turning my face from the smell, I back away. The stench of rotting insides too much to withstand.

I come back a few minutes later, holding a pair of gardening gloves and, with tentative steps, approach him. He watches as I slip them onto his fingers, he even smiles through the shakes. I look away. If he calls me Sara again, I will lose it.

'No more hurting yourself, you can't afford to get an infection.'

Around his wrists, I duct tape the gloves, smiling at the trapped hairs as I smooth it over, knowing how much it will hurt later to remove.

'If you prove you won't, I'll take them off.'

From Sara, I know the rough timeline of withdrawal. He is in the thick of it now, the peak. The first withdrawal symptoms come only six to twelve hours after the last dose, but I kept him medicated for way longer, so when he woke, his body was already fighting the worst. In usual circumstances, withdrawal hits its peak between one to three days. The physical ailments subside after a week.

His top is wringing. I edge over, remove the saturated cloth without a fight. His chest concaves at the sternum to the point it's almost hallowed, his ribs move in and out, violently grasping for breath. If I hadn't seen it before, I would think he is struggling to live. He *is* struggling to live but the fight is internal, from brain running to the nervous system, screaming to escape, to find an exit, rummaging and rampaging inside until it makes its way out of him through tears, or excrement or sweat or even, if needed, blood.

If it was Sara, I would give her something to live for. Line up different activities to pique her interest or keep her hands and mind busy for after the heroin left her body, to distract when she needed something else to replace it. But it's Ryan. There is no plan for recovery.

As the days double, I wonder why I've delayed. Each time I'm handed an opportunity to act, something stops me, as if waiting for the right moment, for some signal, or holding out for something I can't put my finger on, knowing something changed when I saw the picture of Sara, then deepened with the piece of string on Ryan's wrist. Both unlocked something inside I can't understand yet. Both unlocked something I don't want to open in my heart.

Chapter Seventeen

For months after her withdrawal, I would find Sara in some corner, eyes wide and glazed over, staring at nothing in particular. When I called her name, she would shake her head as if she needed to make the gesture to help her snap out of it. Anytime I questioned where her mind had been, she would just say she was daydreaming. It didn't look like daydreaming. Sara stared at empty spaces for minutes, hours even, going vacant, reminding me of when she was using, but this scared me more, because she was vacant while sober and I didn't know how to get through. Drugs I could wean from, but this was different. It made me wonder if the drugs damaged her, whether they burned holes in her prefrontal cortex, sucking her into absent spaces like a vacuum.

X-rays offered no conclusion; the counsellor assured us she was just using silence to work out her next step. I wasn't so sure. Although her inability to focus was a concern. Most of the time, she acted happy, picking up pieces of her previous existence and meshing them back into a life. Each day she came back more. Both needing a distraction, for her twenty-second birthday, I organised a celebration. Sara had been missing for her twenty-first.

Everyone came, even Tim. Bunting decked the house and porch. Streamers streamed from the trees by the woods. Wooden tables and benches dotted either side of the fields, with hired flat floor tiles to serve as a dance floor. It was over the top but I didn't care, my daughter stood beside me when I thought I would never have her next to me again.

It was an evening suited to a party. The sun lingered and even when leaving, still gave off a pleasant heat. I busied myself with the food, staying away from the gossips who had only rocked up to see how the addict coped around temptation. Sara was the picture of health, her red hair long again, cascading midway down her back, the freckles on her arms reawakened from seeing sun, her eyes bright, present. For the first time since her detox, it felt like I could relax.

Later, as the party noise settled into a gentle hum, when the night completely overtook the day and some guests had already left, I weaved through the people, passing by, mingling, picking up empty plates and glasses, not wanting to stop but just take in it all. Sara sat under the tree alone. A girl from her school, Jen, approached. Behind them, I rushed to catch a plastic wrapper that was dancing on the grass by the wind, stopping it with my foot. As I bent to pick it up, I overheard some of the conversation.

'Good party.'

'Thanks.'

'How's it going? Heard you had it rough?'

'You could say that,' Sara said with a chuckle. There was no malice in her voice.

Jen sat next to her. I stayed frozen to the spot, holding the wrapper in my hand.

'You were in the city for a while?'

'For too long.'

'Glad you're back?'

Sara shrugged in answer. 'How's it been here? Did I miss much?'

'You know Carraigshill. Nothing changes here.'

'Yeah, I'm starting to remember that.'

'Can I ask something, if you don't mind, like?'

Sara picked at some grass. 'Fire away.'

'Was it worth it?'

I leant forward, desperate for the answer.

'Heroin?'

Silence.

'It was always worth it.'

'Even now?'

'I'm clean, if that's what you're asking.'

'Not asking. Not like that. It's just... sometimes the lads take stuff. Say I'm missing out. It scares me. How addictive... when they are out of it, I wonder. Must be nice to just escape. Getting away from what is going on in my head... sounds appealing.'

'You're looking for permission?'

'No.' Jen gave a cautious laugh. 'Just wondering what your take on it is now that's all, coming out the other side.'

Sara stayed silent. She ripped clumps of grass from the ground.

'Tonight's a laugh.'

'I guess.'

'Did I offend you?'

'Why would you think anything you could say would offend me?'

Jen stood. 'Sorry for trying.'

Sara tugged on Jen's skirt. 'Sorry. When you live rough, you learn to bite first. Sit again?'

Jen sat back down.

'It must be a lot... to take in.'

Sara picked at her lip, stared into the distance. 'It's not that. It's just...'

She shook her head.

'Tell me,' Jen said.

'I know I should be happy. Like, I see the stuff that should be fun, that should make me laugh like everyone else. It's just... everything is just... boring.'

The wrapper slipped out of my fingers.

I think of that night now and wonder why I didn't question if Sara was missing Ryan. Of course, she must have been. For years, they were inseparable. After her discharge from the hospital, after her detox, she cried for him for months. Although she never went into details, Ryan broke my daughter's heart. When she recovered, once the tears dried, we never spoke about her ex. Afraid to bring him up in case it triggered her back to relapse, I never asked what happened between them, or where he was. If anyone mentioned him in passing, like when a friend of hers bumped into us on the street, Sara straightened and looked like she would burst into tears. That was enough for me to veer the conversation somewhere else, thinking she was too fragile, wanting to protect her from further hurt. Now, I wish I had talked about him. That I'd shown her I cared about how she was feeling. Shown her that she wasn't alone, that missing him would have been natural, that no conversation was off limits. If I had, maybe things would have ended differently. Maybe, maybe, maybe.

Chapter Eighteen

In the night I wake to a noise. A wail. Like what I imagine a banshee sounds like. For a second, I think she's come for me, that old woman who points at death, so I sit up straight and look at the window, but there is no face there.

There it is again.

The sound is coming from inside. Not a banshee, not even from a woman. The sound is from Ryan.

He screams out again. One word. Then again. One word over and over. He isn't crying out for help, which is what I would do in his situation. If it was me, I would plead. If I chose to scream, my one word would be help. Even though the words would be pointless. Here, screams are silent outside the walls.

Ryan's one word is Sara.

He cries out my daughter's name on repeat. Calling her. Begging her.

At first, I want to go in and shake him. Tell him to shut up. Rattle him. Slap him. Tell him no screaming or shouting will ever bring her back, that he made sure of that outcome.

Then a memory comes, forceful and real enough that my shoulders slump and I slide my body back onto the mattress until I'm prone. I clamp my eyes shut, as if that can influence blinding the recollection. Suddenly cold, I pull the bedsheet over my head, wishing it away.

Wishing those images won't come.
   Yet they are all I want.

Chapter Nineteen

Ryan spent every morning having breakfast in my house for a year. At first, he would scoot past with his head down, his hair ruffled and his eyes crusty from sleep, sometimes with lines still indented on his skin from the pillow, not stopping until he joined Sara at the breakfast bar, with answers to my questions so polite it made me laugh. When it became clear that there would be no repercussions for turning up, when the morning ritual turned from a maybe thing to a permanent, I would leave the front door on the latch so he could come in without having to ring the bell. Then, he would run up and nuzzle her on the neck, nodding as he passed, saying a quick, 'Hi Ginger.'

As time went on, I wondered if he even went home, only making a pretence of entering, when really, he was sneaking out the window and walking around the house.

Whatever really happened between them the night before, every morning they would sit side by side on high chairs, scoffing muffins or fruit or cereal, depending on what was on offer. And I would sip my coffee and marvel at how young they were. How free. There was never any annoyance about Ryan, not then, and if you asked me, I would have thought there never could be. From day one they were madly in love but also, and most of all, Ryan was good for Sara. Around him a confidence blossomed that hadn't ever been there, she straightened around him, was less afraid to be who she was. She looked people in the eye when spoken to rather than looking at the floor. Their happiness brought peace to my house. Sara became my friend again.

On the morning the pre-exams for the Leaving Cert began, Sara, having stayed up most of the night studying biology, had been fine all breakfast, cracking jokes and holding Ryan's hand but just before leaving, as we were walking out, she sloped, her body curling, neck to chest, knees and bum to feet.

Ryan steadied her, literally, placing a hand on her back as she was landing, softening her fall.

'It's a waste of time. I'm going to fail. I'm gonna forget everything and I won't be able to do nursing and join you in England and we'll...'

Ryan knelt on the ground, squared his face against Sara's face, holding each cheek, forcing her to look into his eyes.

'None of that is going to happen, OK? Even if you fail today, it's only the pre's, right? They mean nothing. All they do is let you know where you have to study more. They help you, yeah?'

Sara nodded, those green eyes sparkling with tears, childlike in their hope, in her want to believe him.

'You've put in the work. You'll put in more work for the next four months. We will do the things we planned.'

Ryan gave her exactly what she needed. Her breath returned to calm, her eyes never left his, never looked to me, only at him, only wanting Ryan. I saw the shift, the belief in his words, the understanding of the truth in what he said. Sara allowed him to lift her up. It hit me that their roles in the relationship had reversed from the very first day they met. The equality was new to me. When one of them faltered, the other would lift, one of them *could* falter, and they would survive.

To witness this was strange; to have someone else take over the role of pacifier in Sara's life unbalanced the order of my own. Instead of getting jealous, or feeling obsolete, I was relieved. From the day my daughter was born, my biggest wish was that she received the love she deserved, that other people would see her worth and surround her with love. Tim failed many times. Ryan fulfilled that wish. With him, I could be sure someone else loved her, that someone else would fight her corner, would look out for her.

They were inseparable. Sweet. Back then, when I compared their love to what mine and Tim's had turned into, it was the complete opposite. They set a benchmark. They gave an old girl like me hope. The sight of the two of them made even the most pessimistic people believe in love, in soulmates. He must have got stick from the lads, because that wasn't the way lads in Carraigshill acted, but Ryan was that rare breed who didn't follow the crowd, and being the star player meant the crowd followed him.

Being the star player's girlfriend alleviated Sara from hiding in the background of life, to everyone wanting her around, meaning parties and invites, to days out at the beach, or pubs. My only worry back then was if, for some reason they broke up, she would go to pieces after. The longer I was around them, the more I couldn't see that happening at all. Back then, I would never have imagined how it would have turned out, how they would turn out. Nobody could have believed as they watched them feed pieces of muffin into each other's mouth, as they ducked away from thrown crumbs, or heard the laughter that filled every corner of the whole house, the same couple would be strung out, shooting up down a back street only a year later.

Chapter Twenty

When I wake, it is still before dawn. I creep into the room. Ryan is propped up against the corner, sitting on the floor. He is asleep, his eyeballs rolling and flicking, lost to a dream.

As quietly as I can, I tuck a new sheet onto the mattress, picking up the soiled one from where I left it on the floor.

There is nothing I can do about the smell. Opening a window is not an option. Nor is leaving the door ajar.

After I empty the buckets, I leave a banana and a packet of ginger biscuits. The potassium in the banana will help with the cramping muscles. The ginger will help with the nausea.

It is a small thing, a tiny concession, but one that doesn't go by me unnoticed. The dream, the thoughts last night about the Ryan he once was are still present. It doesn't help to go there, for that young man is long gone. The Ryan in front is a different person: manipulative, ruthless, unkind.

I just need to keep reminding myself of that.

Chapter Twenty One

When Sara was young, the two of us loved nothing better than being outside. With her playing in the fields, while I sat on the porch watching. Sometimes she joined me, the two of us listening to birdsong, or waiting for snippets of nature to forget we were real and land near us or pass by. Most of the time, Sara couldn't stay still. Only after she tired of attempting cartwheels, or exploring, or chasing crows, would she sit and just relax.

Or, in those first few weeks after she was born, when I had no clue of what I was doing and quiet moments were out of my reach, I welcomed the peace of the balcony. If I could steal some time, a second even while she slept, or Tim listened to my begging for once and took her for a whole five minutes, I would go to the seat and close my eyes and smell the pine wafting from the woods on my left, from the trees that surrounded the house, their shade blanketed me, shushed my manic brain with their moving branches, reminding me that all loud noises hush eventually, that those precious, crazy moments of looking after a baby would one day pass.

The porch helped me find a rhythm to my breath. There, the silence gave me the reprieve I sought. All I needed was a moment there. A moment in silence returns a person to who they are. Silence separates you from everything. It frees you from guilt, pain, fear. It frees you from the person you think you need to be.

Only five minutes before, the walls had narrowed to the point of suffocation. Desperate, I had tried winding, feeding, rocking, singing. Nothing worked, nothing soothed. Noise like that can make you break. It can make you question what life is worth. How could one tiny being with such a cute mouth create that much sound? The pressure had built until I was afraid of what I could do. On the porch, the tiny distance helped create enough of a gap for me to understand the frustration was down to sleep deprivation and Tim's disinterest, and really, no matter how loud she cried, I loved my baby.

When she stopped crying, everything usually righted. In seconds, I would forget my fragile state. The relief, the reprieve from the grating, tear your hair out noise, alleviated me to a state of bliss.

One particular night that wasn't enough. After days of trying everything, when I was at my wit's end and I was ready to pull out my hair, when tears were a constant and I couldn't understand how heartless Tim was leaving a room when we walked in, when he slammed the door complaining about the noise, when he shouted in the night I was keeping him awake, I gathered up some blankets and sat in the rocking chair. I pulled out my breast, the first time I'd ever exposed myself outside, the skin instantly puckering with a thousand goosebumps. All my life I covered up. There on my porch, I freed my breast from its clothing and offered it to my baby.

Whether she reacted to my calm, or was starving even though she had refused my previous offerings, or the shock of the cold or the sound from outside stilled her, I don't know, but she quietened right down. It became Sara's charm. It turned from *my* sanctuary to *our* place, the place we came to bond, to feed. There I would watch her after she suckled, then slept. Not having to move her, tucked into the crook of my arm, safe on a breast-feeding pillow, cocooned in blankets, I could listen to my favourite sounds: birdsong and baby's breath. There, I could return.

These days, the porch is not my sanctuary. It is a dirty, rundown, dangerous place, not only treacherous to step on with its uneven boards, for to sit is a hazard too, with the rusted, ready to disintegrate metal handles on the rocking chair. Even worse, even more dangerous, are the memories I pull up when I've tried to sit.

I don't want to see Sara laughing in my lap. It hurts too much to feel the empty space of that memory. Yet since I brought Ryan here, they come.

When Sara was about five years old, she used to bring her dolls out and line them on the seat. When I asked her what she was doing, she said, 'Looking after my babies.'

Sara will never have a baby. A grandchild will never swing on the porch.

After she died, I stopped tending to the garden, stopped painting the decking, stopped oiling the metal, or cleaning the cobwebs away from the glass windows. Instead, I invited decay, wanting any visitors to see it and think twice about calling, hoping it would creep them out, so they'd decide to ring instead, muttering that a voicemail or a text was better these days, anyway.

The house contained memories, too. The more the place changed, when I didn't open the curtains or turnover the sheets, when the walls and carpet and tables tarnished from bright to dull, I could pretend it was just my place, happy to live with just a ghost beside me.

It's funny how you become accustomed to smells. How the scent of decay or smoke or rotting rubbish becomes normal. Only when you leave the house, when you walk back in again, does it hit you like a slap, reminding you of what you got used to, of where you allowed yourself to descend.

Chapter Twenty Two

On the fourth morning, Ryan's shivers subside and he sits in the corner against the wall with a blanket wrapped around his legs. Each time I enter this room, even though I expect him, it is still a surprise that it's not Sara. Each time I bristle with resentment, even though I know he didn't ask to be here, that I'm holding him against his will. Despite these facts, he acts uncomfortable but accepting, his hands placed palms upward in his lap, giving off a non-aggressive demeanour. His eyes are alert though, this time looking straight at me, watching like a cat with a mouse, waiting for my next move before he strikes.

This time, he nods in acknowledgement. I place a tray on the floor next to the door, with a bowl of soup, some bread and a drink all in plastic containers, all with plastic cutlery.

'Do you need something to help with sleep?'

It is the first thing I have said to him in days.

He shakes his head.

'OK then.'

I pick up the buckets and am about to leave the room when Ryan clears his throat.

His voice cracks when he speaks, his tongue unused to forming words.

'Why are you helping me?'

I nearly drop the bucket. It takes a second to compose myself. My voice, when it leaves, is husky.

'Is that what you think?'

He looks hopeful, like I am his hero or something, with no fear present, no worry about what I'm going to do. Wariness is there, but also appreciation. Disgust floods me.

'I'm not helping you.'

He blinks a few times, processing the sentence. He opens his mouth but I don't wait for his response. I leave the room, needing to get away as quick as possible. Closing the door, I stop mid-walk, immobilised, until the stench forces me to get rid of the contents of the bucket. In the toilet, I vomit, chunks of vegetable soup mixing with Ryan's faeces. I wipe at my mouth. What am I doing? What am I doing cleaning out Ryan's excrement, serving him soup, checking if he needs anything? When did I change from trying to hurt him to helping him? The resolve I've felt ebbing each day comes back full force. He is the fool, not me.

I gather my keys and wallet and run to my car and drive. No more dawdling, no more softening. I will go to town for supplies. He is well enough to feel the pain, coherent enough to understand the turn, to comprehend why what is to come next is happening.

It is time.

Chapter Twenty Three

At the bottom of the drive, my old neighbour, Barry, steps out, blocking the path. With enough distance not to hit him, I jam on the brakes.

'Not now,' I mutter under my breath.

I roll down my window. 'Hiya, I'm just rushing to the shops.'

He takes forever to come near, strolling head bent, then leans on the window. I don't turn off the engine, keep my foot hovering over the accelerator, ready to go.

He looks in, noticing.

Act normal. Why didn't you say you had to go to work?

Because he might see me come back.

'It'll only take a minute.'

He taps at his ears, indicating the noise is too loud to talk. With a sigh, I turn off the engine.

'Not to be rude Barr but I can only stay a second, I need to get to the chemist to pick up something.'

'Oh?' He looks concerned.

I shake my head. 'Just a headache.'

Remember to buy them so your story checks out.

'I've painkillers up home if you need some?'

'Nah, I've to get a prescription anyway. It just makes me a bit snappy that's all.'

He pats the roof of my car.

'Understandable.'

He stares at the ground for what seems like hours. Stalling. Gearing up to say something big. I want to rush him along but know if he doesn't say what he needs to he will only call later and I can't risk him doing that. I smile and brace myself.

Please don't talk about Sara.

'Thought it best to tell you in person I'm selling the field.'

I drop my shoulders. 'Oh, right.'

I don't know what else to say, or why he's telling me.

He kicks at some dirt on the ground. Sparks up a rollie, his fingers stained yellow from fingertip to past his knuckle.

'It's too much to hold on to these days, the upkeep like, and I could do with a bit extra in my pocket and I was thinking, like, I know you like your privacy and all, so I wanted you to know before I go to the agents, cos there's been some interest before, like.'

Prickles of annoyance rise on my neck. His words jar. The fabricated headache threatens to become real. This is pointless information, nothing to do with me. All I want is for him to disappear, all I want is to just go.

'OK then, thanks for thinking of me.'

I stop from saying, is that all?

He puts a hand on the open window, preventing me from moving.

'I wanted to give you first dibs. It'd be better if it didn't go through those feckers in the bank, grabbing their take like. Prefer to do it private.'

'I don't see what that has to do with me though Barr?'

He takes a long drag, screws up one eye as he inhales. 'Some lads approached me about the land after.'

He stops, hesitating to go on. I sigh, open my eyes wide, sit upright in the chair trying to hurry him on.

'After?'

'After your girl.' He stops, embarrassed.

'Oh. Sorry if they hounded you, I got a lot of that as well... it's just... I wouldn't have the money or the need for more land so there's not much I can do if someone buys it.'

He holds his hands up. Takes a step back.

'Fair enough. I just wanted you to have first go. All of a sudden this feeling come over me that I should say it to you first. Being in the papers a lot, I didn't want some weird fella buying the place next to it, there's some right sorts out there.'

He sparks up another cigarette, while stomping out the other.

'I need the money pretty fast, so, you could have new neighbours fairly lively. Always had time for you, you never gave me grief, thought I'd give you the courtesy like, no offense meant.'

'No offense taken.' I sigh again. 'Thanks Barr.'

In dismissal, he taps the roof of the car, and I drive on slow, hoping he won't hang around or snoop near the house. The mirror reveals him walking away, going home. I breathe.

The conversation flattened the top off my anger but I'm still determined to go through with my plan. On the drive I run through some things I need, the places I have to go. McElherry's for some rope, the common type, one that everyone will have some of hanging around the garage, one that won't get you convicted after. In the true crime shows, it's always the rope that catches the murderer, the blue or yellow fibres only available in a particular place, still hanging in the murderer's workshop or garage. No, any old rope would do for Ryan. The Rohypnol I have will ensure he can't fight back but I can't guarantee it won't wear off. Ryan is stronger than when I first took him. Hence the need for the rope.

Next stop would be Fallon's for the painkillers – so my story to Barry checked out.

Why had I hesitated? For a while I had lost my way, lost track of my focus, been distracted by getting Ryan clean. Over the last few days, I'd felt the softening, the draw to care for him. Like Sara would have. But I'm not Sara, Sara couldn't soften anymore because of him. I need to harden.

In the supermarket, I pick up enough food so I won't need to leave the house again for a few days. No matter where I go people stare. Even strangers. Most are blatant, not even trying to hide, their brows and forehead folding in, wondering, trying to place me, their eyes hazy, trying to focus on how they know my face, how my features have imprinted on their memory. At first, they smile, thinking I'm some long-lost friend, or some old customer, or relation, some part of their past. Then, usually their face drops when the penny does too, when they realise *how* they know me. From a newspaper clipping of my blown up distraught face at the funeral, or my straight backed, trying to keep it together stance, side by side but never as far apart from Tim, as we enter the courthouse, or just me caught in motion, on the TV, never looking straight at the camera, my hollowed cheeks, my pale skin showing the blue of the betraying veins still pumping with blood, highlighted from the flash of cameras, staying on me for a moment as the news reporter painted the sad tale of the grieving mother, then flashing to Sara's face, the girl with the same hair as her mum, the same picture used every time, the one of her at her Debs, shiny, beautiful, in that green dress, before the drugs, before her violent death.

Is that what all fame feels like? Would it feel different if someone came over to say they liked you in this film or request a photograph? Most don't approach when they realise they only know you from your suffering, that the only reason you are famous is because of the nightmare you've been through. From most, in fairness, there is great sympathy.

Fuck their sympathy, I've never wanted it.

What I want is to forget for a moment. What I want is for someone to make me smile for a minute. What I want, is my daughter back. It doesn't matter how much time passes either, when someone meets me all they recall is my misery plastered all over the pages. Even if I'm having one of my better days, their recognition reminds me why I should be miserable.

There isn't a person in Ireland who doesn't know my face. Before Sara died, the sense of community was something I was proud of. When they heard of a senseless, awful, evil murder, the whole country went into mourning. At first, the mass horror gave some comfort; to know a nation was in shock too.

Until they spun a different campaign. The media latched on to Sara's past, implied her guilt, implied she played a role in her own murder. The hate mail started then, the bad mother letters, the ones that began with sentences like, how could you let your daughter... I read every single one. Non stop. They were right. I took each word and drank, smoked, plotted, planned my own death after my revenge because how could I let her die? I *let* her die. *I* let her die. Me, I did, it was me, *I let her die.*

And then time moved on for the TV watchers and the newspaper readers and Sara's face didn't make the news anymore. When another crisis took over, I could feel her slipping away, forgotten about, until I missed the daily reminders, missed seeing her face.

In the hardware store, while I gather the supplies, I make sure to shoot the breeze with Joe the manager, waving the rope at him when I see him eyeing it. Rather highlight and explain what I'm doing then have twenty strangers saying to their friends, 'I saw that poor girl's mother acting weird in McElherry's buying rope today. Can you imagine?'

'Hey Joe, think this will fend off some deer that keep coming on the drive? I'm terrified one of these nights I'll knock one down.'

'What you need is a fence, a rope won't keep anything big out.'

Not what I want to hear Joe.

'Already on it. They can't start till next month so I just want something temporary to give me peace of mind. Figure if I just stagger some wooden spokes and attach some rope it will do the trick for a while. Better to try anyway.'

I turn in the direction of the counter. Job done.

'Be careful,' he calls back.

I cringe. Am I that transparent? I back around to him again, feigning interest.

'Of what?'

He stares at me with a blank expression I can't work out. I stop from squirming.

'The ticks. Don't get too close to those deer if they're wild. Watch out under those trees of yours too. Lyme disease used not be a thing in Ireland, but I'm hearing about it more these days.'

He has been dividing some hooks into trays as we speak. He stops now, for effect.

'One of those feckers lands on you, it's all over. What they do, is burrow in without you ever knowing, until days later, months later, all sorts of symptoms start happening, like headaches or heart palpitations, or your face getting all paralysed and it doesn't go away. One of those can live in you, just squirreling away, sucking on your blood forever while you get sicker and sicker. Not pleasant at all.'

I feign interest. *A tick is the least of my worries, Joe.* 'What should you do?'

He shrugs, his knowledge not going that far. 'If it was me, I'd strip off after I go out there, check your body in a full-length mirror. If you catch them early you'll see the bastard burrowing in.'

I shiver. 'You've got me all nervous now.'

He grins. 'You'll be grand.'

It is only in the pharmacy, as I pay for the painkillers that my mistake dawns. As I hand over the money, a chill runs down my neck. The house. The door. Ryan. In my rush to get away from him I forgot to lock it. The door that stops Ryan from leaving, is open.

Chapter Twenty Four

Before my brain catches up, I'm back in the car. All I can concentrate on is my scattered breath, struggling to catch air. My lungs aren't big enough, closing in, my mouth open wide, trying to swallow some. Still, I drive. At a red light I gather my thoughts, let my breath settle. The red light stays lit forever. I will lose him. All the sneaking, putting Ryan in the trolley, getting him clean, will all be for nothing.

'No.'

I whack my palm on the steering wheel.

The light is still red, the green light for the pedestrian walk turns on instead. An old woman crosses, eyes me suspiciously, probably after seeing or hearing my outburst. I sit straighter, try to calm.

'Get your shit together, Lorna,' I whisper.

Ryan will have known immediately the door wasn't locked. It has a faulty hinge, coming out of its frame, creaking ajar whenever you leave it open. That's why I put him in that room, because of the lock. When I got serious about Sara's detox, I'd attached one to the outside.

And now I'd screwed up and he would be gone.

I scan the streets as I drive on, not knowing what I will do if I see him running. Enough time has passed for him to make headway. Even in the time I talked to Barry, he could have snuck out the back door and hitched a lift, could be out of the county if he wanted. I curse my last words to Ryan for admitting I wasn't helping. Before that, he might not have moved. After, he must know I plan to do him harm. He would be a fool to stay.

The pads of my palms ache from how hard I grip the steering wheel. The thought of him leaving blasts away any doubts I developed while nursing him, the chance he might be gone confirms I want him there. I haven't come this far to let him walk away. It might all end today and I'm fine with that. Out in the open, the slow death I hoped for won't happen. There's no way I'll get him in the car again now that he's recovered. I'll have to use the car as my weapon. If I find him, I will knock him down. And roll over him again and again until I'm sure he is dead.

What about the photo? The bracelet?

I shake my head, trying to reject the memories. It is easy to win my own argument.

How many men hurt the woman they love? Even if he still loves her, it isn't enough reason to let him live. Because of love, girls die every day.

As I pull in from the road, there is no sign of Ryan anywhere. Along my drive, no scuffed earth, no footprints in the mud. I barely let the car stop before I jump out and run for the porch. With trembling hands, I open the front door, the *locked* front door, which means nothing, or could mean everything. Ryan might be hiding in some corner, waiting to hit me over the head, knowing I've come back to do something, wanting revenge himself. I take a deep breath and let the door swing open.

As I step in, I listen. Except for the blood pumping in my ears, the place is silent. Edging in, I keep my back to the wall. The living room is dark as always, the curtains still drawn. At first glance, the room is untouched. The place is still filthy, uncleaned in months: rubbish heaped in piles, food plates sit in stacks, ready meal packets discarded on the table. The couch is three quarters full with newspapers, wrappers, wine bottles and empty glasses.

Something is different in the room though, I can feel it. I scan every nook, checking in case he is crouched down somewhere. Until I find the displacement. The ashtray is empty. I flash back to my last cigarette and remember pushing the butt between a mound of more, an already extinguished one fell onto the table. Did I clean it? I remember thinking I needed to clear the butts out, but afterwards, I still hadn't. When I left, the ashtray was full.

I swivel quickly, hearing a noise, sure that Ryan is behind me. All that is there is an empty hall. Almost on tiptoes, I step back into the hall and listen. There is a clanking coming from the kitchen. The door to the room I'd kept Ryan in is ajar. I nod, my suspicions confirmed. Ryan is out. Picking up an empty vase, my fingers smudge a year's worth of dust, I creep towards the kitchen. Holding my breath, I push the door with one hand, gripping the vase in the other, ready to use it, to crack him over the head.

He is there, his back to me, hunched over the sink, unknowing, unaware I've entered. Instead of launching, my hands go slack and I nearly drop the vase.

Chapter Twenty Five

The kitchen is transformed. Gone are the pile of plates, the stacks of cutlery, the glasses stained with wine, the mouldy pots that took over every available surface. The place smells of bleach mixed with lemon. The image is a replica of before, when Sara was alive. It throws me off my tracks, unsteadies me.

Fresh air blows across my face from the open back door and the window. All evidence of dirt is erased. Only this morning, I ran my finger along the kitchen press and two inches worth of grease sat on my digit.

'What have you done?'

Ryan turns, a kitchen towel in one hand, a cup in another. The scabs on his face have faded, reduced in size, his shaved hair has grown out about an inch, his stubble too, widening his face, filling out and hiding the deep hollows of his cheekbones.

He stands there in Tim's loose clothes, letting me watch him, shifting his weight to the other leg, saying nothing, until I meet his eyes. He keeps looking at me for a second, as if he is searching mine for an answer, then he flicks his to the wall, then downwards to the floor. Submissive was the last reaction I expected.

'Sorry. I shouldn't have left the room.'

With that, he puts the cup down on the scrubbed counter and leaves the kitchen, one leg slightly dragging behind the other. He enters the room, *his* room now. I scan the kitchen, recalling what he must have seen. The clean counter earlier covered with plates and food, dead blue bottles trying to make their escape for freedom, had lain at the closed window sill after butting themselves into unconsciousness. I let the shame settle, feeling how far away I'd moved from who I once was. There was a time that even the thought of not tidying up after dinner would have mortified me but what do I care about cleaning anymore? What was the point? I used to scrub and polish every day of my life and for what? My daughter was still murdered. Nobody spared me any pain because I kept a beautiful house.

I pick up the cup he held, cradled more like. Sara's cup. Given as a present on her sixteenth birthday as a joke, the rim is a tiara, across the middle says princess. Drank from and dropped so often a bit of the tiara chipped, giving it a sharp edge. No matter how much I warned, she refused to dump it, saying she drank from the other side, anyway.

He definitely saw the wall. Four faces stare out, one under the other. My hit list wall. Opposite the kitchen table, I would sit and stare at the images, running through how I would exact my revenge. Had that scared him? Seeing his face directly under the man tried for her murder? Surely that had alerted Ryan of my intentions, that what I was doing was more sinister than getting him clean. Yet he walked back into the room with no suggestion from me.

Ryan's smiling face stares out now from that revenge list. His photo snipped from my daughter in the original, when Sara didn't want him next to her anymore.

Tim, Ryan, Oliver and Scumbag.

Oliver McAllister, the barrister. With his tailored suits and the nodding, scribbling team behind him and his annoying habit of sniffing before he spoke, regular enough to make me question if he partook himself in some drug taking. In the courtroom, he ripped into Sara, made out like it was all her fault, when he didn't have to. With his plea, there was no need to bring in doubt or question the motives of the victim. Until he revealed his own motive.

Some days I've dreamt of getting him disbarred, finding some imprudent action or fraudulent indiscretion I could use against him. Since then, I've followed his trials. He has a penchant for dodgy characters: the accused seem absolute in their guilt, but also show signs of money; he isn't a pro bono lawyer, that's for sure. Over the last year, I have compiled a dossier full of his clients, his horrible friends, the circles he frequents. No matter how much I poke, I can't find any dirt yet to use against him. Yet, is the right word. Killing such a high-profile lawyer would cause mayhem. Some might say he is just doing his job. Nevertheless, he is the guy who hangs around with murderers, wife batterers, child molesters. What a job. How he can look in the mirror? How can he go about his day knowing he's responsible for freeing an evil person? He must know they are guilty. If he can only save someone from prison on a legality, if he has to resort to those measures, that alone speaks of the person's guilt.

Observing him at the trial, I don't think it mattered one bit if Scumbag did it. In public, he treated him as if he were his own son, full of concern, an arm placed on his shoulder when people, the judge in particular, were looking. I hate him, hate everything he stands for but not enough to kill him. Maybe.

Tim, Oliver, Ryan and Scumbag.

The last doesn't get a name. Only referred to as Scumbag, Monster, Murderer, Thug. He doesn't deserve to be humanised. He doesn't deserve to breathe. Him, I cannot follow. Cannot get to. Yet.

I run my fingers along the cup's tiara, faster and faster until I get what I want, the porcelain slicing deep into the grooves of my finger. The blood oozes out, black first, then red. Good. I deserve that. It will serve as a reminder not to mess up again.

Chapter Twenty Six

Every Saturday morning since she was six years old, Sara and I would get up early to bake. At first it was simple things: shop bought pre-packaged ingredients for cupcakes, or chocolate chip cookies, upgrading to sponges and scones, then fancy breads good enough to call artisan. By that stage, Tim and I had split, so I introduced baking as a distraction. On the days her father didn't show for his visit, Sara would set up a table at the end of our long, lonely drive, not stopping until she reached the main road, working on the sign all day, the table banging against her legs as she walked it down. There she would stay, for hours if needed, waiting to sell our wares. It broke my heart that she probably only did it for a valid excuse to watch the road.

Then, the teenage years hit and Sara stayed in bed until after Tim arrived to collect her. If I suggested we bake something, she would pat her sides, saying the carbs would turn her hips even bigger, so I dropped asking, knowing even then by losing the tradition, I lost that part of Sara. Instead of resenting the loss, I understood it was just a natural progression through life, like a toy discarded or grown out of. Back then, I could fast forward the years, picturing Sara coming back to me, in her twenties maybe, looking older, the two of us baking up a storm for some event, an engagement, or a baby shower, or Christmas, the two of us side by side, back together, mother and daughter, best friends again. I kept that day in my mind during the bad ones. Until the day it became a surety that it couldn't happen.

The kitchen, the oven, the house, all lost its appeal after she died. There was no need to be a talented baker or home keeper, there was no reason to keep the place presentable in case my daughter returned. I wanted it to rot. I wanted to rot, too.

The water splashes over my bloody hand. After it runs clear, I sit in the newly clean kitchen for hours. Rolling over what I am feeling and no matter how much I try, I can't work out what is going on inside me.

Feelings are like pounds of flesh – you can learn how to shed them. Since Sara's death, I numbed myself to the point that all I allowed in was anger or indifference. I haven't cared about anything in years, hating anyone that does; making small talk; speaking about the stupid weather as they go about their day. What do I care if it rains? I have no interest if it turns sunny. Nothing matters. The only thing that was important, love, has proven to be a transparent object that can evaporate, that can be lost, or taken.

My gurgling stomach makes me move. This is new, the hunger, something I haven't noticed for some time. I get to work, with nothing fancy, just throwing some pasta on with garlic and tomato. The door stays ajar. Every so often I find an excuse to walk past, like finally remembering the shopping in the boot, making two trips to empty it. The rope stays in the car. Each time I sneak a look in the gap, Ryan stays still, lying on the floor.

When the pasta is ready, I carry a plate to his room. His breathing is ragged, deep in sleep, the kind you can't fake. I lay the plate beside him and back away.

For the longest time, I numbed myself, felt only anger, but as I look down on Ryan as he sleeps, I feel something, something long forgotten. It is far from love, but it isn't anger or hate or repulsion, either, nor pity, which I could understand. Maybe it is due to him lying on the ground, or that his usually tense, in pain face has relaxed in slumber, giving a sense of him being much younger, like a baby even. Maybe I'm feeling this way because he cleaned my kitchen when he could have left. Whatever the instigator, it stirs such motherly affection I urge to stroke his face.

Only now, do I remember the *love*.

The love Ryan had for Sara. The love she had for him. The love *I* felt for him. For a split second, I want to protect him, to make sure he sees no more harm, to tell him everything will be better now. Until I remember who he is, who he was, who I am, what we are doing here. I rush out of the room, throwing my dinner in the bin, my appetite gone as quick as it appeared. No bottle is opened tonight. I head straight to bed, where I lie in the dark, wanting to summon up all the reasons to hate Ryan Howe.

And yet.

He had a chance to run and he didn't take it. Instead of using it to go home, to disappear, he stayed and cleaned my kitchen. I can't work it out. Does he want to be here? Does he want to get clean? And even if he does, what am *I* doing?

Chapter Twenty Seven

At dawn, the streets blur into sameness. When sleep wouldn't come in the night, I gave up trying. Better to drive. Better to get away from Ryan. There are too many conflicting thoughts around him. All this time I believed the love I once had was irretrievable. When I wanted to hurt him, I meant it. How could it be real though, if all it takes is for him to wipe down my kitchen counter and I feel something?

I do not love him. I hate him.

I shake my head. What I need is to sleep. How I feel, what I feel, is unreliable, for I haven't had more than two hours' rest in one go for at least a year.

I'll rest when they're dead.

'Is that true, Lorna? Cos you have a guy in your house that you could kill right now but you're too chicken to do anything about it. The worst thing you've done is spill soup on him, for fuck's sake.' I say out loud.

I drive into Cork City for no reason but distance. It's practically one straight line, and my mind doesn't have to do anything but go on autopilot. When I reach the city, I park the car on the mall, planning to walk up to the quay, or grab a coffee along the dock by the water. South Mall is dotted with solicitor and lawyers' offices. If there was ever a section that could be labelled the business section of Cork City, this would be it: one long street full of banks, estate agents, the passport office and legal establishments. If I was going to see a barrister like

Oliver anywhere, the likelihood of it being there is pretty normal. Still though, when I do, it's a surprise. For months, I followed him, his routine as ingrained into my memory as my own and the only takeaway was the man is as slippery as olive oil. He rarely leaves his office unless he's due in court. Yet here he is now, doing something new, checking both sides of the street before ducking into the Imperial hotel.

I follow.

Too early for the usual doorman to hold the door open, I wait until Oliver has approached the dark wood reception desk before I slip in. The hotel foyer is impressive. Marble floors reflect the light from an elaborate crystal chandelier hanging from the high-ceiling. Ornate panelling surrounds it. The hotel is all plush colours, creams and deep greens. It is fancy, but I've seen it before, well informed of its nooks and crannies, as we spent two days in the hotel for our honeymoon. Thankful for its immense columns, I lean against one and just listen.

'Booking for Humphries.'

There is a clicking noise of fingers padding keys. I try to hold down the excitement that it is a booking and not a breakfast, that it is a room not held in his name.

'Your wife checked in last night, sir. Room 243.'

I don't wait to hear anymore. I enter the lift before he can say thank you. All this time I have found nothing on this man. All the hours I spent looking up court records, going through his history, and this is what I'll do him for. It's so cliché but I'll take it. My luck doesn't end there. Number 243 has a table across from the door. I turn on my phone to video with just enough time to position it properly, nestling it inside a black vase full of green shrubbery. I hear the lift ping and vault to the end of the corridor. All I need to do is wait. I try to calm my erratic heartbeat, my whirring brain. This might not be the time. He may be too clever to say anything at the door, or the video might not catch what I'm after. It doesn't matter. Because now I know his weakness. I rest my head on the wall and listen.

Just one knock, the air suck as the door swooshes open. There is no talking, no casual hellos, only a slurp as they kiss. Then the door closes softly, no slams, just with a light click. I count to a hundred, even though all I want to do is rush to the phone. Terrified he will sense something is off and open the door again. With brisk strides, I pass the door, picking the phone up without pause, forcing myself to wait to watch it until I'm safe behind the corridor.

It's enough. The video catches Oliver in full side profile just before he knocks. The door opens and for a second a blonde woman in a negligee appears. One thing I'm certain of, whoever is behind that door, it sure isn't his wife.

Chapter Twenty Eight

On the day I took Ryan, I had started a compulsory break from work. The thought of staring at the walls for a week forced my decision to act. I couldn't just sit, drink and think, so I decided instead to torture and kill Ryan, with enough time to cover my tracks. The holiday is over. Today, I must return to work.

Before I leave, I slip into Ryan's room and place a bowl of cereal on the floor beside the uneaten pasta. He sleeps on. I pick up the bucket and slosh its remnants down the toilet. It is still dark. After I clean the bucket out, instead of placing it back in the room, without a big conversation in my head or debate, I just don't. Placing it in the shed where it used to be, I get ready, leaving the house knowing I have, again, left Ryan's door unlocked.

This time I have no fear of him leaving, which is irrational because the first thing an addict will do is leave. Still, I do it. The only reason I can put this action down to, is that I am testing Ryan and the decision he makes will be fundamental to the way the rest of the story, our story, will go, leaving destiny in his hands. Maybe in discovering Oliver's infidelity, I have found another outlet for my rage. Or maybe I am forcing an outcome when I know I'm conflicted. For if he runs, I will have to act. If he goes to the guards, what have I done? They can press charges for abduction, but I can argue that all I wanted was to get him clean. For some reason I can't explain, I believe Ryan won't do that.

People recognised me from the papers, but the trial brought a different type of interest all together. Once the details of what Scumbag did to her came out, the insinuations hushed, reduced to one line only in the paper. *A recovering addict*, like that one sentence summed up who Sara was, who she had been. There was no more implied blame, for the list of injuries made it clear. No person, whether an addict or forever clean, deserved what he did to her. It horrified the nation. Letters poured in of another kind then. *I'm so sorry for what you went through...* Those I didn't read.

Being infamous was one reason I switched into care work. I couldn't return to the shop, where each new customer would recognise me. I needed to keep busy, but I couldn't face it anymore. Working with one individual meant having the conversation only once in a while, rather than a hundred times a day.

At Patrick O'Neill's house, I turn the key in the door and call out. 'Only me.'

At the time of keeping Ryan hostage, there are three clients I alternate between, spending the morning with Patrick before moving on to the other two. He is one of the lucky ones, not with his predicament I mean, but for the ability to pay privately for home help, so I can spend the entire morning there making him comfortable.

My other two clients aren't so lucky, it takes longer to travel to their house than the time they have me, only permitted the allocated hour the government appoint. An hour isn't even enough time to wash someone, let alone tend to their needs. My heart breaks every time for Mr Jones. Confined to the bed, he has lost complete use of his right side. How can you look after a person in an hour? I do what I can, washing and changing him, reheating the meals on wheels delivered every day. I never leave on time. Those first few weeks with him, I spent hours cleaning his room, washing his clothes, giving the man back some dignity, not going until I'd exhausted myself. Some days scrubbing an area until my fingers bled. What was time for me, anyway? It was better to spend an extra hour at Mr Jones cleaning or at Mr Bell turning him so he wouldn't get bedsores, rather than going to the off licence to fill up on another bottle. It prevented me from doing anything drastic for work and gripped me somewhat to life.

I walk straight into the living room, now turned into a state-of-the-art bedroom where Mr O'Neill sleeps on a remote-controlled hospital bed that moves up and down, or alternates between lying or sitting. Music plays from an expensive looking antique radio. A wide-screen TV hangs on the wall opposite. His children have made sure that their father has the best tech you can buy and although I've heard him on the phone assuring them he watches it every evening, I have yet to witness him turn it on.

Next to the bed is a locker with everything he could possibly need during the night close at hand. The position of each is important, each one has a place. Losing his sight requires consistency. It is the only way he can keep living alone.

The first time I met Patrick was the only time he seemed unsure or afraid. A man still fit, still strong, standing straight, he is easily 6ft. Impressive, yet his voice was gentle, and he took the time to choose his words. That first day, he had asked one question in the interview. It seemed to be his only requirement for hiring.

'Can you keep me from going into a home?'

The blindness was new. Overnight, the world turned threatening. Before, he had lived a full life by normal standards: golfing, holidays four times a year, work parties, even the occasional date after the love of his life died two years previously.

Instantly, I liked Patrick.

Being blind meant he read no papers. Not turning on the TV meant he hadn't heard my name. Whatever was going on in my life, I knew I could help. Yet, out of all the interviews I'd been to, I knew the family wouldn't hire me. They would demand to hire a strong man, in case the need to lift happened. Knowing I was wasting my time, I told him what I would do.

'Mr O'Neill, first, I will teach you where everything is in your house. We will count the steps. To the bathroom, to the kitchen. We will stock every shelf and cupboard with what you want in order, creating a system. Everything will have a place. After that we will do the same with outside. Around your garden, I noticed you have a lovely spot for listening to the birds. We will set an exercise routine, work on your balance and your core. I'll teach you how to roll if you fall, how to get up when you can't find anything to lever. Then, if you're up for it, we can do the same with the neighbourhood. If what you want is to not go into a home, to not lose your independence, I will do everything in my power to make sure you don't. Forget about going into a home, what I want is to give you your life back.'

I stopped, afraid I'd said or promised too much.

Mr O'Neill gave the widest grin.

'The job was yours when you said "first."'

Since then, we have made headway. Even on the days when I wanted to end it all, I kept my promise, turned up, determined to give Patrick the run of his house again. He's never judged me, even though he must have noticed the smell of alcohol on my breath. For two or three hours a day, I can park my grief and concentrate on someone else. As money is no object, we converted his downstairs to a living quarter, which wasn't hard, with two living rooms that opened into each other. He hired someone to take out the doors the day I suggested it. The space left still bigger than most two bed apartments.

His mind is sharp. He absorbs everything I show him. He went to the bathroom by himself within the first week. With him, we learnt to focus on textures more. Making objects that felt similar stand out by adding a groove to one box, a lump of Velcro to another of the same shape, anything to decipher the difference when he was alone. He told anyone who would listen whether on the phone or a visitor how I was his saviour but I knew the truth; those tasks saved me. Mr O'Neill, became Patrick.

His kids relented with their talk of state of art facilities and settled to waiting and seeing how he got on. After all, they knew their father. He hadn't made his fortune without determination. But, we both knew, one fall, one mess up like a broken bone or an accident like a spill of boiling water would send him straight to pensioners prison, even if it was at a thousand euros a night penthouse at the best old age facility in the country.

'Rise and shine Patrick. You getting lazy in your old age?'

He chuckles. 'Just resting my eyes, dear. How was the break? You back to me all refreshed?'

I pinched the bridge of my nose. 'Refreshed wouldn't be the word. Come on! You slacking on me?'

'I wouldn't dare. What's the plan?'

'Don't pretend you've forgotten. I know you've had a week to doss, but today is *the* day. There's nothing to stop us, the sun is shining, we have a full three hours. You are jumping out of that bed. After you get dressed, we are going to count the steps to your bench so we can eat some breakfast outside in the sun.'

Patrick beamed. For a moment, I even forgot about Ryan.

We have a system. Before we move even a step, I describe what is in front of us. For his willingness alone, I respect him. As a self-made rich man, he could have a carer by his side all day. Despite being blind, it hasn't changed who he is. He wants to learn to take control of his disability, he doesn't want someone else to do it for him, he wants to reclaim his life. In order to do that, all he needs are the tools, which, in this case, is information. Patrick doesn't want me to dress him or spoon food. What Patrick needs most from me are my eyes.

We stand side by side. I hook my elbow, resting it lightly on his hip so he knows it is there. His hand slips under, resting in the crook of the bend.

'It's mostly a straight run. You are in the middle of the room. Hold your left hand straight out by your side.'

He does; grazes the wall. He nods, understands.

'On my side, I am leaning against the end of your bed. If I step away and you put your right hand out, you will reach it.'

He nods again, which is his sign to move on.

'I think it's going to take about twenty-five steps until we come to the back door. You ready?'

He nods. We move, counting each step as we do. It takes twenty-three.

'We are here. The door is about five inches in front. Can you remember it?'

'I think so,' he said. 'Elizabeth bought these great big double door things. Black with spirals. They open out. Finicky if I remember.'

'They were. The key was slightly bent, so I got a new one made. It's a turn key lock. We will keep one in it at all times and if you side step three times to the right.'

We did it now.

'And lift your right hand up to shoulder level.'

His fingers find the area. He taps along, moving his digits over a metal rack. His fingers go slow, stop on the first little metal spoke, rolling the end of it between his thumb and forefinger, then moving on to the left, counting as he does. 'One, two, three.' He reaches the third spoke and his fingers scroll down, touching a key.

'That's the spare. Come back to me.'

He side steps three times.

'Let's get you out there. All you have to do is turn the key and push. There is no drop down on the other side. Just step forward two steps and I'll instruct you from there.'

For a few seconds, he doesn't move. It isn't resistance; Patrick is preparing, getting mentally ready, acting this task out in its completion before he moves one inch. In Patrick's mind, by the time he turns that key, he is already sitting on the bench, having accomplished what he will set out to do.

There are a few stumbles, I won't lie. We navigate a step that threatens to imbalance him but locked onto each other, my grip is strong, so he stays upright. Patrick doesn't get upset; we both know a stumble now will teach us what not to do later. We both know we will learn from our mistakes here, that after more practice, it will imprint in his memory. Before long, we sit on the bench, our chests heaving from the accomplishment and exertion. Patrick takes a deep inhale and stops, taking forever to exhale, to the point of worry. He blows his breath softly out and breathes again, and then I relax.

'I can smell them.'

I smile. 'Describe them.'

'There's lots. Elizabeth's lavender to my left. Roses behind. And another, I can't place coming from the right.'

'Gardenia's, I think they are called?'

He nods. 'That's right. That's exactly what they are.' He takes in a long breath and whispers. 'I can see them. The pink petals... the smell brings it back.'

We sit for a long time. I close my eyes, listen to what Patrick hears, see what the sounds show when the world turns off sight: there are still shadows that cross my eyelids, still reds and oranges. I wonder if Patrick can see shadows, or if everything is completely black, but I don't ask, I don't want to break the silence. Being around another person with no need to speak or entertain is comforting, so I just concentrate on the sound of the insects, the gentle rustle of the grass as it moves in the breeze, the song of the many birds coupled with the content sighs coming from my bench partner. Worry cannot exist here. A strong sense of what will be hovers in the air, tickles my skin and my nose. I know the feeling is temporary, somehow that makes it more special, makes me more eager to relish it because it has been a long time since I've experienced anything remotely like peace, anything at all similar to serenity or just even pleasantness I used to feel on my porch. Being with Patrick, away from my home, away from Ryan, devoid of any memories of Sara and my life, here, I allow it, allow something fragile to penetrate, something that words will ruin or having to explain. Bringing Patrick outside was to better his day, his life. Now that I'm sitting here, I understand I am gaining just as much from it as him.

Despite the calm I felt in the garden, my hands still shake when I turn the key in the lock in my house. Because I know something is about to happen. No matter what it is, there will be no going back. Either way, I will discover what direction this thing with Ryan is turning, what my next move should be, what way my life will go.

My sitting room gleams. The sound of music vibrates throughout the house. The smell of garlic and chicken wafts. I close the door with a thud, disappointed.

'Am I right? Is this the way you want it to go?' I say to Sara.

Ryan is humming. I smile then, with the memory of her spinning to that very song, in the same kitchen he sings in now.

About four years old. Her party dress, lifting up as she twirled, showing her bright yellow knickers and skinny pale legs and the most perfect squeezable bum I ever saw. Sara's laugh returns as if inside my ears, her child laugh, unguarded, unreserved. How is it possible for sound to carry through a memory? Yet it does.

And then there is another memory. After a hard day running around after a three-year-old, after a million tantrums, after I'd avoided fired toys and any other missiles she could find. After I'd exhausted her with trips to the park and playground, read countless stories, answered the many questions before bed, when only she would decide when it was time to give in and close her eyes and once chosen, would fall instantly. In those first precious seconds when the silence took over, when the stress would fizzle from my shoulders and face, and my breathing slowed, I would sit back and watch. All the tantrums forgotten, all the resentment, the frustration, the exhaustion, the need to flee would disappear. Free to admire, enjoy, love. She never looked as peaceful awake. Sara with her red hair splayed on the pillow, her pale skin against that fiery auburn made her cherub like, angelic even, and the sight of her was enough to make me want to take her in my arms and squeeze, to freeze the moment and never forget it. You do forget. You misplace every memory until one day something brings it back, a date on a calendar or a piece of music or a photo or even a smell and all at once the memory hits you and brings that time in your life back as if you were still living it.

Ryan's humming brought that memory back.

'OK then.' I nod. 'I get it. This is what you want. This is your sign. Maybe there are more things I can learn about you, more things he can remind me of. I just hope you know what you're doing.'

And with that, I walk into the kitchen.

II

Part Two

Chapter Twenty Nine

'It wasn't like I gave up cleaning the house,' I say, as he closes the back door.

'Well, I did... I mean, I didn't stop seeing it.'

I click on the kettle, wave a cup to check if he wants one. He nods, then washes his hands in the sink, drying them as he sits on a chair by the kitchen table. He stays silent, as if he knows I have more to say and is waiting for me to elaborate. Once the coffee's made, I hand him a steaming cup and sit opposite. As I speak, I keep watching the dancing swirls.

'It wasn't as if grief blinded me and I went around oblivious to the mess. I saw it. I wanted it. All the grease and dirt and overflowing ashtrays. The grimy windows, the dust on the table, the spiders' webs and the rotting smells from the toppling rubbish. I wished rats would come and nibble at me in my sleep, chew on my face like I dreamt about in my nightmares as a kid.'

I flick my eyes up at him, see understanding.

'Anything opposite to how it was when she was alive. Better to cover the couch with piles of crap than see the empty spot where she used to read. Better to cover the table with an inch worth of dust then see the ring where her favourite cup overheated and left its mark on the wood. Dirt is what I deserve.'

My voice betrays me by cracking. I look out the window.

'Better to only see the grime on the window instead of the swing out the back she would spend hours on as a child, where I would watch her brave going higher and higher, until the seat was nearly over the bar and I would have to grip the sink to stop from rushing out and warning her.'

My mouth gapes now with the refreshed memory. Sara is alive again there. A hand touches mine, warm and soft. I stare at that hand, Ryan's hand, horrified, yet I don't flinch. Instead of recoiling, instead of being disgusted enough to jerk my hand away, I wonder how long it has been since I felt skin on my skin, felt the warmth of human contact outside of my job. We stay that way, both sipping our coffee, with his hand on top of mine and it takes seeing his tears to realise I am crying too.

There is no actual conversation from either of us about ending his forced detox, no stating of our mutual intention takes place. Instead, I just stop locking the door. It should come as a surprise each day he stays, but it doesn't. An unspoken acceptance exists between us that we are in whatever this is together, even though nothing is forcing the union anymore. My intention to hurt Ryan has faded away. Instead of wanting to suffer, now I need him around.

Chapter Thirty

With Ryan loose, the house changes. Beds are made. Dishes cleaned and dried. Ashtrays emptied, bottles recycled. After a couple of days I contribute, finding I want to step up or at least match the tasks Ryan is setting, even though he never announces he's fixing the missing slat on the shed, or cleaning the windows.

The first morning, I take up a sponge and scrub the bathroom, my movement slow, my energy reluctant but as the hours pass and a gleam forms on the tiles, when the grime that rimmed the sink and the bathtub and every surface is replaced with clean lines, or sparkling surfaces, I move faster, wanting more, remembering what it feels like to do this when life was still normal, remembering what it felt like to sit back and look at what I'd done with satisfaction.

Afterwards, each time I walk into the bathroom, a thrill runs up and along my skin because I am taking back control, I am getting my head and my life in order, and without realising I missed that, I see I need it now.

We don't talk. I appreciate that about him; how he's not trying to fix what happened with words. Whatever he says, whatever excuses he concocts, won't bring Sara back and could break this fragile state we've found ourselves in. There is a constant busy determination emanating from Ryan, an infectious energy that at first, I have to force into action, but after a few days, I find easier to break into.

There is a cleansing in cleaning I forgot. At work, I do it without thought, viewing it as a task, as a necessity of the role. What I said to Ryan in the kitchen was true, keeping the place dirty was punishment. Denying myself the satisfaction of fixing, of cleaning, of completing menial tasks. Denying the soothing that comes from the simplicity of the action, from the concentration on one physical thing, from the distraction, meant I also cut off the pride that came after from standing back to see what I accomplished.

Now, whether it is a spotless living room or a decluttered wardrobe, or a pie wafting its scent throughout the house, it leaves me feeling better than sitting on the couch knocking back vodka and going through a pack of cigarettes. In a time in my life when nothing makes sense anymore, I discover a clean room helps. As I wipe counters clean, the fog shifts.

That said, I don't know what to do with this delicate, unexpected softening. Yet, when you have planned for your life to go one way and it surprises you by going another, and you find you like the way it's going, you lean into it.

Having someone in the house makes me want to cook. At first, out of necessity - his gaunt face and thin body still looks fragile enough to snap, urging me on to make something strengthening. As I stir and chop, I listen to the pleasant sound noise can make, from a distant bang from Ryan as he tinkers with who knows what outside. As I search and pull ingredients, recipes come back, of nourishing meals I gave to Sara when she was sick or recovering, ones I'd learned while she went through withdrawal, when I'd wanted to comfort without making her nauseous, finding foods to entice her to eat. Back then, I learnt heroin dulls the taste buds, so I worked out what helped; salty broths were easier to digest, giving her digestive system time to get used to regular meals again. Now it is ideal for Ryan. Ideal for me too. Slowly, our appetite returns.

As I collect dirty clothes, I stop at his bedroom door. Ryan sits hunched over, cross-legged on the floor, writing. It isn't the gesture that halts me, or the fact he is writing, even though I wonder how he got the book. The sight of him makes me nearly drop the dirty sheets on the floor. It is as if I've witnessed a person reverse time. Ryan is younger looking. The hair that has grown is shiny, his face clean. Regular meals have rounded his features only slightly, he is still achingly thin, but he looks healthier. A glint of the athlete Sara fell for peaks through.

'Where did you get that?'

He startles. Looks up sheepishly.

'Sorry. Hope you don't mind. I found it when I was cleaning.'

His face falls, as if worried.

'It was empty.'

He flicks through the pages, proving his point.

'If someone used it, I wouldn't touch it. I needed to get my thoughts down. Things I don't want to forget.'

He points at his head.

'For too long, I tried.'

He scratches at his wrist, his fingers running up his forearm, rubbing the track marks back and forth.

'I relapsed, to erase what happened. It never took the pain away, not fully. Made it worse. No matter how I tried to switch it off, all I could see was her face everywhere, her scared face knowing what he was going to do.'

A flash of anger comes hurtling back. *Good. I hope she haunts you.*

I rush to the kitchen, needing to get away and stuff the bed sheets into the drum. Ryan doesn't get the hint, following me in. He stands with his back to the counter, leaning against it. My hands shake as I pour the washing powder into the drawer. I slam the door of the drum but it doesn't have the effect of shutting him out. Ryan is getting ready to say something. When I turn around, he is holding the open journal in his hands, like an offering.

'I thought remembering would only bring the pain, but the good times are coming back. Could I read the passages to you, if it's not too hard to hear?'

My words come out harsher than I intend.

'Like what?'

He puts the journal down on the table, rubbing his hands on the thighs of his jeans.

'Sorry, it was a stupid idea. It will only bring up too much.'

'Read it.'

He picks up the jotter again, his eyes so hopeful my stomach churns.

'Are you sure?'

'I said to, didn't I?'

I plonk on the chair, acting annoyed but really, it's to steady my legs. Afraid my catching breath will betray me, alert him to how much I want to listen, then out of spite he won't speak, won't share. I tuck my shaking hands under my thighs and wait for him to tell me something about Sara.

'I worked on this one last night, so the writing might still be rough. Anyways.'

He flicks to the start of the book. Takes a breath and reads.

'Sara makes a heavy day lighter. Seeing her gets me through. Although, it's more than that. Before, I hadn't liked my life, not really, even though I'd never said those words, never told anyone. Something was always off, something was always unbalanced. Forever searching for this missing thing that was impossible to find because I didn't know what the hell I was looking for. Back then, before her, I hadn't known how lonely I was, how unsettled. With her, I understand love, I get there isn't a need to change for anyone. I don't need to win for Sara. She couldn't care less what happens in a game as long as I'm safe. I can lose matches. I can miss goals and she'll still love me. That's a new one. All my life, I believed I had to prove myself to everyone: my teachers, my friends, my parents, especially my parents. Like I needed to show them they were right for allowing me to be born, like I hadn't wasted the opportunity. And then I met Sara on that pitch and the first words out of her mouth wasn't a question, wasn't her asking anything of me, or from me. It was a statement. She wiped away my blood and then laid her hand on mine and said, full sure like, as if she knew, as if she understood everything I held inside, like she held secret, insider knowledge, and said, "it doesn't matter what they all think. You don't owe them anything. You're going to get up and finish the game and after that, later, you are going to find me and we'll talk." And the thing was, even though I'd just met her, I believed her more than I believed anyone. In those few sentences I knew she got me, that she wasn't just talking about the bloody nose, she got what it took for me to walk out in front of a new school, in a new team, and she was right, talking to her made everything all right. Everything that comes out of her mouth is the truth. That is Sara.'

I gulp, unable to say a word.

He lays the book on the table, then closes it, running a finger along the edge of the cover. I place a hand on the book, and another on my heart and then stand and run for the door, not wanting any words to ruin the last ones I still hold in my head, wanting to run over them all night, to fall asleep with them, to think of only Sara.

Chapter Thirty One

I may have softened with Ryan, but that is not the case with Oliver. Crossing the road, I hold a thick padded envelope to my chest. With my other hand, I straighten my wig, a brown expensive concoction that you would never believe is fake. The make up on my skin is heavy with layers. As his wife opens her car door, I hand her the envelope. She takes it, then looks up, searching my face, confused that there is no recognition there.

'If I were you, I'd want to know before the tabloids break the story,' I say before turning, before walking away.

There will be no mistaking the man in the film. Or on the other ten clips I included. There was no way I was going to leave it to the one occasion. Once I had a grasp on his infidelity, it didn't take me long to follow the woman to her place of work. Turned out to be quite the scandal. Oliver seemed to get his kicks from sleeping with the powers that be, a judge who sat in front of him many times, for some high-profile cases. Quite the scandal, one sure to cause uproar. In one recording, he says, 'we only have an hour. Darla's only getting laser.'

How humiliating. There his wife is, tidying herself up for her husband while he screws another woman. In another he is holding court documents, while his lover carries a briefcase too. The papers will run with that one, of course.

As I walk away, I feel sorry for the wife. There is no joy taken from her pain. Caught in the massacre, for this is the only way I can get to the man I want to hurt.

A shiver of excitement runs up my arms as I imagine how Oliver will react. His disgrace fills me with more joy than I can put into words. So self-assured always, one of those guys who seems to land standing whatever the obstacle appears before him. Who went to the excellent schools, born into money, had all the connections to always believe he would make it. No, Oliver never doubted his success. Never had a day's trouble in his life. With all his affluence, I don't understand why he would choose to represent the scummiest of people. The company you keep rubs off on you and Oliver walked with the dregs of the earth. That tells me enough about his character. There is no joy in hurting his wife, but there is plenty in imagining how I have demolished the walls to his world. Worth the early mornings staking him out, the late nights trailing the other woman. Even before I see his face across the front pages of the papers, vengeance has been better than I could even imagine. The payoff I'd hoped for with Ryan has come from Oliver. Instead of satiating my need for retribution, it increases. This is only the start. Any pain I can use to destroy Oliver's life, or any of the others, I will take. So far, this is all I've found. Never mind. Patience is my best attribute. In a long queue, when everyone around is fidgety and about to freak out, I'll offer for them to go ahead. Or if I'm sat on a train or in an airport and they announce a delay, I'll just take out a book and knuckle down, happy to have more time to read. Queues never bother me. Time passing doesn't send me into panic, not in the past, anyway. I used to say, before my world upended, that everything happens at exactly the right time. This was my time with Oliver. It was worth the wait.

Next.

Chapter Thirty Two

A piece of notebook paper waits for me on the table by the door.

The first time I woke here, when you stood over me, I thought you were Sara, come to take me with her. When the drugs left my bloodstream, left my brain, I saw it wasn't her, that it was you, I didn't fight it. Even if I'd wanted to, there's no fight left. I couldn't do it anymore. I couldn't live that way for even one more day, but I couldn't quit it either. You took the excuse away. Saved my life, no exaggeration. You know what my plan was that night, I don't need to go on about it. You know there was no coming back for me. Taking me to your house, to Sara's house, took my choice away, which was exactly what I needed. As I sat in the corner, I kept wondering what I could do to thank you. When you left the door open and I saw the kitchen, I thought, well that's one thing I can do, I can clean. Later, when I saw the jotter, I remembered Sara scribbling in one. I thought, well that's something more, maybe I could give you memories? Of times you wouldn't have been there. I can give you what I knew about Sara.

I pick up the note and follow the noise. He is on a ladder, replacing a light. I wave the note in his face.

'You think I didn't know my daughter?'

He steps off the ladder, draws in a breath, wipes at his face, bracing himself for a fight. When he looks at me, his eyes aren't angry, they don't match mine.

'Course you knew her. Just... there were times I was there when you weren't. Telling you about them might give you comfort. Like a gift, I suppose, cos like, I think that would help me. Maybe there are times you can tell me about, like when she was growing up?'

His hands flop to his sides, he tilts his head and for a moment I think he's going to cry. 'I need to remember her, not as the girl who was killed, not the way she left, because that's all I think about. I want to remember Sara as the girl we loved. Both of us, you and me, all we have left of her is her love.'

I stare at him a long time.

'Is that why you didn't run when you saw the door open?'

He shrugs, as if searching for an answer, as if that question was one he had never even contemplated.

'Where would I go that would help me more than here? You're hurting. I'm hurting. There's a reason you brought me here and whatever your plan is, I'm fine with that because I need to make amends.'

'Why haven't you asked to leave?'

He leans against the wall. 'Where would I go?'

'You have a home. Surely you have to pay rent?'

'Long gone, I'd say. The landlord threatened court. You saw what was in the house. All he would have to do was fill a box with the stuff and leave it outside. Do you want me to go? I will, if you do.'

I shake my head.

'I don't want to go back,' he says in a whisper.

He clears his throat. Talks normal.

'Too many triggers. The friends calling who aren't really friends, just people who use together. Here, I'm getting stronger. Each day I'm more able to cope. Not easier or anything like that, it's just... being here, I'm remembering Sara more.'

'Me too.'

He meets my eyes, nods slowly and something passes between us, an understanding that the only person in the world who can understand is facing the other, that we are both here in pain, trying to find a way to cope.

'I have to go to work now.'

'Would you like if I write more? If it hurts too much, I won't.'

I look up at the ceiling, as if Sara is looking down. When I answer, my voice sounds defeated almost.

'I would Ryan. I'd like it very much.'

Chapter Thirty Three

Through Ryan's eyes, I see my house. See the faded, chipped paint on the door, the dust lined up on the skirting boards, notice the general, dishevelled composition. It's funny how you become accustomed to dirt, the same way as a terrible marriage. If you start to accept it, it can build up and take over. Dirt won the battle when Sara died.

Having someone in the house brings other attributes to the surface. Manners for one, for we are polite to the point of falling over each other. Also, it's strange to hear noises coming from another room when I'm not occupying it. In the first few days of his roaming, the sounds put me on high alert, forgetting it was Ryan and going straight to something sinister like it being a robber or, more likely, someone we both knew. Scumbag has many unsavourable acquaintances. I won't admit it to Ryan, but once his stay is a confirmed actuality, I relax, feel safer. Although sleep still evades, my raging mind rests a little. My feminist peers would protest in horror, but I like having a man's presence in the house.

We set to work each morning, rising early, each of us lost to the task we have set. We don't announce what we are doing, neither of us says out loud, *today I'm going to repair the lock* or *I'm going to paint the kitchen*, but it is implied, expected even, that the other is doing *something*.

The paint is only magnolia, the most predictable shade you can paint a wall. I concentrate on the motion, the swish down of the brush, the bristles fanning out like a tongue on the upsweep. I lose myself to it; my only thoughts being where do I need to point the brush, or what places I missed. When I'm done, I step back and survey my accomplishment. The curtains are open; sunlight spews a prism on the wood floor. The air is fresh, the breeze from the open windows swallow the years of stale smoke and stagnant breath. It is as if the room talks to me then. *Welcome back.*

With Ryan's help, the house brightens. At first my work concentrates on the interior, I finish the kitchen Ryan started, scrubbing the oven, cleaning out presses and fridge, all the while working to the sound of a nail being hammered into wood, or the swish of windows being washed, or the thump of a footstep on the roof as he replaces tiles. The image of him catches my breath sometimes, as I watch him work from my window, his top either drenched in sweat or removed. There is nothing sexual in how I view Ryan, but I admire, or feel some kind of motherly pride when I see the chest muscles move and his taut stomach. He is bulking up finally, his energy blossoms.

When the inside is tidy, he sets to work on the porch. Mending bent slacks. Sanding. Reinforcing the seat with wood found in the shed. Then he tackles the fields. He has to hack at the weeds first. That alone takes days. Using an old rusting scythe, even though I offered to buy an electric one. I must admit, when he lifts the tool and whips it across, spraying green, I can't imagine the modern one being as satisfying. Picking up the mess will take days, but Ryan doesn't care. The only thing we have is time.

After that, he builds a bird table and butterfly box. The beauty of it all drags me back outside. In the morning, I sit sipping my coffee and feel the healing happen. I watch the birds, pecking at the seed laid out on the flat wood, drinking from the water at the curved top, marvelling at their colours, my heart doing a little leap if I catch sight of a goldfinch or a blue tit, being careful to stay quiet, so they don't notice me, so they will stay and let me just be around. I'm thankful for Ryan in those moments, because by reclaiming this bit of land he has helped me cope more than he knows. How can watching a bird give me a reason to get up? It has, though, somehow it has. It hasn't taken from the memory of Sara, but added to it, reminding me of happier times, taking me away from the harsh memories, sometimes only for seconds before the guilt of enjoying something after my child died gets too much. Until the next morning when the call of the porch is too loud to ignore, and I trail out there as if I'm pulled by an invisible rope. After I boil the water and stir my instant coffee, barely waiting to add the milk, filling the table with seed, then sighing on sitting, that seat more restful than any attempt of sleep in the bed and I rock, and sip and watch.

Ryan's presence stirs my own memories. Triggered by the tiniest of gestures, like when he bends to pick up a cup, it rockets me back to the day Sara fell over a dip in the gravel, gashing her knee. Ryan picked her up like she was made of fluff. Light and easily transferable. That memory wasn't the nicest, mingled with her pain. Every memory with someone is precious when there will never be any new ones.

The way he pours his tea reminds me of the stacked milkshakes they used to buy from the new café in town. Every Saturday night, that first year when Ryan became a permanent fixture in my house, they would take over my kitchen and make popcorn and homemade versions. Sara would get her face right in the shake and only emerge when her nose was covered in cream. I loved her for not caring. I loved Ryan for the way he looked at her while she goofed.

Most of all, having him around makes me understand I haven't just grieved for Sara. All this time I grieved for Ryan too. So much of a pair they became one, to the point of, if one appeared, I expected to see the other trailing behind. I have missed Ryan, there is no other explanation. Along the way, sadness turned to anger.

When it's clear I won't be going ahead with the original plan or kicking Ryan out either, the fact that he is sleeping on a mattress on the floor after working on my house twelve hours a day can't be ignored.

I set to work on the spare room, which had become a dumping ground for clothes or anything I wished to close the door on. Working steadily, the refreshed room is gifted to him as his, me offering it casually, mumbling, acting as if I don't care either way, just pointing in its direction.

'It's yours if you want it.'

He answers straightaway, two words.

'Thank you.'

His surprise is genuine. Even though we don't say anything else, something inside me dances at his smile, something I haven't felt since before Sara died. Something like joy.

Once a prison, the room I first moved Ryan to, the room I detoxed Sara in, becomes a reading den. Handmade book shelves run floor to ceiling against three of the walls, with a couch against the bare one. All the books I stacked in piles everywhere in the house, find a place to rest. Finally, there's a sanctuary inside the house, a place to get lost in, a place that for a few minutes I can delve into someone else's thoughts, into a character's life. The room is so different, no memory of Sara exists in the space. The door lock unscrewed.

For a long time, I believed the only way I could change the house was to cover it in clutter, to lose the memories to dirt. Now I see you can change it another way. The house comes alive with beauty and I realise, with a lick of paint, with a person humming in the next room, you can make a lonely house love again.

We fall into a routine. Each day, I pick up the jotter left on the side table by the front door, and go to work. Each day, Ryan tackles another part of my house or land. Every lunch break, I pour over his words.

She has a birthmark in the shape of the earth on her left ankle. I say to her, 'you have the whole world on your foot.'

...When she sleeps, her mouth drops open just an inch and on the third breath out, she whistles. I close her mouth every time, knowing her fear of spiders, knowing her terror if she thought there was any possibility one could drop from the ceiling and climb inside. It's a waste of time, though. After a few seconds, her mouth gapes again. I stay awake and watch her, scan the ceiling to make sure it's clear, and she's safe. It feels good to want to protect her, makes me feel useful. I watch her sleep and wonder what she is doing with a loser like me.

...Sara looks at people with no pretence. If she likes you, her face lights up, her eyes widen and her smile takes over. If she doesn't, everyone in the room knows it. I love that about her. Everyone knows where they stand with Sara. I live in a house where you have to pretend in order to survive. If you mention the truth, speak about what happens, there is trouble. Sara shows me the value of being true, of how that opens you up inside.

It becomes the favourite part of my day. Rereading his words, unlocking unknown memories of Sara, remembering her in ways I hadn't known, even though I wasn't there. Reading brings the essence of her back, strong enough to make me hug the jotter to my chest afterwards. Each evening I go home and place the jotter back down and discover another part of my house transformed. The bathroom cracked tile filled in. The grout cleaned. The leaking tap fixed.

...Sara's favourite flower are orchids. 'Not the fancy kind,' she says, 'not the kind you buy in the shop dyed bright green or something.' She says the special ones are the ones you come across, walking along a field or traipsing past someone's garden. She loves them because they are fighters, she says, because they have withstood unnatural weather and have still risen to the top.

'Each one is a victory,' she says.

The shape draws her to them, not the colours. She makes me hold one up close, right to my face, until the spikes nearly unleash its dust on my nose.

'That stuff stains,' I say.

She just laughs and calls me a wuss.

'People say roses are provocative, that they represent a woman's sexual organs, but the orchids do it way more. Look how the petals reach out, wide, suggestive as a pair of splayed legs, and the middle, the column it's called, peaks out like a gem, like a precious pearl. If that's not suggestive, I don't know what is. Even the spikes, the dust, I'm sure you could think of what that represents?'

She laughs at my scrunched-up nose.

'Take your mind from the gutter for a moment, Ryan,' she says. 'Look at the shape of the petals. Orchids are the perfect representation of a woman. Robust, yet holds onto its softness, beautiful. If I can be like an orchid, I'm happy. I could look at them all day. Did you know orchid seeds are the smallest in the world? As tiny as dust particles, easily blown away to the wind. If you break open a seed from a ripe orchid, if you see them drop it will look like a wisp, a puff of smoke, when really it is the life force, the babies of the plant.'

Since the journal, I find I don't linger in work, for I have a reason to leave. Between the visits, if there is a gap, I usually eat my lunch in the car. Since the jotter, I drive to the lake more, at first figuring if I needed to cry I could do it there in private. Now, I go there to dream after reading, to laugh, scream or cry. The place quietens me. Ryan's words give me back my girl for a few minutes. And then I turn on the ignition to go to the next patient.

This evening, the house is quiet as I enter. No clanking or cranking or shuffling or singing, no music plays in the kitchen. I can't say I know instantly that Ryan has left, but at some point, a low feeling in the pit of my stomach digs into me with the wonder whether he's gone, if he's had enough and ran. If he's relapsed. The house feels different, something feels wrong. The back of my neck prickles. I scan the living room. No sign. In his room, there is nothing or no one. The bathroom door is wide open and empty. In the kitchen, there is cutlery in the sink yet unwashed. There are crumbs scattered around the toaster. The back door is ajar.

Has he ran? Has he left me?

My chest is closing in, I take deep breaths, trying to claw back some air. Then I run for the open door.

Outside I see him, lying on his back on the concrete floor, his hand twisted at a funny angle. His eyes are closed but contorted, scrunched in pain.

'No.' I run to him; his skin has drained of all colour.

'Ryan, can you hear me?'

He doesn't move. Doesn't try to speak. I feel for a pulse. Low but there. He doesn't react to my voice or to my touch. He is breathing, but his pallor means there might be internal bleeding.

I speak softly at first.

'Ryan, can you hear me?'

I touch his forehead. It is cold, bringing memories bombing of Sara's skin. There is a light film of sweat. His lips are dry and cracked, not a good sign, he may have been here for hours, the toast remnants on the counter indicate he could be lying here since morning. The ladder laid out beside him suggests he fell. If it was from the top rung, a broken neck can't be ruled out. There is nothing for it, an ambulance has to come.

It isn't lost on me as I dial that I am doing the opposite of what I set out to do when I stalked him all those nights outside his house. Twice now I have purposely tried to save Ryan's life rather than end it. It doesn't make me feel better knowing that, and I don't care about my turnaround. All I want right now is to save him, to keep him with me. I speak out loud to the one being I believe in.

'Help me Sara. Please help him.'

Chapter Thirty Four

On the drive to the hospital, my heart beats fast enough to worry I will need a stretcher alongside Ryan. I hate the hospital. Too many terrible memories, too many fraught journeys to the same building, twice when Sara overdosed, once when all my nightmares came true, when I left stripped of motherhood.

Are you still a mother if you no longer have a child?

I drive with my foot pressed down on the accelerator.

It cannot happen again. I can't deal with another death, another life gone too soon.

This time, what I say is not to any God, not even to Sara. I speak to myself, understanding what I want for the first time in a long time.

'Don't take Ryan away. Let me keep him. Let him live.'

In the hospital, after parking, they make me wait. When I finally walk into his room, Ryan sits up in the bed, a bandage wrapped around his head. On seeing him, my hands go to my face and I can't hold it in any longer.

His smile is a multitude of moves, unsure, trying to keep it together, but as glad to see me as I am to see him.

I go to him then and I can't help it, I rush over, I lay my arms around him, needing to feel his aliveness, to prove he is here, to prove he survived. Careful not to touch his bandaged head, I hug him. When his arms wrap around me, when I feel his jaw lean on my shoulder, I hold back bloated tears.

'Are you OK?'

'Concussion. They don't think there's any bleeds, but they want to keep me in for observation, just in case.'

'You're lucky. You could have broken your neck.'

'Never believed in luck. Guardian angels, now maybe.'

I break away from him.

'You write about her in the present tense.'

He startles. When he registers I'm not angry, he smiles.

'In my memories, she's alive. On the page, I want to keep her that way.'

'Me too.'

'By writing her in the present, she never went away, never goes away.'

There is vulnerability in the way he looks at me. An earnestness that makes me want to stroke his face.

'It comes across that way. When I'm reading, it's like she's here again. Not exactly here, I mean, but somewhere, in a place where I can still see and feel her. It's a gift, Ryan. Each one opens a line, a root which branches out into a memory I'd pushed down. I thought there were no more memories left.'

He shifts in the bed.

'Can you share some? Maybe you could write them down too if you can't talk? The more I write, the more flood in.'

His eagerness is unsettling.

'It's one thing to read someone's memories but another to write down what's in your head.'

He nods, tries to cover the disappointment.

'It's just... it's helping me. Thought it might do the same for you. Although... I keep it to the good times. The dark times can stay gone. I don't want the day to come where all I have left is the nightmare ones.'

He runs his fingers along a crease on the bed sheet.

'Ginger, I know you probably didn't plan on getting me clean. You must hate me. But I don't think the bad memories are helping you. Since it happened, I couldn't think of nothing but Sara in pain. That's not what I want anymore. I can't think of Sara that way.'

Just before I leave, when I'm nearly at the door, he calls out. 'I get about the others, about me, but why is Tim on the wall?'

Every muscle clenches. I turn, seeing him, my body relaxes. There is no more need to hide. With the fright of the day, and now his direct question, I give up the secrecy.

'In fairness, I think Tim would have been on my wall even if Sara lived.'

Ryan laughs first, and I follow, until it turns into a proper belly laugh, my first one in years, the first since.

Alone again in an empty house, I stare at the list. Despite all our cleaning neither of us have touched the pictures.

All stare back.

Ryan's words in the hospital have the opposite of a calming effect. Since he suggested forgetting the bad memories, they are now all I can picture. Sara on the slab. The funeral. The trial. Just because I've softened with Ryan doesn't mean I can't still hold a grudge with the rest. Different quality images on the wall: Tim and Ryan are photo paper, cut out from group ones around the house. Scumbag's face is bigger than the rest, the image grainy, almost pixelated, the newspaper cutting of fragile quality, less prone to surviving being touched. It is the only one I could find that showed his true nature. After that one, he turned savvy, covering his face from the cameras. It is most like him, not the old pictures the tabloids used of his school yearbook where he looked innocent, looked nothing like the thug he turned into. His face stares down at me now.

Starting with Ryan was a mistake, when there were such strong feelings for him still. Reaching up, I lift Ryan's face away, he can come down, but the rest, stay up there, as a reminder I'm not finished. With Ryan I can remember who Sara was. The list will serve as a reminder of what they did.

Chapter Thirty Five

Sara sits on the couch, her small frame right in the middle. She pretends to watch TV although she's really staring out the window. Waiting, all the time waiting for a man who won't come. For Tim, who let her down again, who didn't show at the time he promised, who a few hours later will turn up swearing blind he got called into work, rather than tell her the truth, that he turned over or partied all night with some woman, then slept through his alarm.

As soon as she hears the car pull up, she forgets the hours in between. Forgets the tears she shed, the million questions asked, each one like a knife in my heart. Questions like, 'he's not coming, is he?' disappear like puffs of smoke, leaving no evidence on her face of ever happening. The words she left unsaid are worse. When she bites her nails or picks roughly at her skin, I hear, I see, I know she's thinking: *he doesn't love me.* Sometimes, when I catch her looking at me, her eyes hardened by pain, I can tell she wants to ask: *Why did you pick a man who would let me down?*

And then we hear the gravel scattering from his car and she scrambles to put her shoes on, grabbing her gear as if terrified that if she delays, if she keeps him waiting for more than a few seconds, he will leave. When the door opens, she runs to him without looking back, launching herself from the top step into his arms, wrapping around him like he is everything she's ever wanted, like her wishes have come true.

Tim is the wish granter. I am only ever the bearer of bad news and I don't blame her, for I would run to the person who let me stay up till whatever time I wanted, too. He is the guy who buys the ice cream and takes her on adventures and orders takeaway food; who can afford takeaway when he hasn't paid maintenance, who lets her pick out a toy every Saturday, on the one day he spends with her. All the hours he's not shown up are bribed away and erased. It takes willpower, but I never say a negative word about Tim in her company. Even when she comes home on Sunday, with dark circles under her eyes, grumpy from staying up half the night. I try to be the better person, try to be the one who doesn't taint her vision of him, knowing if he stays the same, one day that will come. When you truly love someone, you don't need to prove you're right. I feel guilty on the days I look forward to the realisation. Through gritted teeth, I will be the one who gives routine. I will be the steadfast one, the one who forces regularity and rules, the one that says no, who tucks her into bed at a reasonable time. I will be the rule maker she fights back against. For her benefit, I will be the one she hates.

Chapter Thirty Six

Once the MRI returns clear and the nausea disappears, they discharge Ryan. I don't tell him what it means to have him back, or how his return brings a giddiness to my heart. I'd forgotten he could do that. In the early years, his presence brought plenty to smile about.

Later, he joins me out on the porch. We sit not saying anything for a long time. It is me who breaks the silence. It is me who needs to.

'Decades I've sat here. Looking at this same view. I could have had a big life, went places, explored the world. All I ever wanted was to stay put. Stay in this house. Stay waiting when Tim left me, waiting for a man who was never going to return. Then I stayed and waited for Sara, for you, to see sense, to get better, to come home. Now what do I stay for? I don't want Tim anymore; Sara can never come back.'

I shift to see him.

'Is it you, Ryan? Am I staying for you? Am I waiting for you?'

He bites his lip as if to stop himself from showing emotion.

'Because I know already that will ruin me. You'll break my heart. You are going to relapse, or move on, or want to put Sara behind you. I wouldn't blame you.'

'I won't.'

'You should. If I could I would.'

He sighs. Looks ahead.

'I still won't.'

I slump in the chair.

'You will and you should and you shouldn't feel guilty about it. At all.'

I wipe roughly at my face, trying to find the words.

'I'm not saying this to leave you feeling responsible for what happens after you go. What I'm saying is about me. About how futile waiting is. Was.'

'What do you want to do, Lorna?'

I look at him more sharply than I intend. More in shock than anger. At his question, at the use of my actual name.

'I can't remember the last time anyone asked me that.'

'Is that what you want for your life, to just wait? For what, anyway? Are you waiting to die?'

'Maybe.' I take a beat. 'No, not yet. After, maybe.'

'After what?'

After I kill who I need to kill.

'After... I'm waiting for something, some kind of feeling I can't explain, some sign to know what to do next. Death? It doesn't scare me, the sooner the better. If I knew for sure it would bring me to Sara, I'd go now, right now. If it doesn't, if there's nothing after this, at least the pain will stop. Before I go, I have to finish something.'

Ryan turns, opens his mouth to speak, but I put a hand in the air to stop him.

'Not now.'

'It's got something to do with the list on your wall, hasn't it? Are you planning to get them back for what they, what we did?'

There is no shock in his features. No disgust present. In fact, there is a glint of excitement. Of compliance. If I tell him, can Ryan help me with my plan?

'Later,' I say. 'I'll explain it all when I get back.'

Chapter Thirty Seven

There isn't one person on this earth who can deny how beautiful Sara was on the night of her Debs. Altered, the green dress fitted her body like it was sprayed on. Sara kept smoothing the fabric down, unable to stop touching it.

The dress would have been fine left plain, the fabric and fit enough to take anyone's breath away. In the end, Sara settled on a smattering of gold beading working along the v of the neckline, ending near the rib cage. With gold, there's a danger of turning tacky so I worried the beading might ruin the dress. When she tried it on, the gold glimmered and reflected the highlights of gold in her own hair. Out of everyone, Ryan's reaction got me most. He looked at Sara like no one had ever looked at me, not even Tim. As if, he had waited for that night; like he'd been gifted, or couldn't quite believe he was there. He kept covering his mouth, as if trying to keep in the moment. And even though it is true that once they saw each other they only had eyes for the other, it was only me that noticed her eyes flicker, every so often to the door, or the slip of frown that would pull at the edges of her smile when she thought no one noticed. I nipped to the kitchen with the excuse to get another bottle, when really it was just to press redial, hissing down the phone, 'Tim, do not let her down tonight.'

As time went on, the fidgets increased. When the limo arrived, after she delayed as much as she could, looking for the clutch I'd watched her stuff down the settee, I followed her into the bathroom, where away from everyone she breathed in heaves. I hugged her, hushed her.

'You are going to have the best night of your life. Don't be sad.'

All gentle words, shushing and soothing, while I rubbed her back, until her rib cage ceased from expanding and her breaths stabilised. When she settled, we broke apart to face each other. There were no tears. I'll never forget the look she gave, never forget the heartbreak behind her made-up lips and eyes. Alone, she couldn't hide it any longer.

'He's not coming, is he?' she asked, her voice breaking.

'Probably delayed. Your dad will make it up to you.'

'How? How can it ever be made up?'

The way she said it dripped with accusation. Up until then, I brushed away all Tim's faults, seeing it as a pointless task to try and change him. That moment was the end of any love left for my ex husband. It was the beginning of my hate for Tim. All my instincts went to jumping to my defence, to ripping into what an awful father he was. That would only help me, not her.

'Ryan is out there and he loves you. He's the only man you need. You're lucky to have found love early.'

All that beauty drained, her soft features turned angular, the plump glossed lips straightened, the big green eyes reduced to slits.

'Look where love got you. Love made you miserable. The last person I want to end up like is you.'

She shoved my hands away. And then she was gone, out of the bathroom, with bag and Ryan in tow, she walked from the house without a goodbye. She climbed into the car and smiled at everyone but me, waved off by all the neighbours and friends.

My eyes stung from holding back the tears. I wanted to cry out, call her, run after the car, tell her I loved her, tell her she was wrong, that the right type of love never made you miserable, that I would never regret loving Tim because that relationship gave me the best type of love. Her love was worth wading through the worst kind.

None of that was what she needed, I understood. What was better for Sara was to let her get out the frustration by unleashing it on me. Better to offload than spend the night with it building and building until it exploded onto someone else.

After they drove off, I sat on the porch with the other guests, most happy to stay and finish off the wine and food. All buoyed up from seeing such youth, such beauty, their conversations floated by. While I pretended the cause of my distraction was from topping up, or refilling, when really, in my head I had stayed in the bathroom with her scathing words repeating what I feared she always thought.

Half an hour later as I stood in the kitchen washing glasses, tyres screeched along the gravel. I didn't hurry, hearing the sing song voices of inebriated guests filling him in on what he'd missed.

'Lorna,' he roared.

Rinsing a glass, I dried it slowly, then headed to the porch, depositing it on the table for anyone who needed it.

He stood in the middle of everyone, his hands flailing to his sides. His eyes held the tell-tale puffy look from sleep or drink or who knows what.

'They're telling me I missed her? Why didn't you get her to wait?'

I searched the sky and took a breath. When I spoke, my voice came out soft, placating a temperamental child.

'The Debs won't wait, even for you. She had to go. You knew this, I told you plenty what time she had to leave for.'

'You told me seven.'

'I told you it started at seven. I also told you everyone would meet for five as she had to leave for six to collect the others and get there on time.'

'She didn't have to collect the others, I could have drove her there.'

'They booked a limo to drop them at the hotel, why wouldn't she ride in it?'

'They could have picked her up last.'

Despite my calm, my voice came out an octave higher.

'Their houses are on the way. You knew this Tim, you knew the plan, she's only been talking about it every day for a year. Christ, even if you'd rang me back and suggested giving her a lift, I bet she would have stayed on. She waited as long as she could.'

He looked around at the other guests, as if hoping for sympathy, or someone to back him up. All avoided him, keeping their heads down, blocking their vision with a tipped glass or concentrating on eating a sandwich. The uncomfortable silence went unbroken until he spoke.

'You did this on purpose.'

I laughed then. 'I can assure you I didn't.'

It wasn't the time to argue or lay out the truth. It was time to save the situation. I checked my watch and ran into the kitchen grabbing the things I needed.

'Come on,' I said to him, as I passed.

'What?' He stepped back, a little unsteadily.

'If we go now, we can catch her. Cat, lock up for me?'

She nodded, lifted her glass in a toast. I apologised to the guests about rushing off, although I wasn't sorry, because now, I could give my daughter the one thing that would make her night. Cat would keep the place safe, would get everyone to leave and would still be sat on the porch no matter what time I arrived back, waiting to see how I got on.

Along slip roads I drove, avoiding the main, avoiding any that might have traffic in the Friday night rush. Tim spent the time on the phone, texting rapidly and except for one 'yes!' he never said a word. We got to the hotel at ten to seven. I stopped the car at the door and ran to one of the girls posing at the entrance with her date.

'Hi Mrs Thomas,' she said. Her name escaped me, it was something

Irish but I didn't have the concentration to summon it.

'Has Sara gone in?'

She scoured the crowd.

'Don't think so. I passed her when I turned onto High Road. She was in a limo with Ryan...'

A car horn beeped.

'Thanks,' I said, running back to the car. I jumped in.

'Get out so she'll see you. I'll park.'

With no thanks, Tim coiled out and slammed the door. I drove off to get parking, the adrenalin high enough I could hear my blood pulsing in my ears. In the mirror's reflection, Tim shoved his hands in the pockets of his jeans, uncomfortable to be standing in a crowd of eighteen-year-olds.

There wasn't a space anywhere. The car park circled the whole hotel, so I drove on planning to go around. At the side of the building, there was only enough space for one row of cars to park. Not one was empty. Out of view, my stomach churned and my hands trembled as they clung to the steering wheel, searching for a space. I needed to get out, to find a spot, so I could just see Sara's face when she spotted her father, to witness her expression change.

At the back, the car park was huge. Also full, with slot after slot taken. I did one whole round, with no luck. When I passed the entrance again, the crowd was too dense to pick anyone I recognised out. There were girls dressed like princesses on the road, preening and checking each other out. Razor rashed boys acting like men in their tux's and suits. The crowd its own life force, pumping with energy. Shrieks of joy at a noise level only teenagers can make, penetrated my open window. Cars beeping forced me to keep going. Finally, at the back of the hotel, one car reversed from the space, then stopped, blocking my entrance into the spot *and* the path in front. A girl in pink satin stepped out and stood in front of my car, hugging another girl who ran towards her. The car behind me almost rammed my bumper, trying to force me forward. The tears prickled. Ready to abandon the car, to leave it as it was, I climbed out. The man behind got out too.

'I need you to move.'

'I need me to move too but as you can see, I'm wedged.'

'We'll see about that,' The man said, his face taking on a purple tone. He stormed up to the girls.

'Move. I have to be in there.'

The girls stepped back, stunned.

A man in the car the girl had left threw open his door and pointed at the other man.

'What's your problem?'

I took a deep breath. *What was it with these men tonight?*

It felt like hours before I got everyone back in their cars and we moved on. As soon as I parked, I barely turned off the engine, leaving the keys in the ignition. I ran as fast as I could without my heart bursting, the spot had to be the furthest away in the whole car park. By then the crowd had reduced to a few stragglers; the late one's, the worse for wear ones trying to gulp back some air to sober them up. Tim stood where I'd left him smoking a cigarette, pacing up and down.

'She hasn't arrived?' I asked.

He took a long drag, then flicked the cigarette away, landing beside me.

'Been. Gone inside.'

The tears prickled but I wouldn't let him have it. 'Was she happy?'

'She was once I gave her five hundred euro and told her there'll be a hummer outside to bring her friends wherever they want after.'

I didn't ask if he told her I drove, or if she had looked for me. I didn't complain that the least he could have done was ask her to wait to say goodbye.

On the drive home, while I listened to Tim bragging to one of his friend's on the phone about his big gesture, I pictured the way one side of Sara's mouth curled inwards when her smile was real, and imagined being there to see it for the first time that night, as she stood in that green dress with the love of her life on one arm and her hero, the first man she loved, on the other.

'That bloody Tim,' I said, taking Cat's held out cigarette and sucking in as much tobacco as possible. I sat on the seat next to her, leaning my head on her shoulder.

'I told you not to marry a flake. This is what happens when you marry a flake.'

I groan. 'What was I thinking?'

She shrugged. 'You weren't. He was handsome. Still is, I'll give him that.'

I handed her back the cigarette. 'You think I was that shallow?'

She takes a puff. 'Not shallow. Horny.'

We laugh.

'Oh, Cat. No matter what happens you make me smile.'

She takes my hand. 'Isn't that what friends are for?'

I could do with her now. Laughter has left me long enough to forget what it feels like. The breath that follows hurts my chest, her loss fresh again. Little did I know sitting on the porch that night that two months later, in the same seat, she would tell me about her diagnosis, or, less than a year after, I would sit on this porch alone, trying and failing to keep it together as I waited for the car to bring me to my best friend's funeral.

'I miss you, Cat. Look after my girl up there.'

Tim's leaving lead Sara into a relationship early, made her desperate for love. Our break up changed the course of her life. It divided her opinions, made her split her views on what it was to love. Inspired her to make choices for love that killed her.

I can't yet go to the unforgivable thing. The thing that puts Tim on the list more than anything else. I could take the lies and the let downs, could ignore the times he was just not a great dad; those traits are not unusual in the scheme of life. There are plenty of shitty fathers. What he did was worse. What he did got her murdered.

Chapter Thirty Eight

At first, when Patrick's grip softens, I think he has stopped to figure out a particular sound. Only when his arm loosens, flops to the side, do I worry. Thinking he's on alert, I look around, trying to decipher the danger. For a second, I wait for him to speak. When I look at him, his face is drooping, the skin slack on one side, the mouth pulled down in a clown's exaggerated sad pose, the bottom lip making a dash for the jaw, the skin under the lid dangles away from the eyeball, revealing red blood vessels. Patrick clutches on to me with his arm that works, clings as if he is underwater, as if he is drowning. His words are useless; they come out only as incomprehensible sounds. Fear in his eyes. It must be terrifying not to see the reassurance from mine.

As time speeds up, the adrenalin and training kick in.

'Patrick, I know you're scared, but I promise I won't leave you. We are going to get you help at the hospital. What I need from you is to stay awake. I'm going to bring you to the car. Before you know it, we'll be there.'

What I don't promise is whether he will be OK. I keep my voice in soothing tones, knowing time now is precious, that every minute counts, that cooperation is key to stop neurological damage.

In the car, I strap him in, then pull away fast. While driving, I ring the hospital, telling the staff in a voice that isn't Lorna the mum, or Patrick's friend, but my carer's voice, that my client is showing signs of an ischemic attack, not wanting to say the word stroke, not wanting to alarm an already alarmed Patrick.

In the car, Patrick slumps in the chair and closes his eyes.

'No sleeping Patrick, try talking to me.'

The words come out like he's singing under water, bubbles of sound. His eyes widen with fright.

Keep saying his name. Anchor him to life, Lorna.

'What's your favourite song, Patrick? I know you are partial to a bit of Sinatra. Can you hum one for me?'

Patrick shakes his head. His hand flops in his lap with the movement. He closes his eyes again. I start humming a song I'm not even sure is Sinatra. Patrick opens his eyes.

'Please Patrick. It's important you don't give in. I know you want to sleep, but I need you to help me.'

And then a glorious sound expels, little more than a groan, but to me, it is the best symphony ever composed.

At the hospital, a team stands ready outside.

Once I know he is in the right hands, once they place him on a gurney and wheel him away, I make the phone calls to his family and then wait. I can't leave, even after they show up. It becomes vital for Patrick to live, as important as it was for Ryan to live. Patrick cannot die. I sit on a plastic chair with Patrick's outcome hanging, balancing literally between life and death. Holding back tears, trying to pretend I never walked down these halls when Sara was alive. Not wanting to remember the day I saw Sara for the last time.

There were many kind nurses when Sara overdosed. Some didn't highlight my failure, some didn't judge.

Being here, I keep my head down. I do not want for them to recognise me. I do not want the awkward conversations, especially when they might tell me I have lost another person I love. The years have passed though, and I am lucky this night. The doctor is young, and unaware of my history with the hospital. Apart from a wave from a nurse who held my hand one time, she leaves me be, which pricks tears in my eyes, for the respect she always gave.

Hours later, when Patrick stabilises, his son places a hand on my shoulder, then thanks me, assuring me I can go, that they will keep me informed, that I've done all I can.

All the major occurrences in my life crept up on me, all the ones that changed my life in an instant. Every one of the life altering, never coming back from situations: the day I realised I was in love with Tim, the day I saw the pregnancy indicator on the stick, the morning Tim's side of the bed was empty and I knew that time he had gone for good, the moment Sara met Ryan, the first night I was called to the hospital after Sara overdosed, and the last day, the nonreturnable day, when I learnt my girl was no more. And then there was this night. When I thought being in the hospital was enough of a life-changing ordeal. With no idea of what was about to happen.

Chapter Thirty Nine

A letter lies propped up against the kettle. I smile at Ryan's logic - knowing after my shift I will go straight for a tea or coffee. Thinking nothing of it, I lob it on the table and continue. Nothing but tea will do, despite the hour of the night. It has been a long, tough day, one I want to forget.

Only after I take the first glorious sip, am I drawn to the envelope. The handwriting isn't familiar. There is no address, so it can't be a bill. Just my name scrawled in black ink, delivered by hand. It isn't a letter, there is no written or typed note. Inside, all it contains is a single newspaper clipping. As soon as I see his face on the page, I dump my cup on the table. The headline reads: 'Out in less than a year.'

He is out.

Concern for Patrick disappears; there is nothing else I can do, but this, this I can change, this I can have a say over, this outcome can have my stamp. I go straight to my room and pull out my bag and strip off my clothes, selecting the items methodically, running through what I will need. Black trousers and top, hair tied back and covered with a black cap, hiding the red with the wig, taking away any noticeable aspect that someone can observe at traffic lights or in passing. I run through what needs to go in the bag, what I will do. I am incredibly calm, too calm. From practice I know what to do, no thought needed. I made my mistakes with Ryan.

There will be no moving Scumbag to my house, no split decisions. The exhausted Lorna that sat on the table five minutes before has disappeared; as if I've stepped out of my body and someone else has taken over. The bad side has taken control and this time even my good side agrees, staying silent. There is no delay, for I made this decision a long time ago.

After the trial, I stopped watching the news or buying papers, knowing how wrong the news can be, how one sided, so I had no way of knowing he was out. There is no choice. If the courts can't keep people safe, I will. I'll rid him from the other girls, I'll take him off the streets, I'll destroy him and be the fucking superhero. After my pleas in the hospital earlier for Patrick to live, after my hope that life would win, death will come tonight after all.

Chapter Forty

One morning, in the middle of the trial, Nick Barratt, the local guard, once a very close friend, once more than a close friend, stood in my kitchen. He fiddled with the top of the chair, taking forever to talk.

'Come on Nick, we both know you're not here for my coffee. Say what you came here to say.'

'Don't attend, Lorna. Not today. Once the image of how a person suffered enters... once they describe it you'll never be the same. It'll be as if it's happening to her that minute. It'll torture you. Once they lay it out it'll be impossible to forget.'

'It is all impossible to forget.'

Nick shook his head, looked at me straight on in the way he'd learnt to win my attention. Just that look said what he didn't say: he had been in this situation many times; he had stood in numerous other kitchens with the deceased's family. Nick understood more than anyone else.

'No, you won't understand until it's too late. What happened to her will take over. The good times will disappear. After you hear what they have to say, it'll only leave you with the images of what Sara went through.'

'You think staying ignorant will help me, Nick? I have to go. There's no choice in it. I need every detail. I need to know every bit of her suffering. I need to learn every minute of the last few hours of her life.'

'Lorna, their words will be cold. They'll act clinical when they're discussing injuries, too clinical to the point you'll want to jump up and throttle one of them. You'll want to scream at them that who they are talking about is your daughter, that she was a person and she was loved. They'll call out what he did as if it is no more than a shopping list. You won't be able to erase it. You'll feel what happened to Sara as if the pain is being inflicted on your body. You'll ask yourself over and over what you should have done to stop it.'

'You think I don't do that anyway?'

He pursed his lips.

'Come on, I know you do Lorna. All our life I've known you. That's normal, a part of grieving. I'm telling you, this will be... irreversible.'

I tapped the side of my temple. 'This never stops. I saw some of the injuries, I know my daughter was given a traumatic death. But do you know what else I know?'

He shook his head.

'That they have sat in that courtroom and talked about my daughter as the victim. They have read out facts as if she is not a real person, just someone a crime happened to.'

I held up the newspaper.

'They talk about my daughter as if she was a low life. Like she is the scum that forms on a decaying pond. Less than bacteria, less than germs. *He* is the scum. He is the problem. Why is it her face that appears on every paper? Why weren't we shown him drugged up? Why isn't he the one hounded with stories of his background? Because they protect the living.'

I throw the paper down.

'No matter what is said today, I will be the reminder to everyone that she was loved. Is loved. Sara wasn't just a nobody, do you understand? They have insinuated she deserved it. Like she was less of a person. Like she played a part in her death. Sara can't be in that courtroom, can't stick up for herself, he made sure of that. My daughter needs me to stick up for her. No matter how hard it is to hear. No matter how many nightmares come after or how much it will haunt me, I will sit in that courtroom and show the world I've shown up, that someone always showed up for her.'

He nodded, his shoulders slumped with acceptance. 'Would it be all right if I walked you in?'

Nick Barrett. A man that held much promise, once. I wished the timing had been better between us. One day I had felt something. One day when I had wanted a life, we had dreamt of one together. That day was gone.

Nick was right though.

They read out the facts in hard sentences. During the description of the attack, each word brought pain. The nouns I knew, but each verb, every adjective, destroyed me.

He dissolved Rohypnol and injected her with enough to keep her docile, but not enough to numb pain. He kept her for three days, raping her, using her skin as an ashtray. The expert listed her injuries off rapidly: broken ribs, broken nose, unattached jawbone, ripped earlobe, broken fingers, dislodged hipbone, bruising to the back, neck, knees, shins, feet. Tears in the vagina and anus. Burnt eyelashes and hair. Clumps missing in part of the scalp. The estimated time of death was only an hour before she was found.

No part of Sara went untouched. As they read out that list, I stared at the man responsible, the one they said did it and he was a nobody. A spotty, lanky, scummy fucker who, left alone in a room with, I could knock out in a second. A half man, half boy of twenty who had turned an apartment into a den. A rich boy who could have been anything, who had the best start in life, went to the best schools, wasn't ever left wanting. Instead of doing good with it, he took his mammy and daddy's money and used it to set himself up dealing, until he got hooked on the gear himself.

Once arrested, mammy and daddy paid for bail, shipped him off to rehab and made sure by the time of the trial a year later he acted like a model citizen. The same guy who each day dressed in a different Armani suit, who used his parents' money to hire the best defence barrister, Oliver McAllister, the guy seen in all the high-profile cases that made the headlines, defending the murderers and most shocking, achieving the impossible by finding the loopholes, finding the argument that got them off.

This time he proved to be worth his weight in gold, as he systematically ripped Sara's reputation apart, implying the rape hadn't happened, that she willingly had sex, that in a drugged state she had burnt herself and tore out her own hair and threw herself around the place, breaking her nose and jaw and the majority of bones in her body. They argued that it couldn't be a murder case because she had died of natural causes. The official cause of death was heart failure.

They rooted out footage of Sara, dirty and dishevelled, begging on the street. Played a video of her drugged and talking nonsense, painting the picture of a woman almost deserving the death she received. The green in her eyes swallowed by the black. Smoking a cigarette, her head bobbing, loose, flopping onto one side of her neck to the other, the cigarette burning down, close to her fingers.

What they were trying to do, hurt. Making a point that when she took drugs, she had the capacity to not know what she was doing, or what she was holding; that she could easily burn herself. Watching that video I felt the guilt, the terrible guilt that I couldn't help her, that no matter how much I searched, no matter how many streets I'd walked down, no matter how many times I'd forced her in a room and made her go into withdrawal, I couldn't save her in the end. I dabbed at my face for I'd been warned the courtroom wasn't the place for tears, then sat straighter, made my face blank because if I couldn't keep composed they would have to stop, or they would make me leave and that I couldn't do, I would stay with Sara until the end, no matter how hard it was to see or hear, I would represent, I would show that despite what they said, despite the picture they painted, Sara was a cherished daughter, and no matter what way they tried to spin it, she didn't deserve her death.

They paused the image when her head slopped back in sleep, when the hidden person with the camera took the cigarette from her without her notice, making their point.

It took every bit of composure to stop from walking over to the large screen and running my fingers along her face. I wanted to hush her, tell her everything would turn around, that even if they ripped her apart in this courtroom, later I would find a way to avenge her.

In that moment, all I wanted was to claw back time, do everything differently. To move her away. To leave Carraigshill and Tim. To never meet Ryan.

After the video stopped, Scumbag's father gripped his wife's hand. I knew what that squeeze meant, how he was telling her they had found the solution. Shown to discredit her, to attack her credibility, to depict how damaged she already was. All I saw was a girl needing help. It was too late. I failed her. Tim failed her. Seeing her alive, hearing what Scumbag had done, how she had suffered, my pain hardened and turned. In the courtroom he took away any power she had as a victim by implying she deserved it; that she wasn't a good person, that she had played a role in her own death. My hate for him, for his parents, for the barrister tightened in my belly. It took all my strength not to react.

After the verdict, I wish I had.

If I'd known how the case would go, I would have launched across the room to claw at him. I would have gouged his eyes out. Back then, I still had hope in justice, still believed in the judicial system. Still believed there was a chance I could find forgiveness.

Scumbag slaughtered her twice. First in his apartment, second in that courtroom. They all did. Oliver, the judge, the papers reporting in it after, they all took part. He hurt her, but after that the others ripped her apart.

They depicted him as an honour student, caught in the trap of meth and harder drugs, delirious enough that he couldn't recall ever meeting Sara. Never mind that he was a known drug dealer supplying the whole area. Never mind that she had been clean for months before he took her, or how his neighbour testified he heard her begging for hours the night she died. Never mind the guards who found her, who wrote in their statement she had been cable tied to a filthy bed with her wrists covered in blood, where she had twisted and fought to free herself.

From him there was no remorse. At first Scumbag denied all responsibility. When the DNA proved his skin was under Sara's fingernails, how his semen was found inside and over her, they pivoted. On the day he was due to take the stand, they changed his plea to not guilty by reason of insanity. His cross examination was a joke. All he repeated was he didn't remember anything. My moment to find out anything disintegrated. And I didn't believe a word.

Oliver was clever. He found a way for Scumbag to admit guilt while still being classed as not guilty. There was too much evidence, so he changed tact and decided if Scumbag would go down, he would land with an easier thud. After the things already said about my daughter, they took away the one chance I had to discover what happened by claiming he couldn't remember.

They flew an expert from America to speak of his psychosis, a psychiatrist and lecturer from Harvard about the break formed in Scumbag's brain from continuous meth use. About how meth affects the same neurotransmitter involved with schizophrenia. He spoke of delusional thoughts, aggressive behaviour, of seeing things that weren't there. The consultant was worth the price to fly over. Assured, well spoken and convincing, the man almost had me feeling sorry for Scumbag.

If he did suffer from some temporary insanity, if he had worked on healing, I could understand. If he had stood in that courtroom and said he was sorry, I could have maybe even forgiven him. Not once did Scumbag look directly at me though, not once did he show any signs of remorse and I checked often, every couple of seconds. Sometimes, when Oliver was talking to his father, before the judge entered, Scumbag would lean his head in my direction, not making eye contact, looking at the table, but he would smirk. When someone is staring at you even if you aren't looking directly at them, you can feel their gaze. That smirk was for me.

Those smirks ignited my plan for revenge.

All I got at the trial was the how's.

How he ended up like he did.

How he hurt her.

What I needed was the why.

A guy like him deserves to die. In fact, erasing him from civilisation will be heroic. What got me through the rest of the trial was the many ways I could kill him: smuggling a gun into the courtroom and pulling the trigger, following him into the bathroom and throttling him with his own tie, grinding glass and putting it in the water jug, or breaking into his house and injecting him with enough drugs to wipe out twenty people, where I would stand over and smirk back as he convulsed and choked on his own vomit. With him, my only regret will be how quick he'll die.

People always talk about time when they speak about death. About time being a healer. I'll tell you now, time heals nothing. Loss doesn't leave you. The only thing it leaves is shock. The pain stays, grips into you. Sometimes you're fooled; when you open your eyes to a bright day and you go to smile, go to feel grateful and then it floods in, the memories infiltrate your skin as much as the sunlight, burning at your treachery for forgetting for even a half of a second, for the time it takes to flicker a crusty eye, for feeling anything other than empty. Because you relinquished all gratitude on the day they informed you that you lost everything. The loss is everywhere, in the moments when you wake, in your nightmares, in the silence of long minutes that drag and multiply, joining into hours, becoming days and nights. There is no point to anything. There is no joy. No enthusiasm. No positivity. Those emotions are gone. You stay alive so one day you will get to them, one day you will hurt them.

One day you will get revenge.

Chapter Forty One

Bringing Ryan home was a mistake. With him I chickened out, hesitated. A total rookie error. Starting with the one I had the most feelings for, who out of everyone was the person I would hesitate with. After that, I let the memories flood in, humanised him by remembering how sweet he could be. Things changed between us and I'm glad.

Ryan would have only been a taster kill. His death was more to see how it felt, to see where it could go wrong. He was an easier target: no parents looking out for him, his body skinny and wasted, not locked away, not protected, drugged up he wouldn't fight.

What I hadn't counted on was how he would grip into me, how the memories he shared with Sara evolved into the only words I needed each day. Finally, there was someone to talk to about her, who wouldn't change the subject or clam up. Who wanted to speak about Sara. Who missed her. That grieved as much. Anyway, there is nothing worse I can do to Ryan than let him live. He suffers as much as I suffer; the suffering is far worse than any pain I inflict.

When I made the hit list, I thought I needed courage to start with the small ones, to see if I could even hurt someone, but that was a stupid idea. Why was I wasting my time with druggie boyfriends or sucky fathers, or dodgy barristers when I could go straight to the big man, the main guy first, the one I really wanted to hurt? With Ryan or Tim, there was always going to be hesitation, too many feelings, too many memories holding me back. Oliver was on it for a little satisfaction, he was never going to die.

The truth is, I created the list because I couldn't get to the one I wanted to kill.

Scumbag has none of my loyalty, none of the memories I have of Ryan and Tim. All I know of him are facts, the despicable things his personality was willing to go and do, or how far he pushed the limits of human existence and, despite the excellent job the lawyer accomplished by discrediting my daughter, I know the truth.

With Scumbag, I will not hesitate.

A force pushes through my body, so I don't walk but glide. I must be moving, putting one foot in front of the other, but I feel nothing, numb to the action of muscles, fear, hesitation. All I see is his face, his smiling smirk surrounded by the words: Out in less than a year.

In the car, I drive on autopilot, not too fast to be stopped for speeding. Tonight, there will be no mistakes. No one will look at my car and sense danger. No one will look at me and know any better. Turning the steering wheel, the newspaper clipping flaps on the dash from the open window. Caught on replay, my mind loops. They reduced the sentence without telling me. Not even Nick, who kept me informed every step of the way, let me know, although after the way I treated the man after Sara died, I don't blame him for avoiding knocking at my door with more bad news.

After the farce of the trial, I hadn't held much hope in the sentencing. McAllister portrayed Scumbag as a vulnerable man who had fought his demons and come out the other side, who slept with a girl lost in her addiction who tragically died while in his company. He even suggested Sara bought him the drugs. Witnesses stated they saw her getting into his car after hanging around the docks, an area known for scoring. They listed the ways he tried to make amends, depicting him as the model citizen, so the sentence came as no surprise. Not guilty by reason of insanity sent him to a cushy mental health unit to be evaluated instead of the prison cell he deserved.

He got years, though.

I laugh in a voice that doesn't sound like mine, that doesn't sound completely sane. Life is so messed up. Him beating the system will make all my dreams come true.

As distracted as I might be, I make sure not to drive past the front of his house, which is usually well lit, with a big open spaced drive. Instead, I drive the back roads. Not one car passes along the blackened, bumpy lanes.

I stop fifty feet away. I lift my hand in front of me. It is still. No shake at all. A complete straight line.

Chapter Forty Two

How many times have I sat in this spot? Enough times to know which bedroom is his, to have learnt the habits of the family. The father, a lean, well groomed, pompous man whose own dealings are of dubious credibility. Legal though; I checked for any flaws in his company. Usually awake until the early hours, with one light on if he is on his own, or more in company. He always retreats to the left of the house, that wing reserved for him. As far as I can tell, Scumbag never steps foot in his father's quarters at night. The mother stays upstairs in the middle of the house; the light turning off early, never past eleven.

Before being sentenced, Scumbag lived in the ground floor to the right of the house. Now that he is out, I can't see any reason for that to change. It is more an extension than the ground floor, slightly separate from the house, like a granny flat lobbed on the side, with its own roof and exit. From my many visits, I know the door opens out, with only a small gap at the back between the wall and the bush. The same bush I will hide behind soon. The space between the two is only a couple of feet wide, perfect for hiding a sneaky smoke or skinning up.

Windows light in all the correct places, the usual night time positions of the family are taking place. Satisfied, I drive on, parking the car a mile up the lane by a forest car park, so they won't hear the wheels scrambling on the gravel, or on the off chance a late night stroller will identify my car later. This time I won't need the car; they'll be no saving this man. I turn off the engine, grab my bag, then creep back to my spot.

From trial and error, I discovered the best gaps in the bush on my previous night visits. Now, I go straight to the slight mound on one part of the ground and sit, eye level with a break in the shrubbery, knowing if he pops out, he won't see me.

There is a light on, the faint beat of a song travels my way. This pleases me, for now I'm sure he is in there. It could have happened; he might have been out partying. He could celebrate his release with loads of people inside the house. Although I doubt it, his parents are too careful for that, too press savvy. Instead, they will keep him close, keep him safe until the press dies down. In all the time I watched the house, his side had very few visitors. Any other person I might have felt sorry for, being lonely up on his separate side, with no friends night after night. Sympathy for him is non-existent. All I care about is how it plays to my advantage. Like now, little do his parents know that keeping him near them means I know where he is, know where to find him. I can't be sure he is alone or has company and the repetitive beat brings on a tiredness in rapid ferocity. It has been a long night, and it is going to get even longer. All I have to do is wait. Now that I am here, it won't matter if I close my eyes, it will be of benefit even, as it is better to strike when the house sleeps. I'm a light sleeper; if he even coughs, I'll hear him. I have all night. Moving my bag to rest my head on it, I lay on my side and stroke it like a cat, the only thing that can give me comfort now.

Chapter Forty Three

A vibration wakes me. I answer my phone on the first ring, not wanting to alert anyone. I sprint up the lane before I say anything.

'Hello?'

'Lorna?' Patrick's son croaks.

My stomach contracts.

'Please, no.'

There is silence except for breathing, ragged and out of control. I can hear the tears laced in them.

'I'm sorry. Sorry for sending you away. We thought he was going to be all right.'

I harden, feel the shell turn to steel.

'What happened?'

'They said it was a massive aneurysm, they swear he wouldn't have felt anything, that he wouldn't have suffered.'

There is a burst of sobs from the other side of the line. My heart aches from hearing his pain.

Patrick, the only person that gave me a reason to smile after Sara died, is gone. He fought to live with his blindness, to learn. A good man. And now he is gone.

'Are they lying Lorna? Are they telling us what they want us to hear? Did he suffer?'

I wipe at my eyes. This answer I know.

'No, James. Your dad wouldn't have suffered. He would have died within seconds.'

What he wants from me is reassurance. I don't go into medical terms, don't go into the accusations like, *you should have left me be there.* It doesn't matter. If I stayed, I would still be in the hospital right now, hugging someone else's family, consoling, grieving again, unaware of any letter, clueless to any release, not sat outside my daughter's murderer's house. And Patrick would have still died anyway.

No, I'm exactly where I need to be.

James sobs on the other side of the line. Aware of what I need to do, I become separate from him, feel distant, cold even. In order to not be discovered, I need to keep my voice quiet, need him to hang up.

'Your father was special. If there's anything I can do.'

The line clicks off far longer than I've left the conversation. I can't think of Patrick now. Tomorrow, I will ring back, see if they need my help, tomorrow I will cry for my friend but right now I need tunnel vision, now I need focus. Because tonight, there will be two deaths.

No more mistakes. I turn the phone off, shove it in my pocket, then stroll back to the perfect spot. If you passed me you would think I was going for a scenic amble along the beach, not walking in the pitch dark along a deserted lane.

I hear him before I see him. Or rather I hear the click of the door from a key turning: the swing as it opens, the plod of shoes as he steps outside. My mouth is dry, my shoulder aches from the angle I've slept but I am on alert now, ready. I clutch the bag closer, settling it on my lap. Even though I have come here for him, the sight of real flesh, of him as a real person, is a shock. I press down on my chest in an attempt to steady my breath.

Through the bushes I can easily watch. The sensor light shines on the floor so he can see, but all it does for him is shine on that spot, making everything outside the dark invisible. He looks up at the sky as he skins up. How could I have compared him to Ryan? Even the way he scans the sky is different, Scumbag looks like he's checking for lightning rather than stars.

Him skinning up is a good sign. It will make him dozy, give him the veil of sleep. I sit and seethe, only a few feet away. So much for being clean. I'm tempted to reach through the bush and grab him while he is still awake, wanting to see his reaction when he sees who is coming for him, wanting to be a witness to his fear, wishing I had brought a gun and could shoot him in the face. Never before have I hated anyone as much. I see now the list was only a game, a way of running through different scenarios, distracting me while the real target for my anger was locked inside, the only person who I seethed at the notion of being alive, who I despised to the point that my own survival depended on him being eradicated, is the guy standing behind the bush.

The trial didn't humanise him. He is the devil. Pure evil. Anyone that can do those things to another living person is sadistic, no matter what drugs he'd taken, he has to be sick inside, twisted. I bristle. Could I taser him through the gap in the bush? My fingers will fit through but not my hand, not the taser. I bite down on my lip hard to remind me to restrain. Waiting is my best bet.

The way he carries himself when no one is around tells multitudes. With his open legged gait, he spits every few seconds gathering his bile, vaulting it through his mouth like a weapon. Spliff rolled, the way he sucks in the smoke is pure attitude, pure scum. You can tell a lot from watching a person when they think they are alone. There is no sign of the heartbroken, sorry boy they depicted him to be in court. The styled hair is gone, shaved again, all pretence of being an upstanding citizen long disappeared. There is a scar on his cheek, not present at the trial and I smile at the thought that someone might have done that to him in punishment for Sara. He smokes with his shoulders back, his legs apart ready to rip into the world or anyone that stands in his way. He taps at a phone and puts it up to his ear.

'You get it?'

There is a pause. He screws up his nose, the hoods of his eyes pulling down as he points at the air even though the person on the receiving line can't see.

'Nah, tell the gomey I said not good enough. Tell him he gets no more slack. Tomorrow, or I'll rip his balls out and watch his bitch of a mother chew them till she chokes. Tell him Ripper's back and I'll use him to make sure everyone knows.'

There is no trace of the private schooling in his accent as he talks. Any northsider would know he isn't one of them, his voice more like an American accent than imitation Knocknaheeny. The boys up there would laugh at him first, then put him in his place. A rich boy playing at running an empire. From his expensive runners and his perfect veneers and his stupid diamond chain and oversized clothes, he is the typical rich kid wannabe gangster. It shows his intellect. Instead of softening at his immaturity, it fuels me, how someone so stupid could take my Sara, take her and do what he did.

I twitch, piano notes play in my head, on my brain, unrelenting, twinkling those keys, not giving any silence, not giving any break, bombarding, making me want to move, making me need to do some-thing, making me crazy. I itch to tear at him, to spit in his face, to claw at his skin. To burn him like he singed Sara. It is better that he acts like this, it turns my heart to steel. He is making it easy to do what I've come for.

With him there will be no prolonging. No getting him clean first and making him suffer. Although I want him to suffer, for that would be right and full of satisfaction, I also just want him gone from this earth. His death matters more than the length of his life.

On one of my many stakeouts, I made a discovery. One time just as I walked up to the house, I heard the rumble of a car. I crouched down into a ball. The car drove past, then stopped outside the house. Full sure the car saw me, I waited, huddled between the bush, frozen to the spot. A young fella of maybe sixteen got out, he didn't even glance over. The light of his phone highlighted his face, his lips moved. Within seconds, the bush pushed out and Scumbag appeared. They didn't talk, a hand slipped into another, like some kind of wonky handshake. Once he'd received the stuff, he disappeared. After they both were long gone, I studied the bush until I worked out which part opened. Lucky for me, it wasn't a swing door pushing out one way that could only be activated from the inside, but pulled both ways. The problem with an easy exit is it's also simple for someone to get in. From that day on, my way in was waiting whenever I needed it.

Only when the lights go out and the beat silences, only after another hour ticks by, as the sun threatens to rise, do I make my move. I won't pretend the time passes smoothly, I wrestle with myself, one side begging the other, *don't do it, go home, it's not too late to turnaround. Sara wouldn't want this.*

I force myself to recall the cigarette burns, the black singe of hair and I clutch the bag tighter.

It is easy to get into a house when the window is a modern full length one, left ajar. I slip in with no problems. The house is quiet. Within seconds I see him. Scumbag is asleep on the couch, sitting upright, his bare arm facing towards the ceiling, giving access to a perfect vein. The pale skin drives me towards him like a magnet. To carry out my plan, I must get close. Too close. With the taser in one hand I try awkwardly to hold the syringe. Prepared hours earlier, to limit the noise, for what do I care if it turns rancid? That is the point, after all. Despite all my training, all the times I've used a needle, both my hands shake. For a second, I wonder if I can do it, if I have it in me to go through with taking a person's life. All the years I worked to prolong, to revive and improve, can I really take an existence away?

I can't. I won't. I lower the syringe.

There is a tattoo on his neck, behind his ear. A tattoo that wasn't there at the trial, not in plain sight anyway, unless he covered it with concealer. The darkness of the ink indicates it's a fairly new addition to the skin. It's just one straight line, or a 1, the red ink giving no misunderstanding to what it's meant to be. Did a line represent my daughter? Was it a statement to the world that he killed one person? That there were more lines to come?

Rage reawakens. It shoots through me, like I imagine heroin feels as it flushes through the veins. I stand over him and hold my breath until I hear his own sleeping intake. All my time as a carer has taught me how to creep into a room without waking a patient.

There are no fresh entry marks on his arm. It doesn't matter to me if he is clean. As much as I want to torture him, or for him to see my face beforehand and know what I am about to do, I won't risk it, can't dare, because there is a ruthlessness in him I can't chance. He has bulked up, looks fitter, if he overpowers me, it will be all over, he won't hesitate in making a few phone calls, or hurting me himself.

I just want him dead.

I want the earth rid of him, to never worry that he is in the same county, where we could bump into each other on the street. It needs to be a fact that he can't ever do the same to another girl.

As soft and as silent as I can manage, I lay the taser on the arm of the chair by his head, close enough that if he wakes, if he reacts, I can grab and administer. This time, there is no delay as I stand over a man, no hesitation. If anything, I hold back from what I want to do. Up close, I hate him more. I am close enough to see the stubble on his chin, the crust hanging off an eyelash. Eyelashes he still has when he left my daughter with barely any. I can hear his breath. I can feel the whoosh of it against my skin, can smell the weed from his disgusting mouth. The same mouth that bit down on my daughter, leaving perfect teeth marks on her bruised skin. It takes everything to stop from doing what I really want which is to beat on his chest, taser him until he convulses, until his brain turns to mush, until he lifts from the ground. I want to rip his eyes from their sockets and smash them on the floor and stomp and squish them.

Using both hands to steady my grip, I slip the long metal syringe at an angle into the crease of his arm. It slides in, the vein blue and prominent, grand and healthy again, no drugs in it awhile, a good thing now, his tolerance of the drug will be low, like a new user, which bodes well for my plans. With no scabs or sores, the needle enters without any resistance. As smooth as it's done, as the plunger pushes down, his eyes open.

Chapter Forty Four

This is my payoff.

A range of emotions run across his face. First, his eyes widen as it dawns that someone is standing over him. Confusion comes next as he tries to work out what is happening, or who I am. Then comprehension. In the last second, horror arrives, because he understands it is too late to shout, or call for help, or fight, because by then the plunger is right down to the very end. Too quick to say anything or grab at me or for a weapon.

Heroin isn't a slow acting drug, especially when it's injected. That's why addicts gravitate towards it, that's why they risk messing with needles, because the high is instant. Anything that goes straight into the bloodstream acts quick. Scumbag doesn't have any time to react, or any time to feel the high even, as there is enough dosage to kill three people.

As he jerks, as the froth streams first from his mouth then his nose, as he lays there choking, and his chest moves with rapid violence until I'm convinced his heart will rip through his skin and bones and explode, I just stand there.

It is over in about ten minutes. In the end, killing him is too easy. It comes quicker than I dreamt. I stand there waiting for what, I don't know, something else, some emotion or feeling to evoke. What I feel is numb, like I am watching a terrible actor die on a low budget TV show, half expecting to see the flicker of an eyelid as he pretends to play dead. It doesn't feel real. There is no vindication, no high, no satisfaction. It is like putting out the washing; a task needed to be done. After the froth spills out, when his pulse stops, when he turns blue, I fold my arms. No naloxone for Scumbag.

After, I place the tiny plastic bag that held the heroin on the couch next to him, along with some foil I kept ready. It is then I remember the spoon. I search around his kitchenette and find one in the sink. It's better if it looks like one of his, if it matches the rest of the set.

There is a noise then, a movement upstairs, coming near. Someone, the father it sounds like, calling his name. 'Troy? You awake? Remember, we've the meeting with the solicitor at nine.'

Troy AKA Scumbag or drug dealer or murderer of my daughter. I want to shout out what I have done.

No need to worry about being late for the solicitor. Your son is dead. Take your farcical trial and your early release and see what you can do with it. Now we are the same. Now we can both be grieving parents.

Instead, I head for the window. Even though I would prefer to stay awhile, to make sure his body turns colder, I'm content with the lack of vitals. Scumbag is as dead as a person can be. Not wanting to be there when the father steps into the scene, in case regret seeps in from witnessing his father's grief, I retreat.

I do not feel sorry for the family. They have forced this outcome, pushed me to the brink, made my justice mandatory. That man, the father, only looked at me sideways in court, always avoiding me, which could have been understandable, seen as respectful even, but the way he cocked his head, held his jaw, bellowed his laugh when the judge wasn't around wasn't from respect. It wasn't because he didn't know how to react over what his son had done. It was because I meant nothing. The trial, Sara, we were only a block in the road to him, an issue to get over, a problem to deal with. And he had, with his expensive lawyer and influence, with their long legal jargon and their demoralising statements.

The mother was just as bad. With her designer clothes and impeccable makeup, you'd swear she was going to a business meeting rather than her son's trial. Always tapping away on her phone, always chatting to someone between breaks. 'It's awful, just awful.' I wanted to run up to her and smash that phone. They were a disgusting family, truly they were.

The papers claimed shock with the ruling but I wasn't. Being at the trial I had expected it. I would have accepted the verdict if it was fair. Or if the mother had shown compassion, or if the father apologised for what I'd gone through, if Troy AKA drug dealer AKA dead person had tried to explain, or shown any remorse, then maybe, I'd like to believe, I might have found a way to forgive. The father, his son, his mother, not one of them had and now because of that, Scumbag lies dead on his couch.

I give him one last look before I leave. His hands are palm up as if stretching out to me. There is a wet patch on his jeans. Dead eyes that stay vacant forever more. He does not look like a murderer now. His features have softened as if asleep, becoming a twenty-one-year-old boy again. A stupid, vicious boy that can never play at being a gangster again.

I slip out the window and after I pull the bush aside, I run as fast as I can away from the sight I've just caused.

Chapter Forty Five

There is no blood; nothing on my clothes or hands to hide or clean. There is no evidence to get rid of; apart from the syringe pricking his skin, I didn't touch him. Anything I did pick up, like the spoon, I used gloves. The taser was sterilised beforehand, so there is nothing to worry about there.

My hands are steady and I am calm, too calm even, it is like driving away from a work shift. Except, all I can see is the look in his eyes as the needle went in. I run over it to make sense of what I saw in them, what they held in their split-second of meeting my own. There wasn't fear there, as much as it might feel good to imagine there was, not acceptance either, the widening of his eyes was more like recognition, that he recognised who I was and what I was doing. There was no shock at all.

If any surprise comes, it's from the lack of satisfaction I feel. When I imagined how I'd react, I thought the thrill would carry me for days, that retribution would feel more pleasurable, give more gratification, or, at least, make me feel a little better. I do not feel better. I do not feel the buzz I did exposing Oliver. Guilt isn't coming through either. Maybe I am numb, maybe it is shock.

I killed a man. I took a life.

My hand slams the steering wheel.

'Stop it, Lorna. Don't feel sorry for him. He was evil. He deserved to die.'

I run through the reasons I did it, the list of reasons that kept me on this path. The bruises, the burns. All the injuries I couldn't see.

Turning on the radio, I hum, not in tune with the song, more to block out the thoughts that are trying to creep in. The streets blend, the sun is rising now; on another day, the oranges on the skyline would look beautiful but I don't stop to admire it, today the hue has lost its value. Home arrives in no time. Careful to not wake Ryan, I creep out of the car. In the house, the silence brings relief, for Ryan must still be asleep. I tip toe to the shower. There is no blood, yet still I try but fail to wash death away.

Chapter Forty Six

Death is often present when you work as a carer. Working alongside it, I discovered its ways, its rhythms. Never afraid of dying before Sara passed, I saw that time as an end to a well-worn life, a departure from a full, stretched out existence where the deceased had the chance to love and learn from their mistakes, to rectify them if needed. And if they didn't, if they messed up their life, it was their own fault, for they had their shot.

Death, for the chronically ill, is about acceptance; there is always time to recognise their mistakes, to forgive, to mend the life they fractured.

Most clients are elderly or terminal. I learn their traits, their pain, the quirks of their illness. When I notice the turn, I'm the one who makes the phone call. I watch the family gather; there is peace in that type of leaving; as perfect a death as you can hope for. I envy the people able to die surrounded by love, with all the family and friends that matter holding hands around, brought together by their mutual grief. Who drip tears like leaking taps, their anguish evident, not wanting the loved one to go, yet they stay until they pass, until they take their final breath. Sometimes, I am the only one to hold their hand. Each person means something. Their death stays beside me, as I carry on with my day, as I visit the next client or buy dinner or drive home.

Back in my twenties, during my arguments with Tim, I would have given anything to escape. Back then, when I discovered yet another woman in my bed, or secret messages on his phone, death didn't seem the worst thing in the world. The only light, the reason I kept living, was Sara.

Before Sara died, I believed we all went somewhere. That all our suffering happened on soil and by the time we reached the other side, all was forgiven. After Sara, I couldn't keep that belief. How could the same man who murdered her join her? Hell had to exist for people like him. There had to be a place where you could suffer for eternity. After Sara, the only thing that kept me alive was revenge.

And now he's dead. The reason I stayed alive is gone. Now, the rest of the list doesn't matter. The one I wanted to hurt, has.

I shut my eyes tight. 'I'm glad he's dead.'

The shower's hot water pummels my neck. My pale skin blazes red. It doesn't matter if it burns.

Will I burn in hell?

I killed just like he killed. It wasn't peaceful or enlightening. With that act have I separated Sara and I? Have I now determined my outcome, to spend eternity with him instead of joining Sara?

I slip to the floor of the shower.

'No.'

The sounds come out in whooshes,

'No. No.'

An expulsion of the words, a release. The numbness is gone and the positives I've wished for aren't coming. How could I believe I would find peace in killing someone? I took a life into my own hands and extinguished it. Against my entire philosophy and character and better judgement, with my own actions, I betrayed everything I stand for. Who am I if I do that? What do we know about ourselves except what we stand for, what we will do once pushed? I have gone against what I knew about myself and found I am bereft. I don't want to know this new person. I don't like her one bit.

What I've done sits on my chest like tainted food. Everything is clear. Like a fog lifting, I understand my naivety, how I believed it would unleash the pain, or at least release some of the hurt. Instead, it adds to it.

He was a son. Until I removed him from his life. Even if he wasn't a good one, even if his parents were disgusting people, I still did to them what their son had done to me.

Maybe I feel this way because there is no closure. Would it feel better if I'd confronted him? It was quick, over as soon as I'd entered the needle. I needed to do it fast so I wouldn't stop. Hesitating would get *me* killed. Going fast got *him* killed. Now that it is done, the acknowledgement is there. I took the coward's way.

All they will find in the autopsy is bad heroin. Making sure to use his own supply, I mixed it with isotonitazene which I'd read were linked to a spat of overdoses. Bought before the trial, with his trademark insignia stamped on each bag. Even if he was clean, like he claimed, who could argue that the guilt hadn't got to him?

Had he felt any guilt?

I wish I asked him; I wish I discovered if there was any regret in that boy. Now there is no return. I understand what I was looking for was his remorse. If he'd admitted what he'd done instead of denying it, if he'd explained why, apologised even, or testified that he didn't mean to hurt her, I could have taken some solace.

I had to sit through the trial listening to his sob story of a good guy ravaged by drugs trying to claw a life back, asking for another chance, all the while walking to the courtroom with his head cocked, no shame from him, laughing with his father before the judge arrived, talking with his mother as if nothing had changed. A girl dying hadn't altered his life in the slightest.

Now, I know. I understand how he could act that way at the trial. A person can survive after committing a despicable act.

I can pretend. No one will ever know I've killed someone. It will be easy to act like nothing happened. All I need to do is close the door on that part of the brain and move on. This is the truth: killing him hasn't, can't, won't, bring Sara home.

Chapter Forty Seven

Sara visits me in a dream. Her face takes up my whole viewpoint. Her red hair, each freckle, those vivid green eyes twinkle with aliveness. In 3D, I am sure if I stroke her face, I will touch actual skin. Overjoyed to see her, I don't pay attention to her expression, too busy taking in the strands of her hair, no clumps this time, no singed stubs. It is only when one teardrop slides down her cheek that I notice the way she looks at *me*. She shakes her head, silent yet communicating. No.

Side to side, the shakes go. No. No. Before I wake, her tears have turned to rivers.

In the darkness, her sadness stays. For the rest of the night, sleep alludes me. I can't forget how close I was to my daughter. It felt real. Sara was there, letting me know she didn't agree with what I did. As if she was passing on a message, telling me the only way she could, she was not happy. She was not happy with me.

Sara never appeared before. All the times I begged before trying to sleep. All the times I cried her name, I felt nothing, dreamt of nothing. Yet, after what I did, she appeared. There could only be one explanation.

'Sara, I had to. What if he hurt someone else? He would, you know he would. Are you OK? Please be OK. What he did to you.' I wipe at my face. 'Sara, I couldn't let him get away. He was free and you are dead. I couldn't let him live, I couldn't.'

A memory comes to me of Sara, no more than seven years old. Her red hair almost turned to dreadlocks from a summer of running around, avoiding showers, playing. The previous two months spent in the garden discovering all different lifeforms. We had set up an area along the wall, as an animal and insect sanctuary, where she nursed beetles and broken winged butterflies.

One day, I found her near the swings, sitting on the grass, hunched over, crying.

'What's wrong?'

'They're all dead.'

'Who?'

'The caterpillars. I gave them a home in the jar, I put leaves in and food and when I went they're all dead. I killt them.'

'Did you close the lid?'

She nodded, bit down on her lip, the tears welling.

'Oh honey, you didn't know.'

'I killt them. If you kill someone, you go to hell. Your soul never goes to heaven.'

'That's not true. You didn't mean to kill anyone. There's a difference.'

She straightened to reach my sitting height, her eyes as wide as they could open.

'There isn't. If you kill someone, you can't take it back. They died cos of me. I'm going to hell.'

I held her, stroking her hair and knowing the best thing I could do was be there, to just hold her and talk again when she calmed and the right words came. She cried for hours, and I let her. It took weeks for her to get over it.

I sit upright in the bed. My breath stops for a second, winding me.

I've made a massive mistake. A huge, irreversible, unerasable mistake.

You cannot take back death. You cannot unsyringe someone. Right at this moment, I wish I could suck back time, to reverse the actions I performed. Convinced it was the right thing to do, that there were no other options, that it was the only way to get vengeance.

But it has only left me empty. Emptier. Because, before I acted, I was the victim. Now, I've proven I am the same as him, as ruthless, as calculating, as heartless, as capable of taking a life without thought. I am a killer, just like him. In the bed, I curl into a ball, catching my legs with my hands, and weep.

Chapter Forty Eight

Lifting my head isn't an option. If I open my eyes it conjures images I don't want to see; waking brings forth facts I can't take. It is like my brain has finally cracked; everything I thought about life has flipped over and reversed: I am no longer the person in the right, I am the wrong doer, the one that should be punished. Waking brings only one word on repeat. MURDERER.

The sleeping tablets I kept stock of for my plan come to good use. I take them as soon as I wake, not even looking for water, hoping I will die from dehydration, from starvation, from bed sores.

Hours or days later, Ryan leans over.

'Are you unwell? Do you need anything?'

I turn my back in answer, wanting sleep, wanting death, wanting escape from what I did.

The next sight is Ryan again. This time he holds up my neck so I can sit, and drip feeds me some water. I close my mouth, letting the liquid spill, so it dribbles down my chin and pools in my neck.

'Ginger, I'll have to ring the doctor if you don't drink something.'

He holds the glass up to my mouth and waits, tips the water again when I part my lips. And that is it, Ryan saves my life.

He forces me to drink and then a few hours later feeds me soup. He props me up, moves pillows so I can swallow without choking. My hands sit immobile in my lap. Even though I want to refuse, my functions betray my wishes: I open my mouth, I swallow, I digest. The only thing that gets me through is knowing after, once I get some strength back, once the lethargy leaves, I can take my stash of pills all at once.

Killing him was meant to rid me of the pain from Sara's death, but now two people haunt me, two very different ghosts. Sara, all loving, reminding me of what I lost, of what life could have been like, and him, Scumbag, now just plain Troy, reminding me of what I am capable of, of my mistakes.

Even though I take the water, I refuse to leave the bed or get dressed or wash. The next time Ryan appears, he brings his journal. He gestures towards it, asking permission to open. I nod, afraid if I speak, he will want to talk instead, he will probe why I'm acting the way I am. He smiles, looks blankly in the distance, as if trying to remember the scene, back once more with Sara, then he speaks.

'Sara feeds me when I'm ill. The sickness is coming from my arm, hot to touch, I shiver everywhere else. Infected from a needle, the skin around my vein turns scarlet, the colour spreading over my skin, like a spillage. Blisters form there too. When I can't move without crying out, when one blister turns into a pus-filled boil, Sara insists I go to hospital. I tell her I won't leave her but she makes Tommo and Finky carry me after I pass out. When I wake in The Mercy, I'm soaking in sweat. Withdrawal, but also I am shit scared cos Sara isn't beside me. She is all alone.'

He flicks his eyes to me, checking if I'm angry, I think, I shrug in response. *Carry on.*

'They say it's cellulitis, and if I hadn't come to the hospital, it could've got worse, I could've lost the whole arm. There are streaks around the skin and the boil is the size of a satsuma, bright red just past my elbow to nearly my shoulder. Once they give me the antibiotics and lance the boil, I ask them to let me out. They don't argue too much, they keep looking at me sideways, checking on me, burnt in the past by addicts only checking in to get to the drugs, to rob them of something they can sell or take. I want to get out. Itching for a fix but worse than that I need to find Sara. I've never left her side and it's not safe to be alone where we're staying. It would be nicer to stay longer. Here, I lie on a mattress with springs. Clean sheets, warm food, fresh water. These are essential things for most people. We have none of them, have had none of them for a very long time. We've sunk low now and seeing how life goes on for others here I want to change it, I want us to go home, get better. They send me on my way with a warning: no injecting in that arm, bandaged up as a reminder. The nurse is sound. Genuine. She looks at me as if it matters to her that I listen, that what she is saying is important, but not in a giving out way, more like she cares, I guess. She reminds me of Ginger who is the closest person to a mother I ever got but I can't go back to her, can't ask her for help because she would keel over if she saw us. Worse, she would blame herself. Even though the arm hasn't healed and still hurts, the thought of Sara won't leave. Afraid it's some premonition or something, I have to go. As I make my way from the hospital, I break into a run cos I need to find Sara. On the streets we are a team, always watching out for the other and now the vultures who waited for an opportunity to get her alone would have swooped, could have got to her. Sick upchucks in my mouth as I run. Part withdrawal, part fear that I left her. For hours she has had to fend for herself. Although near enough, the place we sleep is still too far. What if she's hurt? What if someone's hurt her? What if she went for a fix and they made her do things to get it?

Then I'm there, in the place we've been using, a derelict warehouse that others use too. The people aren't too bad, are like us, once decent. I nearly cry when I see her, she is balled up, sleeping. When I curl next to her, she doesn't look up or check it's me, she just knows, puts an arm around me, snuggles in, whispers she missed me. I can't help it, I cry. Sara opens those green eyes, kisses my face.

'I was worried about you,' she says.

'Did everyone leave you alone?'

'Shush,' she says. 'Don't ever worry about me. I can look after myself.'

'I don't want to do this anymore.' I say into her hair.

'Me too,' she says.

'You mean it?' I ask.

She nods.

Addiction plays people against each other. Makes them see the worst in others, in themselves. Shows others the worst in them. The cravings mean you would climb over your best friend to fix the itching inside, to calm the storm in your body. It hurts. It gnaws, aches, scratches, churns. We are no different to any other addict. We have tried to give up many times. One declaring they'd had enough, one relenting when the other suffered too much, wanting to take the pain away but dragging us back in. It is why all addiction clinics recommend separation from the people you used with because seeing them makes you fall back. Habits die hard. We both know we can't quit around the other. I would give up the drug before her. Always. Will I go on?'

I incline my head. *Don't stop.*

'Later, Sara feeds me again. I tell her she should be a nurse and we both cry at that, for the life we should have had. Each time she gives me a bite, she lays the food on my tongue barely touching it. When I close my mouth, she strokes my cheek and smiles. That's the image I keep. Her face is full of a breakout and her hair is greasy and I feel guilty because I did that to her, because of me she lives this way but at the same time I've never been as hopeful or feel more love for her. Or from her. We have lost everything; we have nothing to our name, yet we love each other more than anything. Our love can survive heroin and sleeping on the streets, it can outlive poverty and sickness and still in spite of all this, she loves me enough to feed me and stroke my cheek.'

His eyes are wet when he stops and I realise I have held my breath for the last few sentences.

'I'm sorry Ginger. She thought she could take care of herself but she couldn't. I don't blame you for wanting to give up, for it getting too much but I don't think Sara would want you like this.'

I close my eyes. How can I tell him that it isn't depression but guilt? He is waiting for my response when I open them again.

'Why aren't you angry?'

He shakes his head, unsure of what to say. So, I talk instead.

'I feel anger. All the time. I've never been good at letting it out, so it builds until it needs to explode. That's what the list was for. Once I had that, the anger simmered with promise, because one day it would be satisfied. Time didn't help the anger go. I often wondered if I might combust, you hear of that don't you? People just bursting into flames. Bet you anything they were fuming, that something made their blood boil until it sparked fire.'

'I'm angry all the time too.'

I smile. 'Ryan, you are the opposite of angry.'

He shifts on the bed. 'Why do you think I went back on the gear? When you can't let it out, it's better to go inwards, to disappear inside.'

His hands turn to fists. Spit flies from his mouth. 'Ginger, he took Sara away from us. I would have given anything, anything for ten minutes in a room with him. He destroyed us, destroyed her, he took her and made sure he couldn't give her back, made sure she couldn't come back to anyone.'

His voice cracks, he rubs at his skin with violent swipes, then cups his whole face, breathing deeply. I wait, knowing he needs a moment, knowing he hasn't finished, knowing I need to hear what he has to say just as much as he needs to say it.

'If he'd just given her back. If he'd just let her live, no matter how broken she was we could have fixed her. We could have pieced her together. He didn't allow us even that. He never gave us a chance to save her.'

He places his hand on mine, a warm, alive hand. 'I know something is going on with you but you have to stay strong. You have to keep going.'

I stare at his hand. A hand that once held my daughter's.

'I don't think I can.'

'You have to.'

I pull my hand away. Sit back to look him right in the eye.

'That's where you're wrong, I don't. There's nothing here for me anymore, I want Sara.'

'What about me?' He stares. 'I need you. You are the only thing getting me through. You go, I go. Sara wants us together for what I don't know, I feel it, in here.' He thumps his chest. 'Please Ginger, let it play out. Can you just try and live for her?'

I nod, with eyes full of tears, because I understand what he's talking about, for I've felt it too. In the dream Sara was telling me what I chose to do was wrong. That there was another way.

'I'll try.'

Chapter Forty Nine

Tensions were high during the last game of the season. We were thrashing the opposition, a feat unaccomplished in ten years. As the neighbouring team, both existing in the same town, the rivalry between them was of legendary status, so much so, any stranger was asked: Carraigshill or Cusdearg? If they found you supported the other side, it was enough for them to screech the seat away, or turn their back and never look at you again. Punch ups happened often on the pitch, from the supporters just as much as the players. With stakes that high, trouble was written all over the game.

Ryan was the star of the show. Four goals in fifty minutes. The other team scored three. On the pitch, he was beautiful. With him, soccer never looked like moving or running, but dancing. Sometimes when he dribbled the ball, a hush fell over the pitch, just watching the beauty of his play. I sound biased, but strangers agreed. Ryan's life was about to change. Already playing for the juniors, all the whispers said he was one to watch, that one day he would wear the Ireland jersey. A legend in the making, down the field, they all spoke of the career he'd have, of what was to come for the boy from Carrigshill. This was his last game on Irish soil. Four months earlier he'd signed for Brentford but, on my insistence, stayed to finish his Leaving Cert. Two weeks after the match they were moving.

The problem with being a rising star is the opposition knows this too. Every player on the other team made a beeline to take him out. This game was no different. Expecting it, Ryan avoided every tackle, jumping over legs and side-stepping elbows like he was on an obstacle course all too easy to predict. Which only infuriated the other team more. As a guy on his left grabbed his collar, Ryan jerked to avoid being pulled back, then glided past a guy on the other side who dived at him, jumping just before the point of contact and landing behind the ball again, then carrying on. Shouts of 'Ref! Ref!' were the norm, but all of Carraigshill shouted it now, wanting to stop it before it was too late. Did we contribute to the energy that day? Out to cause damage, by any means necessary was the accepted motto.

In the middle of the match, an uneasiness came over me. I kept checking the time, wishing the minutes would hurry by, wanting the game over, wanting him to be safe. I saw it happening before it did. Saw the culprit, saw his face, saw the determination before he even moved. A tall, stocky defender bolted towards Ryan. There was something in the way the guy ran at him. All in, no surrender. From the way Ryan quickly passed the ball sideways to his teammate, Donal, he sensed this, too. Donal vaulted ahead. Always the priority, Ryan kept his eye on the ball, waiting for the next opportunity. All eyes watched Donal, watched for the possibility for a goal, all eyes it seemed, but me and Sara. The defender didn't change direction, just kept going, straight for Ryan. Sara stood, shouted. 'Stop him!'

It was too late. Ryan, hearing Sara's voice, turned to see what was wrong. The defender leaped, legs first, straight out like arrows, aiming for only one target: Ryan's leg. My head spun from such a blatant act to destroy. As his team mate scored, over the roars from the crowd, Ryan's bone broke. He flew back, landing straight down. Sara jumped out of her seat. The guy walked away, his face still seething. No one yet had noticed. I shouted, screamed, trying to get someone's attention.

'His leg! Ryan's leg. Someone help him. Medic! Medic! Ryan's leg!'

And the guys next to me looked at me as if I was stupid at first. The words I screeched settled. They looked again at the pitch, searching the ground until they saw Ryan, lying there. Their shouts joined my shouts. The medic ran to Ryan. In all that time, he hadn't moved, passed out. Then Sara was on the pitch and when she wasn't allowed near Ryan, she ran at the player, shoved him, pummelled her hands on his chest. They stretchered Ryan off, his leg hanging from the stretcher at an awkward angle. I ran then, to my daughter who had dropped onto the floor. The pitch echoed with the sound of her wail.

It didn't matter what disciplinary act the defender got, or whether they banned for life. With two straight legs into a shin, he destroyed Ryan. Destroyed his leg, his career, his future. As Ryan fell down, I knew already. Once seen, everyone in the stadium did too. You wouldn't have to study biology to know. All you had to do was witness the injury, see the split bone rip out of his skin, see the leg bend where it should stay straight.

He was never the same after that. They won the game, but everyone knew before the final whistle that Ryan's football career was over. Everyone except Ryan, that is.

Chapter Fifty

At first Ryan stayed optimistic. He spoke in the hospital about healing in record time. Spoke about signing for the team and what was to come in the following year. Each time some visitor or nurse examined the floor or stayed quiet, his confidence chipped. Until the end of the week, when the doctor explained the severity, when the email came through that the club were sorry to hear he couldn't join them. When the amount of visitors petered out because they couldn't stand the awkwardness, his resolve ebbed away until he couldn't lift his head. Depression swallowed him. Ryan gave up.

Sara did not. She stayed by his side. It was as if she did all her crying on the pitch that day. The times when there was only one visitor allowed, the seat fell without question to her. Ryan's upbringing was tough – his father was a soldier, active, away for six months of the year, keeping the peace in a war-torn country which was ironic, as he was the least peaceful person I'd ever met. From the brief times Ryan confided in me, I knew his mother, Susan, disappeared from his life long before. Ryan's brother died suddenly in his sleep when Ryan was two years old. From that day on, she gave up. Ryan worried about her in the hospital, wanting to leave to check on her, fretting that she wouldn't feed or wash if he wasn't around, only calming when I promised to visit each day. The first time she wouldn't answer the door or phone, so the next time I arrived with Ryan's key.

I found Susan in bed, not lying but sitting on the edge, staring out facing the wall with her hands in her lap. Her gaze didn't falter from the spot, oblivious to shadows and figures, she never looked in my direction. All the time I sat with her, I don't believe she even noticed I was there. When I called her name, she didn't react. The woman hardly blinked. I told her Ryan was in the hospital recovering from a leg break, that she wasn't to worry. If she needed me, I would be there. I left my number on her bedside locker and told her anytime night or day she could ring and I would try to help. After I fed and washed her, I gave the place a clean. I didn't force her to talk or insist she go to the hospital as the woman wasn't there. Mrs Howe wouldn't help Ryan. As much as I wanted to shake her to wake up and be there for her only *living* son, I couldn't push or force her because there was a part of me that agreed with her reaction. Even then I understood my life would end too if my child died.

With Ryan, the drugs started in the hospital, I think. Not so much the strong drugs, but the turning away from life, from wanting to have a normal existence. I could see Ryan was hurting and the pain medication gave him a taste, numbed it, numbed him. Heroin is processed from morphine, the strongest painkiller you can get. Before heroin, he already handed himself over to addiction. He gave up that day on the pitch.

Sara changed, too. They had such an instinctive love, a natural bond that usually came easy. Faced with this situation, she felt lost.

'What should I do?' She asked me one time while drinking coffee in the canteen after the nurses kicked us out of the room so they could change his dressing.

'Do exactly what you're doing.'

'I'm doing nothing.'

'You're doing everything. Ryan feels your strength, and that will give him strength over time. He's mourning his dreams at the moment.

For years, he thought his life was going to amount to one thing and now something out of his control has changed it all. Just be there like you are. Show up every day and sit with him. Listen to what he wants to say. If he shows an interest in anything, develop it, run with it.'

'I'm trying to be positive, but it's like I'm in mourning as well. It's changed my life too.'

I sipped my coffee.

'It doesn't have to. You can both still go to college.'

Sara grimaced; her jaw tightened, her teeth clenching.

'What? What is it?'

'I deferred.'

She wouldn't look at me, kept her eyes on the ground.

'What?'

'You hardly think I was still going to college in England while Ryan stays here? We're a team. Wherever we go, we go together.'

She wrapped around me, all arms and hair everywhere, and I hugged her back and held her until she broke away. I couldn't be angry. A part of me knew she would stay. Back when Tim and I first fell in love, I would have followed him anywhere. And that was with doomed love, a one-sided relationship, an infatuation I should have known better about. Ryan and Sara's love was different, had been different, both loving with their arms wide open, unafraid of being hurt. So far, the other hadn't let them down.

For the first time in their relationship, I saw the change hanging over them like a black cloud, felt the division of equality in that room. All connections eventually lose their balance, when life shifts the boundaries and tests you. Back then I didn't doubt them, although I worried about their relationship for sure, but they were both loyal, they were both fighters, so I knew their bond would survive.

It would have been easy for Ryan to push Sara away, to take it out on her but he didn't. Instead, he leant on her, relied on her, closing off from everyone else, letting her answer the questions, hiding behind his pain. That's when I really became concerned, because he became identical to his mother: there but not there, unreactive, unresponsive.

For a while, there was a real danger of him losing his leg. Even though the leg had set, the break had been severe, and an infection threatened its healing. Ryan and Sara were distraught, Sara repeating, 'Who heard of someone losing their leg from a break?'

I didn't answer that according to my research, it was more common than you would think.

After the infection healed, a little spark of the old Ryan flared. Thinking the worst had happened, a little hope appeared through the darkness.

'I can still walk. With therapy, I'll get my full range back.'

When it was time to leave the hospital, there was no conversation about him coming back to ours. Already decided when the nurse required an address for the release forms, I gave ours instead of his, looking at him to see if there was any resistance, but he had nodded his head, relieved. Sara placed a hand on mine and squeezed.

After that, a different phase of our life started when Sara and I became a carer for two people. Each day, I set off for Ryan's house, checking on Susan, whereas Sara took over the intimate tasks for Ryan: the getting dressed, the awkward, necessary, impossible things when your leg is in a cast, like pulling up underwear, putting on socks and shoes. More than that, there was a necessary faffing. A soothing, stroking, caring, going on. They lay for hours on the couch, talking, watching comedies, snacking on foods high in sugar or salt. As the days turned into weeks, I took comfort when I heard laughter again. Even when I heard soft moans at night coming from their room, my first reaction was to smile. Never squeamish, those types of things didn't embarrass me; it was natural for them to heal what had broken that way. Still, hearing them make love wasn't what I wanted to listen to. Instead, I would jump out of bed, get in the shower or away from the noise by retreating to the kitchen, flicking the kettle on, blocking out the images.

Often, when the creaks of the bed started, I made my way to the porch, sipping my tea. On those days, in the early hours of the morning, I would watch the sun rise, thanking the sky for letting them find a way back to each other through love; for helping Ryan to heal. I honestly believed as the horizon blossomed that we were over the worst, not knowing, not having a clue that our problems hadn't even begun.

Chapter Fifty One

In the papers there is nothing. No article on Troy's death, no headlines that the man that killed Sara got his comeuppance, no newsflash on the radio announcing he passed away. This strikes me as very strange. As a high-profile case, there is still interest. Nothing online either. The obituary columns are free of his name. When I see Patrick's photo there, I wince, for I missed his funeral. I promise to make it up to the family.

No articles about Troy makes me nervous. Are the family keeping his death secret? Or as each hour passes, a much more terrifying thought creeps up on me: could they have saved him? If they did, if he is alive, he saw me. Every sound, every phone call causes me to jump.

Ryan is cleaning up the remnants of breakfast.

'I did something.'

He stops what he is doing, as if he has been waiting all this time for me to finally speak. He places the tea towel on the counter, smoothing it flat before he sits at the table. Staying silent, he waits. I sit across from him, take a breath.

'I did something to someone that there is no coming back from.'

He nods, his head hangs down, not looking at me. His finger traces a groove in the wood table. There is no shock. It makes me want to say more.

'When I used to plan, the pleasure of it, the thought of the act got me through. It was the only way I found I could get any relief. To imagine hurting someone like they hurt Sara. First it was anyone, then it was a specific set of people.'

Ryan's head shoots up at that and I see the revelation in his eyes, the confirmation that this is what the list was for.

'Revenge was the only way. Planning every scenario lifted the dark thoughts. I believed if I carried it out, I would feel better.'

I lay my hands on my cheeks, to keep my voice steady.

'I was wrong. There's no better. It's left me empty.'

I drop my hands, lay them on the table, stare at them rather than Ryan.

'That's not true, I'm not empty. Shame replaced the pain. I've made the biggest mistake. Even though he deserved it, even though far worse should have been done to him so that he suffered like Sara did. It isn't about him. It's about me. I let myself down by doing it. Hurting him hasn't made me feel any better. All it did was make me more like him. It hasn't changed the fact that Sara is dead.'

My voice comes out uneven, with little rasps of breath in between until I steady. Ryan doesn't make a sound.

'It wasn't a moment of insanity, or like I believed she'd come back from the dead or anything. It's just... I thought I'd feel different. Get a sign or some type of message and I don't, if anything I feel like I did the wrong thing altogether.'

Only then do I dare look at him. His hands lean on the table, his arms vertical, rigid. His head hangs down, his features out of range. Ryan doesn't ask who I'm talking about, he doesn't need to ask. Then he looks right at me. When he speaks his mouth stays in a straight line.

'You did it for Sara.'

I swallow.

'Did I? You said it yourself, Sara didn't believe in hurting a fly. She wouldn't have wanted me to do that in her name, to be remembered that way.'

'Is he dead?'

'He looked that way, when I left. There's been nothing in the papers. In here...'

I beat my chest.

'...he's dead. There was no pulse, I waited. He was dead.'

'Good.'

He doesn't flinch, doesn't look away or hesitate. His eyes bore into me.

'Sara shouldn't have suffered; she shouldn't have died suffering. Ginger, I know anger, I *know* anger. I've dreamt of hurting him every day since. Before the trial, I was afraid I'd jeopardise the case, didn't touch anything, stayed clean, even when they said they didn't need me, even though all I wanted was oblivion. During the trial, I kept it together, even though I wanted to vault the bars outside the court and stab him in the heart.'

'You were outside?'

There is a flicker of a nod. He squirms with the revelation.

A wave of nausea washes over. *He was outside.*

'Why didn't you come over?'

He tilts his head, either dumbfounded or wondering am I being serious.

'Tim warned me off. The solicitor said it would work against Sara's case, make her look bad.'

'You could have still let me know you were there.'

'Don't you think I tried? Tim said you were fragile, seeing me would make you worse, make you lose it and they needed you to stay strong.'

'What? He never said a word. Did he tell you I was looking for you?'

Ryan shakes his head.

'What was Tim playing at? I couldn't understand why you didn't show. The way you used to love her, I was sure you'd be there to show us support and you were nowhere to be found, I believed you abandoned Sara. You not being there changed how I saw you. Do you understand that?'

His eyes go to the list. He nods.

'First day of the trial, I walked in, all suited up. Tim was waiting, grabbed me by the arm and escorted me out the building by the side door so the photographers didn't see. I told him you'd want me there, that I could help. Begged him Lorna. He wouldn't listen. Nobody listened. Nobody wanted to know what I had to say. He said it would hurt Sara if a junkie got on the stand, it would only remind people what she had been like. I swore on my life I was clean, they could test me. I don't think he was even listening, just said our history would work against her, that no judge in the country would believe a junkie over an honour student. I pushed past him, said I was going, swore I wouldn't say a word I just needed to be there for Sara. He lost it. Picked me up by my suit collar and held me there, choking me till I nearly blacked out. Told me if I made a scene I would destroy the case before it even began. Told me it was my fault his daughter died. When he put me down I said I wanted to be there for you. He laughed. Said, "Lorna told me she doesn't want to ever see you again."'

'I never.'

Ryan shakes his head. 'After that I didn't fight him. Because it was true. It was my fault.'

'Where was I when he did this?'

'Ahead of him. He came back out after sitting you in the courtroom, I think.'

There was a vague recollection of Tim seating me then saying he needed the bathroom.

'Tim found you shooting up in a den in Cork City. He went to you, asked you to attend, you said you'd come but you didn't show up.'

Ryan shakes his head again.

'Why? Why would Tim do that?'

'I don't know. Protecting you maybe? It's not the truth, I promise.'

'That Tim.'

I beat the table with my fist. Ryan doesn't flinch, as if expecting it, as if ready to speak.

'Your hate broke me, you know? The one person who believed in me as much as Sara, hated me. You say you needed me, well, I needed you just as much. Being without her, I couldn't... the only thing that kept me alive was justice, was hope that even though they didn't know the full details, no human with an ounce of decency could hear what happened to her and not find him guilty. The only thing that kept me breathing was imagining him rotting behind bars for the rest of his life. When they announced the verdict, my body shut down. Faster, worse than any comedown or cold turkey withdrawal, my insides turned to liquid, my skin crawled, I itched until my skin was raw. I should've made a scene, should've hid in the bathroom one of the days. Should've strangled him, should've choked him with my bare hands because what did it matter if I mourned her in prison or out on the streets? Every day he'd gone in to use the toilet. Each day I watched him, too scared to take a chance and follow. Until I couldn't. I failed again. Failed to kill him. Failed to keep Sara safe.'

He makes rough strokes at his eyes as if trying to remind them to stay dry.

'After that there was no point living, so I ruined myself rather than lash out at a guy I couldn't get to. I wanted to join her.'

'Why didn't you call me Ryan? You knew where I lived.'

'Are you serious Ginger? I rang and rang. Left messages every day. Asking, begging, crying down the phone, pleading with you to just pick up. Saying if we could only speak, we could help each other. How do you think I spoke to Tim first? He answered your phone, hung up on me, opened your door, slammed it into my face. '

I try to retrace that time, to figure out what he is saying.

'All the people calling, I couldn't handle it. Tim diverted the cranks, deleted the abusive messages. There were too many, I couldn't listen. In the end he bought me a new phone. He promised me he'd answer if you rang, he knew I needed to talk to you.'

'You never answered the door. Even before the trial.'

'The reporters drove me crazy so Tim dealt with them. By the time I asked him to leave, I thought you had no interest, thought you had said you didn't care so I refused to answer the door. To anyone. Who did I want to see? Just drank or slept there. Most of the time I was out stalking Troy.'

He runs his hands through his hair.

'Makes sense. I thought you didn't want me near you.'

He sits.

'I'm guessing then Tim didn't tell you what I said happened?'

I shake my head. His words pop like bubbles against my subconscious, they jumble and move and I can't make sense of them, they won't settle or stay still.

'It was me who rang the guards. I told them who he was, gave them a list of places he might've took her. Lorna, I begged them to let me tell the court. Yeah, we made mistakes but that wasn't who we were, that was just part of the story. A part she conquered. I wanted them to see Sara as a girl who would wake up and want to do good, who even at her worst, even strung out, looking for a fix would share whatever we had with whoever needed it. I wanted them to see she was loved, not the pathetic character they made her out to be. So many false statements and no one corrected them, nobody told the truth about her.'

I close my eyes at this, because I argued the same at the time. I pinch the skin between my eyebrows.

'How do you know what was said at the trial? You weren't inside, I looked around.'

'An old school mate got me in. He's a cleaner in the courthouse. Remember Johnno?'

I show recognition with a movement of head.

'He always had time for Sara, didn't feel Tim banishing me was right. Snuck me into a side room off the judges' quarters, then left the door open so I could listen. Made me promise not to cause a scene or bother anyone and believe me it came close. Do you know how many times I nearly ran out? I wanted to kill him.'

He wraps his arms around his chest.

'Never did though. Took the coward's way. Just sat there listening to them destroy Sara. Told myself I couldn't get Johnno in trouble, that he would get what he deserved. We both know he didn't. We both know that trial was a joke, that sentence was an insult. And now you're here telling me you got to him and I tell you Lorna, I'm glad he's dead. I'm glad it was one of us that killed him. For what he did to her he deserves to die a thousand lives over.'

His voice cracks; his open mouth tries to make sound but nothing comes out but pain. I step out from my chair and walk over to his side of the table and rub his back, but it isn't enough, he turns, holds me, clings, I try and fail to hold in my cry, and then I let the tears come, for what I had to do instead of leaving it in the hands of justice, for Ryan being glad I did it, for how my daughter, the love of this man's life that I am clinging onto now, died, for Ryan not being there when he wanted to stand beside me, for the new knowledge that maybe back then we could have helped each other, maybe we wouldn't have felt as alone.

'Did he suffer?' He asks through our sobs.

'No.'

'I wish he did.'

'He saw me Ryan, he knew what was happening.'

'Good. That's good,' he says.

Chapter Fifty Two

When we stop crying, I return to my seat.

'It isn't a good thing, I don't feel better. What I did makes me as bad as him, made me the same, I played God when I had no right. I should go to the guards and confess.'

'Confess? Where will that get you? Did that murderer getting arrested change what happened to Sara?'

'I went against nature, against universal laws, I changed His plan.'

'You keep talking like there could be a God, after what happened to Sara. Maybe that *was* God's plan. Maybe you're a hero. Maybe you saved a hundred innocent women by doing what you did. You can't wallow in this Lorna. It will drag you down. And if you do that, he still wins.'

'I don't know if I can live with it. Live with what I did. Maybe if I go to his house, check if he's alive, or talk to his family?'

'What good will that do? He's ruled our lives since the day he took her. We need to forget him, dead or alive. Hopefully, dead.'

He leans back in his chair and appraises me. Clears his throat.

'Let's talk about God's plan. About the night you found me. That week I gave away what little I had, my way of saying goodbye. Two of the girls came back to mine, wanting to continue partying. I let them, thinking what was another hour? By the morning I'd be dead. I couldn't wait till they went. All week the lads commented on how chill I was. It was because I'd decided to check out, that the peace they noticed was because the fight inside was over, that I was going to my girl, I was going wherever she was. I thought I'd left no way to come back. After I took the pills, I looked at Sara's photo and this calm poured in. I felt her with me. And then I woke up, to you, to this house, and I didn't get it, didn't get why anyone wanted me to live. Sara made you come to me, Sara found a way for us to find each other.'

I stare out the window at the trees in the distance.

'Sara is gone, Ryan. Sara is dead. She has no say in anything anymore.'

'Do you really believe that?'

I think of how I speak to her. About asking her for a sign. About the decision I made to walk into the kitchen, believing it was Sara guiding me.

I shake my head.

'Dying is easy. Apart from suicide, there's no choice involved. If you're lucky, your exit is swift, over before you know it, but even the dragged out exits end, eventually. Living is harder. What am I living for? There's no reason to keep ploughing on. Revenge kept me here, kept me focused. Once I had that list, there was a point to it all. It was a lie. Revenge doesn't feel any better than grief. It's worse. Because the guilt has coupled with the grief. Why haven't we been told he's dead? Why isn't it in the papers?'

'Did you make it look like an accident?'

I shrug. 'I'd prefer you don't know the details in case you're implicated.'

'Don't worry about me. Worrying about any of that won't help us. We have to figure out a way of living through this.'

'How can I live knowing what I know? How can I live with who I have become?'

He shrugs. Stands. Flicks the kettle. Rummages through the cups.

Picks up Sara's one and examines it, turning it around in his palm. After a few full turns, he places it back in the cupboard, boiling kettle forgotten, he sits back at the table.

'By honouring her.'

I shake my head, confused.

'What if you got your revenge another way?'

'I don't get you.'

'Whenever anyone did us wrong, Sara would say, "don't get them back, show them."'

I screw up my nose and his head tilts back, laughing.

'Whenever someone fouled me, Sara would walk down to the line. She'd call me over and say those words. She'd say, "don't get even, don't become them, show them who you are."'

I tilt my head to the ceiling with the memory. I remember her words.

'Maybe revenge doesn't feel good because it goes against who *you* really are. Maybe you need a different type of revenge, a revenge that you're comfortable with. The best revenge of all is finding a reason to live, no? Wouldn't that be a total stick two fingers up at death, at that scumbag and what he did to you... to us? Maybe that type of revenge is all we need.'

He sets about making tea. I let his words settle, wait for him to speak again. He talks after he hands me a steaming cup.

'After we got clean, Sara read this book about giving back to feel better, how you could heal yourself by helping others. You know Sara, it was hard to not get fired up when she got excited about anything. So we tried it out, doing random stuff like paying for the car behind us at the drive in, bringing grub to the homeless. We'd sit with some old folks who needed company. When we were leaving, seeing the smiles on them, you'd swear we'd gave them a winning lottery ticket. It made me feel something, like a buzzing. Not the same as gear, not anywhere near, but it got my heart pumping, made me think there was a whole other way of life undiscovered. For the first time since quitting, I felt... hopeful. This time, we would do it. There were ways to feel better. Those peaks could be a different type of reward. A substitution.'

'You and Sara *did* get back together?'

He sips at his tea, doesn't look at me. Doesn't answer.

'Why did you hide it?'

'They tell you in NA to cut ties with anyone who can trigger you, anyone you associated with while taking. It was one step too far. We could give up drugs, just not each other.'

'You think I would have stopped you?'

'Back then, I wasn't your favourite person.'

He stops talking. I appreciate him more for it. I change the subject.

'So, what are you suggesting? We go around doing good deeds?'

'It can't hurt, can it? Even cleaning this place, doing some bits around the house, it's helped. It doesn't heal, that would be dumb... I don't know, it just kind of clears space in my head, distracts me.'

He brushes his hand over his face roughly, making a swishing noise.

'The regret is unreal. Why did I ever touch it? I wish I'd got clean right away, I wish I'd never taken in the first place, maybe I could have got her off it, maybe she would still be here.'

'But you can't.'

'No, I can't.'

I stand, wanting to leave the room.

'When we were helping people, Sara would break out into a before drugs smile, like when we first met smile and I thought we're gonna be OK, cos if the past can erase this quickly, just by doing these things, I'll do them every day for the rest of my life. If it puts that expression on her face. She was happy before he took her, the happiest she'd been in years.'

'I know.'

'You know how he found her, right?'

I take a deep breath, the thought of why hitting me in the chest like a punch.

'Yes. She was trying to score.'

He shakes his head. 'That's not true.'

'It is.'

'That's the way his team spun it. She never went there to score.'

'Why else would she be hanging around there, Ryan? There were witnesses that said she approached them, asked them. Come on. You don't have to do this, you don't have to lie to protect her. I'll still love her. I've always loved her, no matter what.'

He sizes me up as if he's only just seeing me. 'You have it all wrong. You have Sara all wrong. We went...'

'We?' I croak.

He nods, his eyes wide, sincere.

'Lorna, I was with Sara when he took her.'

Chapter Fifty Three

My legs go. I sit with a thud.

'You were at the docks?'

'*We* were. That morning Sara bought a scratch card. For ages she just stared after she rubbed away the foil, until I had to ask her was something wrong. She handed me the card. 100 three times. She said to me, "I've never won anything." I said, "your luck is changing." Sara went quiet over that.'

Ryan looks out the window, bites down on his lip.

'She spoke after a while, saying if it had been the year before there would have been only one thing we'd spend the money on. I said, "last year we wouldn't have even bought the scratch card." She seemed sad about that. Regretful. So, I cupped her under the chin. "Not now though," I said. She said something like her luck wasn't changing, that she'd always been the luckiest girl for ending up with me.'

Ryan's cheeks darken.

'Sara kissed me. She said, "you know what Ryan? There's not one thing I can think of that I need to buy. We have everything. We're sober." I said, "and loved. I've never loved you as much as I do now." I...'

His voice cracks, he taps his fist against his mouth, waiting to compose himself.

'That's the one thing I'm thankful about that day, that this was our last conversation alone. That I got to say that to her before... that her day started off being good.'

The tap drips. I don't get up to turn it off. Instead I listen to it for a moment. Take comfort in Ryan's words.

'How did ye end up at the docks?'

'Sara knew what she wanted to do with the money. She wanted to visit our old haunts with some treats. Charities hand out soup and sandwiches or hot meals but we often were hanging for some sugar. We went to the shop and made up clear bags with the things we used to crave. Chocolate bars, muffins, crisps, toffees. Bottles of fizz. Things to brighten a day. Being around the others felt weird. They acted different with us too, like we weren't one of them any more. The treats went down well though. At one stage I looked at Sara and I could tell she was thinking the same, that we had nothing in common with the lads anymore. The bags were nearly gone, when I spotted him. In his car, doing one of his drops, in the back seat, his driver smoking a spliff, so I tugged on Sara's sleeve, whispered to her that we should dodge, careful not to draw attention. Still, something made him turn. Sara didn't notice, handed out the last two bags, laughed when one of the old guys told her she'd turned into a model. My stomach flipped. I just stood there frozen, afraid to move. He stared and stared at Sara but then it looked like he was telling the driver to move on, and the car started. As he drove, I turned my face away, in case I riled him, all that time he passed I don't think I breathed once. It happened quickly. His driver stopped in front of us, blocking us from getting away. Next a door opened, and she was in the car before I could stop her, I grabbed onto her legs as he bundled her in, he was sitting in the back, shouting at his driver to go.'

'Wait. Are you saying someone else helped him?'

'Someone else was driving, yes, someone else helped him. There were loads watching Lorna, loads of people saw him take her. I nearly made it, nearly pulled her back out, the car was moving but I held her tight. I promise you Lorna I wouldn't have let go, he could have dragged me alongside the car and I wouldn't. The car stopped and I stumbled. The driver jumped out, hit me with a baseball bat, again and again on the hands. Then he cracked me on the bad leg and I roared with the pain but I didn't let go. He knew he had me then. He kept hitting me on the leg. Then the others were behind me, pulling at me to stop, breaking my grip and then I did, forgive me... I let go.'

He rocks in the chair.

'I let go. I should have held on, should have got up and fought him, should have rolled under the car to block it, should have done something, anything and I didn't. Every morning the first sound I hear is her screams as he pulled her in, I see her terrified face as he took her and I did nothing.'

The room is spinning. I need to move, need to do something. I get up, pace the kitchen, pull at my hair.

'Why didn't you make a statement?'

He stops rocking.

'I did. They threatened to throw me in the cells if I didn't calm down. You can go check, there has to be some kind of public record. I described what they looked like, who they were, gave them the driving licence of the car. I showed them my bust up hands, my leg's been banjaxed since. They took me seriously, Lorna, the guards believed me.'

'Why didn't any of this go to court?'

'After I left the station I couldn't go home, I went straight to the spot we handed out the bags, hounded the lads to tell the truth, showed them pictures of Sara, to guilt them into it but they blanked me, wouldn't even look at her image, couldn't. Some of these guys knew Sara years. While I was at the station he got to them. Or paid someone to. If you're looking for someone, it's easy to find where the homeless lads are. There's nowhere to hide when you live on the streets, no walls, no doors to close on threats. If you need something from them, all you have to do to get them on side is promise them drugs. Or the honest ones, well, they get hurt. What could I offer them that would help? Money or drugs wouldn't protect them. When you go up against a guy that knows the exact spot where you close your eyes at night you don't feel protected. Total amnesia. Every one of the other witnesses stated I was lying. A few of them made a statement I was the dealer. You must've wondered why I wasn't at the funeral?'

'I looked for you. Made Tim bring me to your house. It was boarded up. Someone said your mother died.'

Ryan hangs his head.

'Remember when my Dad came home after my leg break? When he told you to stay away, that he didn't need your help?'

I nod.

'After I went away, he put her straight in a nursing home. Found out after I got clean she died, in lockdown. Do you know he married a woman the following month?'

I shook my head.

'Turned out he hadn't paid the mortgage in years, mum's disability payments had paid the minimum. When she went into the home, dad transferred her money to paying for that instead. He did it on purpose, made sure I couldn't fight it. The bank repossessed the house without even contacting me.'

'I'm sorry.'

'Yeah, me too.' He sighs.

The answers keep coming to questions I haven't asked. A memory sizzles. Nick Barrett, standing there with his hat in his hand. *'Something doesn't add up Lorna.'*

'They said she willingly got into the car.'

'Not true. I told your barrister, the guards, Tim. The guards knew him though, knew of him, anyone on the streets heard what he was capable of. They followed up, that's how they found Sara. The guards saw what he did to her, saw my hands all bust up. There was no proof he took her except my statement. One guard took me to the side, said he knew I was telling the truth but they had to be careful, if they proceeded with the charge of him taking her and all the witnesses said the opposite, it could damage the case, could even lose it and he would be free to walk the streets. One detail could convince the judge he was innocent or that they arrested the wrong person. The case had to be rock solid.'

'But if the guards knew she was taken, why didn't they tell me?'

Ryan shrugged. 'Did you talk to any guard but Nick?'

I shook my head.

'The guard who believed me, swore he told Tim.'

'Why would Tim hold that from me?'

'You'd have to ask him.'

Ryan throws his arms out as if he's just as confused.

'Probably protecting you. How would knowing Sara was taken help you? I wish I didn't know.'

'Why tell me now then?'

'Because you need to know she wasn't back on the gear. You need to know that day started out happy. That I tried to save her. I need you to know I tried. Someone was there that day, someone who loved her, someone fought for her.'

I nod even though I can't see him through the built up tears.

'As soon as I left the guards I searched the docks, every alley, every dark place. Back then, I hoped he'd just drop her somewhere, throw her out of the car. I was frantic. Scared he'd inject her get her hooked again, cos it's easier to control a junkie. My heart was in my mouth. I would have done anything. I would have swapped places, I would have told him hurt me, told him rape me, kill me.'

He is crying. I don't console him, for his tears only match mine. They are unstoppable. They are a dam that needs to break. They are too long held onto, too long hidden. Our tears need to flow alongside words badly needed.

'That's the last time I felt hope. I walked around asking questions, for days, asking and asking not knowing Sara was dead. Until I asked the wrong people the right question. They nearly killed me. Once I woke up in the hospital and found out she was gone, I wished they had.'

Ryan sucks in a breath, long and deep.

'Even after, when they knew he killed her. Even after they heard what that monster did, they wouldn't change their story. Some of them denied even being there, some said they were too out of it to remember anything, some flat out refused. Troy had links with other guys, bigger guys that were worried he'd make a plea if he got caught. On the streets you don't snitch, you can't grass no matter how wrong or bad it is, you don't bite the hand that feeds you.'

After our conversation ends, I go to the porch and mull on Ryan's words for a long time, long enough for the day to turn to evening, for the sun to leave my view.

Troy was even worse than I thought. He took her. He got to the others and terrorised them until they were too scared to testify. It is because of him that the whole world thought my daughter went back on drugs. It is because of him that everyone thought she was a failure. Even me.

I stop then. For I don't want what Ryan said to be about Troy. It needs to be about Sara.

Sara had not gone there to score.

Sara's last actions had been to give.

Sara had known that day she was loved.

It is only when the chill in the air forces me to look for a warm cover that I move. I knock on Ryan's door and wait for him to say I can enter. He is doing what he always seems to do when he is in his room now: writing.

I run my hand along the ridge of the door frame, searching for the right words.

'The night before Sara died, I heard her talking on the phone. I heard her speak your name. It made me smile for a second. Next, I worried. Being together could trigger a relapse, could encourage ye to start taking again. When she left for a walk, I searched her room. Under her bed, I found a box. Inside was a needle, a spoon, a lighter. I flipped. Told her she was forbidden from seeing you, that I was sending her straight to rehab that morning. When I said she was never to talk to you again, she lost it, screamed she was a grown woman, she wouldn't give you up, she loved you. I asked, more than me? Her silence was her answer.'

I pull my cardigan closer to my chest, even though I've come inside, the chill has followed me.

'You were the love of her life, of course she would choose you. In any normal situation, I wouldn't have asked. The question was never about you, should never have been about you. She left saying she couldn't live with me if I didn't believe her. She left without looking back. That is the last image I have of my daughter alive. Her back disappearing down that long drive. Do you know how many minutes it takes to walk that? I could have stopped her, could have chosen to believe her, could have given her the benefit of the doubt. But I didn't. I didn't know the truth from lies with her anymore. How bad is that? You say I knew my daughter but in the end I didn't even know when she was telling the truth.'

'We warranted that doubt.'

'When she woke up after her last overdose, she became hysterical. I thought it was because of the room, because she knew I was going to force her to get clean. After, she said she'd wanted that. She was crying out for you Ryan. "He left me, he left me on my own. He doesn't love me anymore." You broke her heart. I thought detoxing would shed more than drugs, I thought Sara would lose the loss of you. The drugs left her system but she never recovered from you. I should have embraced that. I should have invited you back in.'

'Don't blame yourself. Sara asked me over, but until I could make you proud again, I wasn't calling to your door.'

'On the porch, I was thinking about sides. About the amount of different sides every person has. How, we only see the side of the person that faces us at that time. Since you've came, you've shown me more sides to Sara than I could have known. Even now, years later, I only know some of the story. Going on that... seeing you know a lot more than me, I'm willing to try your way because my way clearly isn't working.'

His pen doesn't move. He stares at me.

'Ryan, you said before that I should try and live, that Sara would want that. Can you help me?'

He lays the notebook on the bed, breaks into a smile as if he has been waiting for that question for a very long time.

'First step is to change everything.'

Chapter Fifty Four

There are six shades of green in Sara's eyes. I search the internet for the exact colours. Sage and seaweed, with particles of emerald that hide amongst shamrock and mint pigments that glitter like tiny gems. Tiny slivers of lime pop out in the sunlight. When she turns sideways, her eyes are like marbles. Iridescent, as if the different colours hide behind glass. Someone once called them cat's eyes, but I disagree. Cat's eyes have slits for pupils. The end raises upwards, giving the portrayal of being sly, whereas there is no slyness in Sara's. Only kindness and truth. Her love staring back.

Every time I read those lines, I see Sara's colours again. As clear as if she is standing in front of me. Ryan's words are like a drug. I crave them, need more.

Her hair is waist length, although she never leaves it down. I beg her to. I long to see the soft strands frame her face. When she does, that is Sara. When she sleeps, her hair fans out on the pillow; she calls it a bird nest when she wakes up but I call it spun sugar, because in the summer the auburn, kissed by the sun, streaks the strands with highlights the colour of caramel, that glint in the light. She tells me she hates her hair and I tell her back I can't understand that, how she can hate something that makes up the essence of her, because that hair tells any stranger everything about Sara. When I say this, she makes me list the ways and I rattle them off easily. Her hair makes her unique. In a crowd of mousey browns and dull blondes she blazes, just like the sun. And the sun is the most powerful asset to the earth.

It can be our enricher or our destroyer; if it burns too hot for too long, we all scald. The water in the rivers and lakes will dry out. If the sun moved nearer, grew hotter still, eventually the sea would reduce to nothing too. Every living thing would die: animals, plants, humans would perish. I tell her to be proud of what her hair represents. It is the hair carried down from warriors, from queens and Vikings. Recorded in paintings. Unforgettable amongst a sea of ordinary. It is only right that she should have hair like that, because she is all those things to me, and she will live a life where people will remember her and talk about her long after she is gone. When I say these words to her, I see her straighten, her profile turns almost regal and I smile. I want to always make her feel this way. I want her to see what I see, for the rest of our lives.

For years, botanists tried to grow orchids in Europe. Thousands of seeds might only produce one seedling. All that work, all that effort. Ireland isn't the ideal country for planting these flowers. There is too much rain, not enough continued heat or sun. Only when a fungus attacked the flower, did the botanists discover the orchid thrived. Sara tells me all this. Tells me that is why the orchid is her favourite flower. She tells me she wants to plant them in a line at home, framing the drive and dreams that one day, when someone visits, the colours will line the way to the porch. She says she closes her eyes and sees it sometimes, as if it's already done. I laugh and say she hasn't a green finger in her. She says it doesn't matter; she's still going to try. Even if the rain comes and drowns the buds or the sun doesn't and they never break through the soil, she says in her head, she's already experienced it. She says the ones that survive can take a long time to grow. Some only take a month, whereas some need six months to a year to produce even a root, spending another two years underground.

After reading that, orchids become my mission. I learn about the fungus, about the type needed and what to look out for. I spend more time on them than is healthy, but it is the closest I get to Sara. Being with the soil, touching the earth, it evokes a feeling in me that isn't there at any other time. No meditation or prayer can bring that level of closeness. Orchids dislike disturbance, so when I finish a section, I sit beside the soil, the gravel on my drive makes temporary dents on the skin on my thighs. There, I talk to her. Better than any altar, any grave. If Sara is anywhere, it is here. Troy's shadow darkens my view.

I plant cymbidium along the border of the fields, as out of all the orchids they survive the best outside in the summer and can bear the light the most.

I plant the Marsh Helleborine in the woods, as it favours more alkaline groundwater. They will take time, sometimes as much as eight years, to flower. Those I am happy to wait for, each day I walk through looking for the buds, the white and pink against green grass. None so far.

This is where my patience kicks in. Other gardeners might fiddle with the soil to dig up the root, but they are delicate, precious plants. Until they flower, they need time and love and patience. Like Ryan and I.

Chapter Fifty Five

The dead can live in a memory. Anyone, even people you've never met, can come alive in your thoughts. There, the dead can come back. A reminder, like a scent or a saying, can trigger you to step back into the recollection. There, they will meet you. For a second, or even a minute, they will stay.

With Troy, my guilt keeps him alive, drapes over my shoulders. He sits on the windowsill of every room I walk into, the cocked head gone, silent. Anything that could relight my reasons, stagnate. His potential stays. His possibility is what I see now. His eyes watch me wherever I go. The person who looks at me is just a child.

Chapter Fifty Six

Carraigshill is a dead-end town. On one side, the area drops off into a quarry of old mining pits, leaving nowhere else to go in that direction. Not as scenic as some neighbouring towns, like Knockfarraig, which stole Carraigshill from the coast, locking it into land, swallowing it whole.

In Carraigshill, you would never think the Atlantic was only a twenty-minute drive away. Back in the eighties, before the big American factory cut loose once the Irish tax incentives ran out, money circulated easy. Back then, the town used to be pretty: the shop fronts could afford new paint jobs, could afford to open, the pockets of the workers rattled with money to spend, the restaurants and pubs packed every night. The town had plenty customers then.

Once the big factory closed, the town lay abandoned. Overnight, thousands of households became unemployed. The cleverest or youngest got out using the pitiful redundancy to start a new life somewhere far away. Most of the older employees died young from shock or boredom from forced retirement, leaving the town full of middle aged couples who couldn't run, most with families to feed and full mortgages to pay, who scrounged for work or drank to forget their frustration. Never a college town, most Carraigshill residents left secondary school and went straight to the factory, the allure of instant extra income with annual leave, insurance and other perks too much. Why would anyone want to go to college when a job on your doorstep awaited? No commute, no university fees, no worries. No qualifications either. And so it was, how a whole town became completely independent on one business. Until that business left.

As I drive past the big factory, I shudder. The walls are at least twenty feet tall, it's shadow on the pavement dark, foreboding. In its boom, the walls were whitewashed every six months, now every available space is covered in graffiti. A constant reminder of the town's failure, it hardened most to never trust again. The closure soured the area, gave a rotting edge, not just in aesthetics but in attitude as well. Newcomers were eyed with openly hostile scrutiny because who would choose to live there?

This is where it started.

On I drive, but my thoughts stay on the damage one building can make.

In the years since, parents attempts to make life a little better for their children fell short. After petitions were signed and councillors promised change, every hurdle ended in a letter of apology that funding wasn't there. The result is a town full of half measures: a field turned into a pitch for sport, an old barn converted into a community hall so there is somewhere at least for a children's disco or karate classes. For some in the town, the hour they go to bingo, or play darts or bridge or whatever, is the only time they interact with other people.

On the corner of the street, I pass a young girl, her arms wrapped around her waist as if trying to generate some heat. She nudges her shoulder against a guy. He pinches her bum. She doesn't flinch or walk away. The girl is thirteen at most, her smudged black kohl eyeliner resembles a panda. The guy is a man, full goatee, at least eighteen. I shudder at the thought.

One community hall can't save a town. In a forgotten place, the teenagers lose most of all. With nothing to do but get in trouble they meet the expectation. Once unheard of when I was growing up, people shrug now when they hear of some incident, muttering the town is going to hell, but mostly there is acceptance, a weariness full of sighs. Everyone knows what went wrong but no one knows how to fix it.

Every pub I pass is full, on main street the men stand in lines smoking outside. Once you turn adult that's where most are found. The Covid lockdown dispersed some. Dead probably, but there are plenty more to take their space. Covid savaged some people, made them live in fear, when afraid, people turn to stronger distractions to block out worry. Covid savaged the once healthy also. The ones whose diagnosis was delayed, whose appointments were postponed while their illness festered and grew until it was too far gone to cure. The pubs offer light relief after a shit few years, until the money and sober thoughts run out.

Around the shopping centre, teens hang around on every corner, all carrying the same lethargic, bored expression. Nothing strange in that, you find teens in every town. In Carraigshill though, there is something missing from all their faces: there's no spark, no animation, no loud noises, no energy. Hostile, yes. Aggressive, definitely. The hung heads eyeball as I pass. It's hope that's missing, the hope I remember from when I was a teen.

There is nothing to do in this town. No incentives for the youths. No funding for the sports team. Even this section I drive along, which used to be an expensive part is worn, the buildings left to rot with the people in it. House prices soared anyway, meaning only people with surplus cash like landlords could afford to snap them up, then charge more than the average wage to privately rent them. All available money went on living accommodation.

I saw it coming even before the factory closed. How can one town survive on one company? That's why I drilled it into Sara how important it was for her to go to college. Education was the key to a better life. Or sport. Her and Ryan were going to get out. They had known this too, Sara studied every moment she could, Ryan trained first, then studied every spare hour to get his scholarship. He hadn't been a bad student, not by a far stretch, but once the offer of the club came, he was happy to just pass his exams. He would have still been accepted with his grades. All the physiotherapist, or personal trainer college brochures I sent away for became dogeared and ripped, not from being looked at, but walked on; the information inside untouched. I worried about him constantly. The boy that skipped into my kitchen each morning was gone. The drag of the leg a constant reminder. The drive that pushed him, from what time he rose each day, to what he ate, to what he spoke about, left. None of us knew how to handle it.

Sara worried too. Each time I brought up the conversation about college she changed the subject. As the summer months laboured on, as Ryan fell deeper into a black depression, she became quieter and withdrew. They hung around with their friends more, stayed around the corners of the town they used to avoid. If I mentioned college, she shushed me, as if even speaking about it betrayed Ryan. Knowing this, it should have come as no surprise when she refused to start the next September. No begging or reasoning worked. Sara was adamant. Ryan and herself were going travelling around Ireland and figuring out what they wanted for a few months. I was so naïve. Delighted to see a bit of excitement again, I encouraged them to go, to follow their hunches, to have a big adventure. A dream I'd never been brave enough to try, I did everything to help, even bought an old van we converted, then waved them off with hopeful trepidation, praying a few months would clear their heads.

Each night I would hold my phone and wait, the calls getting less and less frequent until they stopped altogether. Straight to voicemail when tried. When the days turned into weeks, when the conversation came it was vague, distracted, not them. Then, I started to worry. There was something wrong. They would never tell me what they were up to, or where they were. With some high fetched, *you won't believe what happened* story that meant I needed to deposit money into her account. Panicky calls. Urgent and quick where I could almost hear her bouncing on the balls of her feet. Hanging up when I'd beg her to just come home.

When the phone calls stopped, when my calls didn't connect, I lived in dread, on alert for any beep on the phone, ringing the hospitals daily, checking if there were any sign of them anywhere. That's when Nick came to my door. That's when I let him in to my life. He was solace during the dark moments, distracting the lonely nights. During the day he asked around, made calls in different towns. I loved him more for that.

It was the not knowing that drove me crazy. When Covid hit, I still had to work, as a shopkeeper I worked harder than ever, leaving notes on the door in case they turned up.

My panic settled to a constant unrest, bubbling in me all the time. One day they were just there, dropped home by Nick, two figures huddled together in my sitting room. Everything made sense then; who they were the last time I had said goodbye had left completely, the two people in front of me had lost all reason to wash or feed themselves or want to live.

Without question, I took them in. I'll never forget the relief of knowing they were alive. Again, I was so naïve. For me, once I had them back, I thought the hard part was over, figuring they had returned to get clean. It was later it dawned they needed to get away from where they had been; that they weren't running to me but running away. Neither had any intention of giving up. Back then, I resolved I would get them both through. How wrong I was.

Chapter Fifty Seven

Sara's friend forces me out of old memories. Carmel is as thin as a pencil, no curves at all. From behind, she could pass for a ten year old, not the woman of twenty-three I know she must be. Her hair, black and straggly, flicks out in different directions, resting on her shoulders. She looks unsteady on her feet. I pull over.

'Need a lift?' I call.

She staggers slightly, leans on my rolled down window for a better look. There is something in the gesture that makes me slightly sick, it's her familiarity with the act: she is used to leaning onto rolled down windows.

'Hey Ginger, how's it going?'

Her mascara has dried onto her eyelids. Her lips are cracked and dry. From the front, Carmel could pass for a much older woman.

'I'm good, you want a lift?'

'Ah, you're grand, I'm gonna get the bus later.'

I make a point of looking at the sky. 'It'll rain I'd say.'

She looks around, bites down on her lip. 'I just... I need to meet with someone.'

'I can wait, I'm not in a rush. It would be nice to catch up.'

'Serious?' She cups her arms around her tiny frame.

I nod in answer.

Carmel bounces on the spot and I nearly cry for how alive she is.

'You were always sound. Give me a sec, yeah?'

Again, I nod, pretending to fiddle with my radio instead of watching her disappear behind the derelict old warehouse. The nausea is back. We failed these kids.

After only a minute, Carmel slides into my passenger seat, more upbeat than before. I know those mood changes; she has a score in her pocket and all she wants now is to get far away and find somewhere safe to use it.

'Where to? You still living in Cresdon Avenue?'

Carmel wipes at her nose.

'Nah. Parents kicked me out a few years ago. I'm kipping at Joes now, down in Mount Pleasant.'

'Down by Connolly's shop?'

'On the right.'

'Mount Pleasant it is then.'

I drive.

Carmel rests one hand constantly on her shoulder strap bag, protecting it, stroking it. Addicts are so obvious, they think their actions are undetectable, but they move with such predictability. Once you understand, you can pinpoint their next action, almost step by step. With Sara I could anyway.

Once we are driving, Carmel relaxes, only then does she remember about Sara. Her eyes flash once the penny drops. She turns to me as if she has been electrocuted.

'You know, I'm real sorry for what happened with your Sara. What he did to her was messed up.'

Coming from her I don't flinch. From her, I know she means it.

'Yeah, it was. Are you,' I stop, trying to think of the right word, 'looking after yourself?'

'Oh yeah,' she says straightening up. 'I can take care of myself, don't worry.'

The same words Sara used. There's no point saying this. I drive, flashing back to Sara and her in her bedroom, trying out different make up brands.

'Tell me, what was that song the two of you used to always play, I can't place it?'

She screws up her nose, confused.

'When you used to come over to ours to get ready. There was a song you played all the time. The two of you would go out and it would be stuck in my head for the rest of the night. In bed I'd still hear it. I can't believe I can't remember.'

Carmel shakes her head, looks out the window, but I can tell she is thinking, going through songs one by one. I let her have some peace. Suddenly the song has become very important to both of us.

'Was it catching stars?' she says, clicking her fingers.

'Nope. Although now you said it that one was just as repetitive. No, the one I'm talking about had numbers in it... I think.'

Carmel chews on one of her nails.

As I turn into Mount Pleasant the rain starts, big drops hit the window, quickly turning torrential, the wipers not working fast enough to see. Cans are strewn over the grass areas. Every second house is boarded up. A car with no remaining glass sits abandoned blocking our side of the road. I drive around.

'It's number ten, down towards the end.'

Mount Pleasant looks anything but pleasant.

She slaps her thighs, making me jump.

'Got it. Ten reasons to love.'

It's my turn to screw my eyes. I can't match the title to the song. Carmel rolls her eyes and laughs. The voice that sings isn't the voice it once was, but it will do.

'One, you're always there, two, you always care, three, your kind to me, four, you let me be.'

'That might be it.'

Carmel scrolls on her phone. A few seconds later music plays.

I tap on the steering wheel, a million memories coming back at once. Little prickles spike in my eyes.

'That's the one.'

Even though I'm parked outside number ten, neither of us move. Both of us are back in the days that song played constantly. Carmel and Sara getting ready in front of her vanity table, singing to that song, me at the door, humming too, glad to catch the moment, glad to be allowed view a glimpse into my teenage daughter's life.

Five, you get me hot, six, you love me when I'm not, seven, you're always true, eight, I can be real with you.

'Nine. you're my best friend, ten, until the end. Here's my reasons to love, ten reasons to love.' Carmel sings at full blast.

I'm crying and I don't know how to stop. Carmel cups her mouth.

'Sorry, I'm such a fool like, I shouldn't have sang it, acting all happy and that.'

I wipe away my tears.

'No, you gave me back a good memory. That's what keeps me going.'

'Really?'

'Really.'

We listen to the rest of the song but the moment has turned somber.

'I wasn't just crying for Sara; I was crying for you too.'

She folds her arms.

'I don't get you.'

'There's nothing around here is there? What is someone your age meant to do with their life?'

Carmel shrugs.

'I've an interview next week for that new burger place opening up, you never know, fingers crossed.'

'Would you not move away, get out of here?'

We both look at the grotty house she is planning to go into.

Carmel turns sideways in her seat.

'There's no houses. I've tried. Only one's available are more than two wages. Or sharing with some creep who wants you to pay for a bed with more than rent.'

She shivers.

'What happened to college? Weren't you going to do something really good?'

She shifts, defensive looking. 'I did. Was in my first year when lockdown happened. Was meant to do it remote but my computer broke and I couldn't afford a new one and being in that house all day... I just kind of lost track.'

She scratches hard at her wrist.

'Could you go back now?'

Her eyes are like saucers when she looks at me, the black rim making them pop out. 'I don't think I'd remember any of it. Too much has happened, I'm not the same.'

I sigh. 'None of us are Carmel.'

She places a hand on the handle, ready to open. The rain lashes against the window.

'Wait,' I say. 'Just till it calms.'

She shrugs as if she doesn't mind but I can see I have lost her, she wants out, wants to get to what is in her bag. All my reminders of her failures have just made her want to bury her head in drugs.

'In an ideal world, if money was no problem, if nothing held you back, what would you do?'

Carmel sits back in the chair, stumped for a minute, and I smile at the amount of consideration she gives the question.

She turns her body towards me again, a flush to her cheeks this time. 'You won't laugh?'

'No laughing, cross my heart.'

'I'd become a tattoo artist. Have my own shop in town, with a huge window covered with designs.'

I smile. 'You always had a pen in your hand. Always doodling. Sounds like a perfect career.'

'One day maybe.'

'What do you have to do to start?'

She shrugs. 'Dunno.' She scrunches her nose. 'Bet it'd be hard though.'

'You should check it out. How do you know you'd like it?'

'Been messing with ideas for years.'

She takes out her phone, the screen broken but working, selects a file, then hands it to me. I scroll through her work. The pieces are intricate, the lines weaved around each other, reminding me of Celtic symbols like a Triquetra or a Dara knot.

'These are good.'

She holds up her left arm, pushes her sleeve back.

'I did this too. It's a bit wonky, it's hard to do a good piece on yourself. Learnt it online.'

There is an insignia on her forearm, an emblem I recognise. An interloping S with a T through it.

'It was the first thing I wanted to try. For Sara.'

I hover my finger over her skin. Carmel nods, so I run my fingers along the S.

'I'm sorry Ginger. For what Sara went through. It was my fault, I should never have given it to her.'

I continue to run my finger, starting at the top, making the shape as if I am writing the S with a magic pen. Afraid if I pause Carmel will stop talking.

'Given her what?'

She hesitates, her eyes flickering to my hand and her exit. I adjust my features to the least hostile I can make it. I smile. It works.

'It was meant to be temporary, only to be snorted. If I'd known what would happen, how hooked her and Ryan would get, I wouldn't have.'

Still my fingers move, two semi circles joined together. 'I thought Ryan got her started on all that.'

Carmel flinches. Scared now, my fingers making her uncomfortable. I don't stop.

'I'm sorry.'

Raging at her would be easy. I could dig my nails into her skin and rip. A few months ago, it would have come naturally. Instead, my finger stalls and I take my hand away, letting it rest in my lap.

'It doesn't matter. Whoever gave it to her wasn't the problem. Sara would have always become an addict. Even if you didn't, someone else in this town would've offered her at some stage. It's not your fault.'

What is shocking is I really mean it.

Carmel looks at me for a long time, long enough for the rain to cease and the dark clouds to clear.

'That means alot,' she says finally, opening the door.

'Wait.' I tug at her pants. 'Look, I'll do you a deal. Find out where and when, the cost of a course, details like that. When you do, I'll sort it yeah?'

'You serious?' she says, bouncing in the seat.

'Only if you get clean though. For Sara.'

Carmel gives me a quick hug, then gets out, closes the door. She motions to roll down the window, then leans on it. I hope she will never lean on another window like that again. Her face is solemn, sincere. It doesn't matter that the rain has started again, is now pelting her, making her skin blotch with red from the impact.

'I will , I promise.'

'Come to me with the details. If you don't have the money to get to mine, get in a cab and I'll pay the driver. OK?'

She beams, salutes me. 'You got it.'

I pull away before she starts to thank me.

The probability that she will put the work in and get clean is slim. Carmel might never show up at my door, never again dream of becoming a tattoo artist, or if she does show up, she might just take the money and spend it on gear instead. All of this I know as I drive away. Still, the thought of it, the little hope, the chance that I might give her a different option than what was available, makes my heart feel thicker, fuller. I smile the whole way home.

Chapter Fifty Eight

Before Sara died, anger was never my style. After discovering their drug taking, I didn't scream or rage. Protecting them, caring for them took over. Even when Nick warned me how common relapse was.

When Sara died, at first I didn't get angry. Reeling from the shock, I did all I could to numb. Life turned pointless. The only thing that made sense was discovering who Troy was. With enough money to pay the bail, he got to stay at home on the run up to the trial. Which meant I got to spy on the house. The more I learnt, the less I liked. Troy became Scumbag.

The trial brought a new feeling. In the courtroom, a heat rose, a fire that turned my skin red in patches, a bubbling popped over my skin, prickling and running, burning against the dermis. Every hurtful thing, every letdown, condensed into one throbbing mass of hate. All the times I found Tim had cheated, all the times Sara stole, every broken promise, every wound or slant came back in those few weeks. Her death, her face, her scabs, that singed hair. All of it came to the surface, until I was a walking mound of rage. From that pain, I made the hit list.

Spending hours pouring over their faces, staking out their houses, getting to know their routines, finding the exit and entry points I'd need when the time came. Because by that stage, even though I still held on to hope, I needed a backup plan to handle an unfair verdict.

By the time the courts confirmed justice wouldn't be served, I was already thick in my plan, convinced I would be the one to serve it. The plan got me through. It got me up in the morning, kept me occupied in the early hours. The only way to shut off was with alcohol, where I would collapse on the sofa or fall asleep in the car and start it all again the next day.

I see now I never dealt with my anger. All those years of repression had to go somewhere. Killing Troy has dissipated that feeling like popping a balloon. It was never anger I held onto, or kept. Could I have let that anger go safely? Could I have healed a different way if I sought help? Guilt has replaced the anger now. Sorrow and grief never leave. Suggesting to Carmel that I can help lets a fraction of lightness in. I want more. Ryan's words go around in my head. About Sara and what she would want, about how she would have liked to help. An idea bubbles.

Chapter Fifty Nine

At ten, Sara blurted out she wanted a cremation when she died, but when the time came, I couldn't take the chance. What if we needed to exhume her body for more evidence? You hear of it happening, of later breakthroughs with new procedures.

Sara will forgive me for that. Burials aren't for the dead, anyway. The rituals are for the living, for the people left to grieve, to distract for a while from their loss by keeping them busy. Making them chose one coffin from the other or what clothes to dress them in, what readings, music they'd like, their last wishes met. Afterwards, the grave gives you somewhere to visit. Before her death, graveyards seemed pointless. Why visit a place where no souls exist? There is more chance of Sara being around our house, or next to Ryan, or sitting on the porch, then hanging around where we buried her dead body. Still. I come every week. I tend to her patch of grass. Leave flowers and pictures, sit and talk. To her, I never mentioned my revenge plans, for even then I knew Sara wouldn't approve. Mostly I told her about my day, speaking to her about my clients, and then I always asked for her help. Today, that is my intention too.

Every time I visit, I carry my gardening set, and if there is a stray weed, I cut it down. I kneel beside the headstone, take out my two spray bottles, one soapy, one plain water. Spraying the headstone with the soap, I rub the granite with a cloth until the suds cover the entirety, then spray the water, watching bubbles run down and land on the grass. Then I buff the granite until it sparkles. Sitting back on my knees, I take in the sight.

'That's better Sara.'

The grave next to her is in a bad way. It is a man's grave, young too. At forty-two, he was almost double Sara's age, but still. One day, as I left Sara's grave, I passed the wife, struggling to hold the hands of two small shrieking boys. Only then did I realise I had known her around town, in another life, when I was still a mother and her not yet a widow. She had seemed carefree then, full of fun and laughter, and I had admired the shiny life she seemed to have. Her skin had become pinched since then, as if it folded in on itself; origami of the flesh. He dropped dead from a heart attack. A widow maker, they called it and it was just what it made her. That day and since, I felt for the woman, I could see she just needed a moment, needed to see her husband's grave. Often I thought about approaching her, to offer to bring the kids to the shop or something, to give her a few minutes reprieve but thought better of it, for who was I but a stranger to her? My grief stopped me. It must be hard enough to get out here with kids. Was it harder or easier to cope with grief with children? Would there be comfort in their love or would you have to bury your grief like the dead person? Would you have to carry it with no outlet, like a noose around your neck?

I kneel beside my daughter's grave. I came to tell her about Ryan, about his ideas to help people in her name, hoping it will help us, too. Now I'm here, I find I don't need to tell her. Sara knows it all anyway. Without having to ask, the answer has shown itself. Instead, I stand, gardening set in hand, and walk to the next grave, kneeling beside it. On the headstone, I lay my hand. I know he can't hear me, but I introduce myself anyway.

'Martin, my name is Lorna and if it's all right with you, I'd like to clean your grave. Your wife's having a hard time and I'd like to give her this gift, make her smile the next time she visits.'

I set to work. Wiping first the debris and cobwebs from the grooves gathered in the lettering. Spraying and massaging the suds into the granite, it strikes me again how a dirty task can soothe you. Again, I'm thankful for Ryan, for what he has peeled back and revealed. I tug out the weeds, then clip the long grass around the bottom of the headstone. It doesn't take long, thirty minutes at the most, but as I sit back and survey what I have accomplished, I know I've gained more in that time than if I'd volunteered. Because I know grief. When that woman visits, she will notice someone cleaned the headstone. Maybe, for an hour or even that day, it will remind her she isn't alone, that someone else cares too. Before leaving, I take one of the flowerpots on Sara's and place it beside his. Not for credit, I don't want Martin's wife driven crazy wondering who did it, or why. I'd hate if my gesture caused unease.

'Here you go Martin. All beautiful now.'

Ryan is right. We should remember Sara this way. Little gestures help. If little gestures make me feel lifted, how good will big gestures feel? What else can I do? I think about meeting Carmel. How many hopeless people did I pass on that same drive? When had it become normal to see homelessness and evidence of drugs on Cork streets? It seems futile even to contemplate. Trying to help is like pouring a thimble of fresh water into a contaminated lake. Whatever I do will be insignificant. But the niggle of good feeling I get even thinking of helping people is worth pursuing. It stays with me for the drive home.

Once there, I rummage around in the drawer by the door until I find an old copybook and a pen. On the couch I sit, resting the copy on my lap. On the top of the page, I write: *Things we can do.*

My pen hovers over the paper. What can I do? My mind returns to Carmel. Since Sara died, the surplus of my wages has gone untouched. I write:

Pay for someone to go to college.
Set up a fund each year in Sara's name?
Pay for meals for homeless.
Rent out hotel rooms for them.
Write thank you letters to all the people who sent condolence cards.
Clean all the graves around Sara's.
Set up a tidy town type thing?
Make the town good again.

My pen taps the page. I wrote that last sentence without thinking. How do you make a town good? How do you clean up the scum, erase the rot? I could kill every drug dealer in Cork, but another up and coming would just take their place. It has to start with incentives to reach for better, to offer an alternative. Start from the ground up, with the youngsters, or even before that, with the adults rearing those youngsters. It is deep layered, multi-faceted, and how can I expect to do something about it when my daughter succumbed to drugs herself?

A voice speaks to me, a clear voice from inside, different from mine.

You thought you failed with her, but now you know you didn't. She didn't go back on heroin. You helped her kick it and you helped Ryan, too. Start there.

III

Part Three

Chapter Sixty

Three boxes lie under Sara's bed. One is the box I confronted her with, the box with the needle. Another I do not touch. I lift the lid off the last, full to the brim with notebooks. On the bed, I lay them in a row, then wait until my chest stops heaving. One by one, I open them. Some are sketchbooks, full of doodles that make me gasp, cry, laugh. A few are of me caught in a moment, sitting on the porch looking out at the distance. Some, most, are of Ryan. Ryan sitting for her, looking straight out from the page, while others are of him sleeping, or the two of them, taken from a photograph. Also, there are sketches of her father, of flowers, mainly orchids, of birds copied from the fields. They are all excellent. Frame worthy. I hold the sketchbooks to my chest and want to weep at the loss of those talented hands, of that creative being.

The rest isn't as easy to rifle through. Her diaries. Her inner thoughts. One box is full of notepads dated when she was away with Ryan, when she lost to her addiction. Those will stay untouched. I keep to the diaries before she left. Before heroin. Before Ryan even. I open one. As I expect, it is full of teenage angst. Raging at me. I flick. Settle on a page written in red.

Dad left a nodge in his drawer. Normally, I wouldn't go through his stuff, but he pissed me off by ducking me to head to the pub with Marie. Serves him right for leaving.

I flick again. Stop at another passage written in red.

Got plastered last night. What a howl. Can't even remember going to bed.
Another one.

He's so lazy where he hides them. It's like he doesn't even remember. Hit the jackpot and found some uppers. What a night.

Red writing after red writing litters the pages. All entries were on a Friday or Saturday night, times she stayed with Tim.

Rubbed some white powder on my teeth. Mouth went numb. As I did it, I wondered what was wrong with me that I didn't even stop to wonder what it was.

Pages and pages.

Dad says if I ever touch his things again, he'll ban me from staying over. I shouted at him that he's a hypocrite. If he can buy the stuff, who is he to say I can't take it? Not like he's trying to win father of the year or anything. He said when I'm an adult I can do whatever I want, but before that I have to follow his rules. Mum's rules. He threatened to tell her, but I know he won't. He still went out, didn't get rid of his stash either. I messed up, got sloppy the last few times, got greedy. He'll never notice one pill.

She was fifteen.

Chapter Sixty One

Before Ryan, we went through tough times, Sara and I. Overnight, at fifteen, she turned into a mother's nightmare. Divided by two houses taught her how to deceive easily, knowing her dad would cover for her if it meant going against me. He never backed me up, never stood beside me if I needed to correct her, always seeing her point of view, always excusing her behaviour. Sara wasn't a bad kid. Rebellious was normal - I understood that. Even though I knew it was a rite of passage, I still had to address her mistakes. I still had to point out when she crossed a line, highlight what was acceptable and what wasn't. That's what a parent is meant to do. Tim never did. If I asked for help, he brushed it off, or if he did, he did it with such false actions his talk had the opposite effect.

So, curfews got broken and screaming matches became more frequent, doors were slammed. Street corners were hung around. Strange people pulled up in my drive, beeping the horn to see her, people she wouldn't explain who they were after they accelerated off. At the time, I wondered whether she was using, or drinking, but I never found anything. The niggles stayed unconfirmed. Tim hung up most times I rang, laughed or called me paranoid, told me to get my own life. The same words my teenage daughter screamed. Those days, I swung on the porch waiting, not wanting Sara to walk up the isolated pitch-black drive on her own, hoping the porch light would guide her, hoping she was sober, alive, in one piece.

Tim would just wave my concerns off, saying, 'kids will be kids.'

He had a point. Sometimes, though, it felt like he used her to get a rise, which didn't make sense because it was him who left. Tim hadn't wanted me, so why the resentment still?

And then Ryan strolled onto that pitch, and everything changed. The staying out ended, replaced with them staying in. She talked again, looked me straight in the eyes, the same girl who I hadn't recognised, who I had tiptoed around, tried to understand, tried still to love. With Ryan, Sara became my daughter again.

Until she didn't.

And now I know what was the cause for the mood swings at fifteen. Now I know what part Tim played.

Keeping silent or being a flake of a father would be forgivable if she lived, for they are all things that wouldn't kill a girl. Wouldn't put him on a hit list.

Here is the second worst thing Tim did:

After Sara died, after the trial, I called to his house. He had been drinking, but so had I, thinking it was just a requisite for survival.

When I told him I wanted to appeal, he caught me by the throat and pushed me against the wall. He scrunched up the skin of my face, then slapped me on the forehead so it whacked the wall.

When he spoke, spittle flew into my face.

'Never say her name to me again.'

He lifted the shoulders of my shirt and threw me onto the grass. He stood with his hands on his hips as I got to my knees.

'We have to do something,' I said.

He ran straight at me, slamming me on the ground, then he knelt over me, caught my jaw, pinching it, hurting me.

'We do nothing. She is dead. Do you understand what I'm saying? Dead. In the ground like the worms. Gone, finito, extinct, our daughter does not exist anymore. I do not want to hear her name. Don't call to remind me who she was, or who we were to her. Don't ring, don't write, don't you dare drag it all out again with an appeal. Understand? Understand?' He roared.

'Yes,' I said, whimpering.

'She is dead. From now on, keep her that way.'

He shoved my head into the moist dirt. He walked away without a glance and slammed his front door hard enough the wood sounded as if it splintered. I had not seen him since.

My ex husband was many things before that night but violent wasn't one of them.

Looking at the list, Tim's face stares down at me. Then I think of the worst thing he did.

'We're not finished,' I say.

Chapter Sixty Two

Tim swings the door open and reels back when he sees who is knocking, then straightens. I straighten too.

'I forgot what colour your eyes were.'

His laugh sounds uncomfortable, sarcastic even, but I am relieved no anger is evident in the tone.

It is true. I forgot that Tim has green eyes as well. Some of the same colours recorded by Ryan.

'Can I come in?'

He lets out a massive, reluctant breath, then swings the door wide. In his living room, he flops down on the battered couch. I sit in the hard chair opposite. There is no offer of refreshments. He waits, eyes me suspiciously. The house is clean, sparse, but kept together. I wonder does someone help him keep it that way, as he never lifted a finger to help when we were together.

Stop it Lorna.

I get back to the point, to the reason I came.

'Tim, I know you asked me to never speak of her again but you need to hear this.'

'Look Lorna, I...'

'Please Tim, let me say what I need to.'

He shifts in the chair but stays silent.

'I've been thinking about what I should hold on to. What I need to give up, to let go of. In order to let go, I need to release it.'

'Here we go,' Tim says, crossing his arms.

'Meeting you made me see how simple life should be. Love was all that mattered back then. The first time we kissed, I thought no one has ever looked at me like this, no one else ever will. At seventeen, I saw my whole life. Our wedding, our children, sitting around the fire at Christmas, the porch I sit at now, you holding my hand on my death bed. That's how much you meant to me, still, I forgot the colour of your eyes. We stopped looking at each other. You stopped looking first, you stopped loving me. Did you ever love me?'

He ruffles his hair.

'Why are you doing this now?'

'Because I'm trying to heal and you are part of my brokenness. You were the start of my breaking.'

He puckers his lips, ready for an onslaught.

'I'm not here for an argument, I just... I'm tired of carrying all this around. Can you help me find peace?'

We stare at each other.

'For a long time I wondered, just... if I wasn't pregnant, would you still have married...'

'I would have.'

He is solemn. He is genuine.

'Did you love me?'

He tilts his head, really looking at me now.

'How can you ask me that? Why would you need to?'

I slide from the chair, then crawl over to him. On my knees, I tuck two fingers into the gap in his shirt, holding it there, my face following my fingers, leaning on warm chest, hearing beating heart.

'There are times I know from deep inside that you loved me and then there are other times when I remember words said, or the women who were always around, all the women Tim, or that way you used to put your hands on your hips and look at me like I was the dumbest person, like you didn't know what to say, like no matter what you said you'd never get through. Those times compete. I don't know which one should win the argument.'

He rests his hand on my back.

'I loved you.'

I snuggle in, close my eyes, breathe in how wonderful he smells. I miss being with a man, even if it's Tim.

'Thank you for answering.'

He strokes my hair, holds up a strand of red.

'Your hair always reminded me of fire. Our love was like that, made from too much heat. You were quiet with everyone else but around me, oh boy. We were both fiery, both passionate, neither wanting to back down, I loved having that effect on you, having that power to turn your mood. Then you gave birth to Sara and all went calm. The fire extinguished.'

He drops the strand, smooths it to join the rest of my hair.

'Back then I was too stupid to understand fire burns out, that it's meant to burn out. If I'd given it a chance, a new type of love could have grown. Love for me, was all about the spark.'

He waves his hands in the air.

'Look, we both know it was me who screwed it all up. On purpose. I wasn't a good husband. No matter what you would have done, even if you'd been a saint, I would have made sure it messed up. All me.'

'How many years did I need to hear that? Tim, I don't want to carry these feelings anymore but I can't get rid of them unless I say it to your face.'

He lifts my chin so I can look at him. For a second I think he is about to kiss me.

'Permission granted to unleash.'

I unfurl from him. Sit on the couch.

'Most of Sara's childhood I held in my resentment, repressed a huge stack of frustration and disappointment. All the times you said you were calling and you didn't. All the missed parent teacher meetings or Christmas plays, all the times she came back from yours and told me how cool the babysitter was. When I rang worried that she might be using, you hung up on me. How could you hide her drug use when she was younger Tim? I could have helped her.'

'Like you helped her at twenty?'

I reel back. Tim ruffles his hair again.

'Sorry, low blow. Look it's no secret how much...'

'I wasn't finished.'

He closes his mouth, gestures he is zipping it shut. I gulp at air, trying to find words, trying to find the things I've buried.

'What I blame you most for, the worst thing you ever did in the long list of things, is how Sara called to you, asking for a place to stay. When she ran from me and went to yours.'

My voice cracks. 'You turned her away and then she died.'

'Whoa now, hold it there. You've got that last bit wrong Lorna, I sent her back, to you.'

I shake my head, not caring about the tears that line my face, needing them to prove what I am feeling is real.

'She messaged, saying you wouldn't let her stay.'

He shakes his head. 'She wanted you to feel guilty. We talked, I sent her back to you.'

I sob. 'I never saw her again, not alive. She never came back.'

'Sara never came back to either of us.'

'The last words I said to her were in anger.'

He trails one of my tears with his finger.

'Sara got why you were angry. She understood. It just upset her that you believed she could go back on it.'

'But I found the stuff, the drugs.'

'There were no drugs. Sara kept them in her room as a reminder.'

'Why didn't she tell me? Why are you only telling me now?'

'Because I couldn't talk about her,' he says, raising his voice to a roar.

I step back.

'I'm sorry.' He spreads his hands out wide. 'For it all. For the things I never told you, for the things I hid, for hurting you the last time we saw each other. I just went crazy, couldn't handle it. Seeing you that day on my doorstep was like Sara was there again. I flipped.'

He holds onto his chest.

'This shit hurts, Lorna. I'm trying, I really am. I want to do better, want to give you what you need now but my head was all over the place, same as yours. You weren't exactly holding it together back then. Why are you only asking me about sending her away now? Because this hurts.'

I fold my arms.

'The last time I tried to say anything, you put me up against the wall.'

He cups his mouth with his hands.

'I did. God help me, I did. When you needed me most, I hurt you. You have to understand I was crazy with grief.' He taps at his temple. 'The only way to cope was to push our daughter out of my head. Every time I looked at you it was like she was there again. You had to go.'

I lean forward in the chair.

'Thank you.'

'The last day, *her* last day, I didn't think telling you would help. That kind of information... finding out she was telling the truth about not going back on the gear, then hearing she went to the docks to buy some, I thought it would do you more harm, that you would harm yourself, make you carry guilt for pushing her into taking it again when you didn't have anything to feel guilty for and I knew you would, if you heard. You were a good mother to our girl.'

I gulp at his admission.

'When she was gone you were, we both were... fragile.'

'That's what you said to Ryan. Why Tim? Why tell him I didn't want him in court?'

He curls his hands into fists.

'You want to blame me for sending away our daughter but it was him that should have protected her. If he was a man he would have done anything to look after her.'

'Like you did, with me?'

He bites down on his fist. Puffs out his chest.

'Ryan was meant to be better than me. He was meant to do what I couldn't. He let go of her, do you know that? He let her go.'

'Tim, how could he hold on?'

My ex-husband deflates.

'Why all the secrets?'

He shakes his head.

'When I lived my whole life that way, how could I change? Your nerves were frayed, I was scared you'd do something stupid, something that would get you in trouble if you knew everything.'

'Too late.'

He narrows his eyes.

'What do you mean?'

I stand, then walk over to the window. I will not tell Tim.

'What I couldn't figure out is why she didn't go home. I know I'd stuck the knife in before, stirring up trouble but I had a proper talk with her that day, told her you were just worried. Told her how much she gave me a fright getting hooked on that stuff. She got it, she knew you were trying to protect her. She promised me she'd go straight home.'

'She went to Ryan. He said they were helping give out food.'

'Yeah, that's what he said at the time.'

'I believe him.'

'Look, I can see what hiding it looks like now but I honestly thought I was doing the right thing. You were a risk to yourself. Ryan was a junkie. When he came to me he was bust up, I thought he was lying or maybe I wanted someone to blame? Look, I'm sorry, I'll spend my life being sorry OK? I'm trying. Seventy days sober. Off alcohol, all the other stuff. '

He tries to cover his face in his hands, I peel his fingers away.

'Nearly there.'

He braces.

'Don't worry, the worst is over. Before I go, I'll leave you with something positive. What you did for me after, when you took over and managed the funeral and let me just grieve? Thank you. That is one thing I can say about you Tim, you stepped up for Sara when she died.'

His eyes film and he swallows rapidly, his Adam's apple moving up and down. His voice is as soft as a little boy when he speaks.

'What good did it do? It was too late. For Sara, for us. I always thought there was time, that I'd get round to it, become more regular, make it up to her and then she died. You can't take back time. I wasted years, decades and for what?'

I don't tell him about the list, or how close I came to doing the opposite of what I'm doing now, sitting here talking to him rather than exacting a revenge that could never have felt as good, could never have felt warm inside, healing and mending, memory by memory. Instead, I look around the room. There are photos of Sara everywhere. On the main wall, on the mantelpiece, dotted around in random frames on lockers and tables, all of her from about ten onwards, some alone with her smiling into the camera, some with him, arms wrapped around each other.

'Sara drew sketches of you. If you want I can drop them over with photos from when she was small? We never divided them.'

He inhales deeply, cupping his mouth.

'You'd do that?'

'They're your memories too.'

When I leave the house, I leave not as a friend but as someone who once shared a life with someone else. Who once loved a man with all her heart but was hurt by him. Who still wanted him in her life, who wasn't afraid anymore of him hurting her still.

There is nothing left of the old me. I am a starting board, a fresh slate. Beginning over, building blocks, after what we've been through, it doesn't matter if those blocks will one day collapse or come crashing down because they have already, the very worst happened and I survived. After Sara, I can survive anything.

Chapter Sixty Three

The list

  1) Clean the graves that haven't had any visitors for years.

  2) Hand out food

  3) Set up account for Carmel.

  4) Paint wall of old factory.

  5) Drop a bag of shopping to Mrs Parks.

  6) Call to Mr Travis. Sit and listen.

  7) Offer to help Mrs Doyle around the house.

  8) Set up a tab in the coffee shop for next twenty people.

  9) Leave my favourite self help books in random places.

  10) Contact rehab programs about what training I need to become a counsellor.

  11) Help Ryan heal.

  12) Call to Tim with the pictures.

  13) Learn to forgive myself.

Chapter Sixty Four

'You writing about Sara?'

Ryan leans on the doorway.

'No. Still can't, sorry. I'm not there yet.'

He runs his fingers along the door frame, shifting the weight to his good leg.

'What I have been doing, is thinking about what you said, about honouring Sara.'

'Me too.'

'How would you help?'

He sweeps his hands on his thighs once, then makes his way to the armchair opposite. His leg drags more today than usual, the activity outside taking its toll.

'We start with the town. There needs to be something, anything, to stop the boredom. When I moved here there was nothing, no youth clubs, no opportunities, nothing to get a teen interested and there still isn't. Something like an arcade or a café.'

'That would take a lot of work.'

'Work doesn't bother me. Keeps me from thinking, or doing worse. It's when I'm idle I get in trouble. It's when teenagers are idle, they do too.'

'You think boredom is the issue?'

He shrugs. 'For some. Some know no other way. With me it was not having anything to focus on anymore. Pain was the instigator, for sure. That's what everyone thinks, that the pain drove me, but I would have got over that. It was the giving up, the having nothing to live for, or thinking there wasn't. That's why I think it's important to start with teenagers. Drug use or whether they are accepting of it is anyway. Catch them young. Show them there's another way, a healthy option. You're going to get experimentation but that's all it will be if they have a solid base. If they know there's a safe place to talk, that there's another way to deal with their issues then maybe we can stop them going further down the path we took.'

'What would have helped you?'

'There's nothing in this town if you don't study or play sport or have money to leave. Everything's depressing. The area's run down, there's teens hanging around the streets in the safe parts and homeless sleeping rough in the rough. Both lead to trouble. They have nowhere to go.'

'My teenage years were full of boredom and I didn't take drugs.'

'Were you ever offered?' Ryan asks raising an eyebrow.

'Course I was.' I splutter. 'Not hard drugs, but I tried spliffs back in the day.'

'Oh yeah? And what did you think?'

'Did nothing for me.'

He nods as if that makes sense. Was the only reason I hadn't tried anything stronger because I had never been offered them? I had no scruples about drinking alcohol.

'How would you get through?'

He answers quick enough that I smile. This is a subject he has thought about.

'I'd visit the schools, speak to the students, tell how I messed up, how they could avoid it, offer them an alternative. Show how sport can get them out. Just because I can never play professionally, I can still train others, I can still show how. I've missed it, the team mentality, the sport. For others, it would have to be on their level. Everyone these days wants to be an influencer or an entrepreneur. Maybe we could show them how to set up a business online, have a place that gives introduction courses on coding, managing money? I'm telling you, most kids look for trouble when they've nothing better to do, when they aren't shown a different way. Give them a better alternative, make them feel worthwhile.'

'How do we do that?'

'Not sure yet. Campaign? Go to the council with a plan for a basketball court, a proper football stadium or sports centre and I don't mean just for the rich kids but have them in areas that anyone can use them for free.'

'Putting up areas like that just gives teens a place to hang around. It could turn out worse. All our hard work could be for nothing and it wouldn't be easy, it wouldn't be easy at all.'

'When have you ever shied away from hard work? Everything worthwhile takes work, you told us that back in the day. That's what makes the payback feel even better. What does it even matter if it fails? We both need something, we both need a goal, I don't know if you looked at yourself lately but we both need something.' He laughs, then turns serious. 'The thing is we'd be trying. We'd be living.'

'I don't know if I can work with teenagers. I don't know if that will be too painful.'

'Maybe you need to do something for the parents then?'

I think on this a minute. A niggling sensation fires up but it's too early to say anything.

'OK. Let's start with looking at places we could recommend for the basketball court. If being around teenagers is too much, I'll look at doing something else.'

'Ah see, I'm a few steps ahead of you. I already have the perfect place.'

'Where?'

'The old factory. It's right in the middle of the town so there's access. And the car park is concrete and flat, so it's ideal. It's already set up.'

'Who owns the land?'

'Who cares? It's idle the last ten years. Isn't there like squatting rights? Couldn't we just erect some basketball nets and get on with it?'

'We could, but aren't we then getting people's hopes up? Why don't we check if it could be done properly or if there's a plan in place for the spot?'

I smile. 'Look at us all fired up. We've come a long way in a few minutes.'

Ryan hands move to his pockets, he shakes his head. 'We have.'

'It's good to see you happy.'

'Happy is too big a word. At least I'm feeling something, you know?'

He tilts towards me wanting an answer. All I can manage is a nod.

* * *

Later, Ryan is replacing a rusty lock in the shed when I find him.

'I've been thinking about what Sara would like to do in her honour.'

He stops what he is doing. Leans back on his heels. Listening.

'Sara loved to do random acts of kindness, yeah?'

He smiles. 'That she did.'

'What if we set up a charity or a trust in her name?'

I wiggle the piece of paper, open it out to show a new list of names, complete with a new line of faces.

'OK,' Ryan says, warily, rubbing his hands first before taking the page.

I grin; I can't help it.

'This time I want to help the people on here. Some need to change the path of their lives, some just need a helping hand, a talk or a gesture.'

'I'm on the list.'

'I know. So am I. We need to start with us, then maybe help others.'

He stares at the page, then shrugs, hands it back.

'I'm in.'

'Before I hurt Troy... it was like a temporary madness that went on far longer than an episode. It was a prolonged mental crack, an obsession, the only way I could cope. By thinking only of those on the list, of the wrongs done, not questioning if they should be on there, or if the facts were correct, or about the repercussions after. I was wrong to think revenge would help. There should be someone to talk to, after a family member has been murdered.'

'Like a counsellor?'

'Kind of. More than that. Someone assigned to you. Not any old eejit, someone that looks after you, like when you have a baby and the HSE comes out to the house to check how the baby is, like how she's feeding when what they're really there for is to check on you, check how mum is coping, how you're treating the baby.'

'Like a social worker?'

'Yeah. At the time it's an inconvenience, but you know it's also important. They should have someone like that for people going through trauma in the system.'

He arches an eyebrow. 'You're telling me you would have let some HSE guy in?'

I smile. 'Probably not. If it was court appointed though I would have had to.'

'You wouldn't have trusted anyone.'

'I might have.'

Even though I know he is right, I can't help sound affronted.

'You're a better person than me. I wouldn't. I needed this time.'

'That's my point, though. What if an expert recognised the signs, saw the way you would have handled your grief beforehand than gave you an alternative?'

The skin around his eyes crinkles up with confusion.

'I mean, what if someone had said: "Ryan you are showing signs of having a relapse. If you follow our steps we can help." Wouldn't it have saved you months of pain?'

He tilts his head, as if contemplating.

'Honestly, I don't know. Did I listen when you tried to help me after my leg break? Did I listen to my NA sponsor after the trial? He tried to get through but I didn't care.'

'Maybe there was a better way to handle it. You were young. If someone knew exactly how to unlock that pain, maybe it would have got through.'

'It would have to be a plausible alternative. After the trial, I don't know if anything could have convinced me not to use. Maybe... if someone had forced rehab or something.'

'After the trial we were too far gone, the damage already set in. We were left with no outlet, no closure with the result. We were just left to get over it, left in limbo. No wonder we went in on ourselves, how else could we cope?'

He nods, I have his full attention now.

'What if we'd been helped straight after the murder? By someone like us that had gone through it before. What if we were given the tools to cope, at least told of the pitfalls, about what we could have expected from the trial?'

'We'll never know, I guess.'

I leave it there because I haven't the answer. But it sits with me, that thought, drifting in and out randomly, just before sleep, on waking. It niggles and I don't know why or what I am meant to do with it. It stays until it becomes a comfort, a blanket I shroud myself on the days all I can see is a frothing mouth and a boy turning blue, becoming a mantra.

If you'd known better you would have done it differently.

Some days I manage to almost believe it.

Chapter Sixty Five

Only one name continues to appear each time someone mentions the old factory.

Councillor Pat Adley is a hard person to track down. There is no information online about where his office is located and his voice machine is permanently full. Hanging on the line to the council, I lose hours, where the girl on the phone tells me she can't find any address, but yes, he is the right person assigned to that area.

Everyone I speak with is polite, offering to help, but they keep giving me the same numbers, keep giving me the runaround until I feel like I'm spinning. Typical council behaviour. After finally finding a number with a working voicemail, I leave a message.

'Mr Adley, this is my seventh day trying to get hold of you. Could you at least answer your phone? Although, I'm sure if we speak about the proposed plan for the basketball courts, you'll only say you'll look into it.'

I laugh. It takes this voicemail to understand my effort is futile. I speak to myself rather than to him.

'Even if you think it's a good idea, even if you think it's worth campaigning, nothing gets done fast with ye. The powers that be have to go away and talk and talk until they do nothing and the idea gets moved around and sat on for years before they give permission.'

I hang up.

On the porch, with coffee in hand, I notice the flat slats as I step on them. The wood feels smooth from being sanded down, revarnished. Each day I gravitate to it at some stage, for it is the perfect place to sit and think. If I'm lucky, my thoughts will calm. Never alone, Troy and Sara sit on either side. One reminds me of what I should have done, the other reminds me of what I need to do.

I try to imagine what the orchids will look like when they flower. I think of the plan Ryan has sown. Are teenagers like flowers? Once you tend to them and plant their seeds right, will they continue to grow year after year?

I close my eyes, trying to picture the fields full of flowers this time next year. What I see is an entirely different image. My breath catches. *All this land is wasted.*

Back when Sara just died, I wanted the weeds to take over, watched as they grew strong, grew thick, expanded until dense, reaching for the woods until they were nearly part of it. They represented my thoughts: overgrown, gnarly, poisonous.

There is a place in the woods just after the entrance, as you walk along the dirt path made by our many trails, that opens into a clearing. Entirely covered by trees; even on the hottest days in summer, only flickers of light win through. When she was young, this was where you would find Sara, taking refuge from the heat, searching for bugs or small creatures to save. She never ventured further, that was the deal, only allowed to go in but not past the open clearing where the border of our land finished and anyone could enter. The clearing was my favourite spot in the world I think, back then anyway, where after braving the imposing dark of the trees, the shadows and hush would fan out into open space and the sunlight would touch your skin again. In the summer, both sides of the path bloomed with wildflowers. When I was a little girl, I had seen a picture in a magazine of multiple coloured flowers in a field and the image stayed. After buying the house, I set to work, sowing red, then purple, then yellow. Sara never picked them. It was enough to look, for to pick one would ruin the perfect symmetry. Picking meant condemning the flower's beauty to death. Much better alive, vibrant in the earth, such a stunning sight that greeted you after the haunting darkness of the woods.

Out of the clearing, if you follow the path, there are other sights. Open to the public, you often see hikers mounting the high hills behind or fishermen casting along the river bed. More a creek, the water shallow enough in parts to walk across, although there are sections that can deceive, can trick you, deepening to over a six-foot drop, with lost logs at the bottom that can trap a foot if not careful, or stones covered with moss that are slippy, or sly. If you keep to the banks and throw a line in those parts, you can hit the jackpot. On good days, the poachers catch salmon, on a slow day a catfish.

I stand, excited.

All this time, the solution has been right here.

Chapter Sixty Six

When I find Ryan in the kitchen, he is waiting. Pacing. I close my mouth, my sudden idea on hold. This is not the time to speak of dreams. Before dreams can manifest, the nightmares have to leave.

'I need to talk to you about Sara. About how I let her down.'

'You don't. That's in...'

'I do. Like what you did to Troy. I have to let it out.'

I breathe. I understand.

'It was me that screwed us.'

'How?'

'Sara met Troy because of me.'

My heart turns cold. 'You knew him?'

He picks at a groove on the table.

'We had this old guy who used to supply us. Sound, as far as these guys go, just supporting his own habit. But I heard about this new gear. Stronger. Sara didn't want to mess with someone new, but I kept at her, chipping away, pushing. Met him once, that was enough. He was young, younger than us, straight off you could tell he was ruthless, though. Made you feel uneasy, as if you were below him, under him. Most drug dealers act hard, you expect it, comes with the territory, but he freaked me out. He had this cold way of looking, of assessing your weakness, of getting under your skin.'

Ryan shifts on his feet, looks sheepish.

'He called her *yer one*. Seeing us together, when he was handing the gear to me, he took it back at the last second, and said I could only have it if "yer one" did something first. He looked straight at me as he said it and I knew before anything else, he was trying to come between us, that he wanted to destroy what we had. Right in front of her, he said it, but said it to me, like what happened to her was my choice, like I told her what to do, like I owned her.'

Ryan's body shakes, as if trying to remove the thought.

'What did he want her to do?'

'It doesn't matter.'

'It does. It will help me understand.'

Ryan shakes his head, embarrassed, pleading.

'Please. I want to know it all.'

He hesitates, taking a minute to work up to speaking.

'He said, "get her to suck me off." Sorry.' He rakes his fingers through his hair as if trying to erase the memory.

'I'm a big girl Ryan, I can take it.'

'I couldn't answer, in shock like, I think he took that lapse as weakness, as if I was considering it or something, but I swear to you I wasn't. I would never have let anyone touch a hair on Sara's head.'

I nod, urging him to carry on.

'All the lads around him laughed at Sara, too. He laughed for ages, proper howls, and it kind of stunned us into not moving. Unhinged, I'd call him, tapped. I wanted to get away, but didn't want to provoke him. I gave him back the bag and placed a hand on Sara's, trying to guide her away. I could feel her resistance. It didn't matter how strung out we were, or that we'd paid for the bag, I just wanted to get out of there in one piece. He stopped laughing, his eyes went cold again, he sucked air through his teeth and said, "I wouldn't let that dirty scabby mouth around my knob. Bet her flaps are crusty. The only place I'd stick it is in her hole." Then he dangled the bag. "What a bargain. All this for a go at destroying her." You know Sara, she flipped at that. She didn't care about him mocking her, but she couldn't ignore the unfairness. She never could. "We've paid you," she said. He leaned into her, jabbed her chin. "You want it? Bend over."'

'Bastard,' I say.

'He was testing us, trying to get a rise, laughing as we squirmed, getting off on it. He was waiting for us to answer, wanting to get between us, wanting to rip us right through. Lorna, I swear, no matter how bad it hurt to go without, I know what people think about addicts. I would have died instead of making Sara do anything like that.'

'I know Ryan.'

There was the truth. I knew. Ryan hadn't ever tried to hurt Sara, wouldn't have known how to even. Her protector, her love, her soulmate, her life. Her ruination.

'He thought he had us summed up. He thought he was better than us. Even though we were addicted, we never sunk as low as some others. We never stole, never hurt anyone except ourselves. As long as we kept two euro, we could buy some beads and string and we'd make bracelets.'

'Like the ones Sara used to make?'

'Yeah. She showed me how. We'd lay out a blanket and sell them. Not to pretty up what happened or anything, just so you know we didn't forget completely who we were. Yet here he was, this disgusting prick making out I would swap the love of my life for a score. I lost it, went for him. Sara dragged me away. When we reached the corner and I'd calmed, she tapped my arm and said wait and trotted back before I could stop her. He let her approach. Sara leant over, whispered something in his ear. I nearly vomited with the fear that she might agree, that she might do what he asked. His body language changed. He stepped back as if she burnt him. Then I felt scared, because he had this wild, mad look in his eyes but he didn't attack, just pointed, kept jabbing his finger at the air between them, his teeth baring, biting down on his lips. She backed away without the bag. I knew then something between the two of them was unfinished, and that from then on we'd have to look over our shoulder with him. We had always kept out of trouble, always slipped away or under the radar. This was different. Straightaway, I knew I couldn't do any of it anymore. I was sick of the threat of violence, the worry, the need to hustle every waking hour. For what? For the pain we went through, put our body through, put ourselves in danger for? I couldn't do it to Sara anymore. Meeting Troy was a wake-up call, my lowest point. I told Sara I was done, that I would only go through this pain once more. Sara needed a last goodbye she said, and I didn't blame her cos when that itchiness starts you'd climb over your mother to stop it. This time, though... no drug was worth what he could have done. By the shelter, there were a few people we knew hanging around. Sara dropped my arm.'

He shifts his leg, winces.

'I kissed her face and whispered in her ear. "One more Sara? And then we go home?" And I stayed with her as she got the gear ready and I rocked, strung out. All I wanted was a hit, and I knew I had to get away, but I couldn't leave her either. And there was something about that day that was off, I'd felt it since that morning, had a bad feeling and thought it was just that guy, like I'd known we'd meet him, and that it would lead me to want to give up but then I saw it was like I'd had a premonition or something because Sara was fitting, looking funny, overdosing. I picked her up, ran through the streets. At the hospital, they took her, then wouldn't let me in. It was me who gave them your phone number. I waited outside, watched you run in and only then I left, because by then I was hurting. You would look after her.'

'Why didn't you come up to me? I could have helped you too.'

'It was my fault. We needed to get clean separately, do things differently. After I came home, when she spoke to me again, she told me you'd brought her back, got her clean. We talked about that day a lot. About Ripper, Troy, I mean, about the lead up to getting clean. We didn't know he would find us, but I knew after what she said he wouldn't leave it go. It's all about reputation with these guys. Out of all the things we did on drugs, he was the one I kept an eye out for. The one I worried about. That's why I knew straight away when he saw her that day, he was gonna do something. He would prove what she said wasn't true.'

'What did she say?'

'As soon as it was out of her mouth, she regretted it, said she shouldn't have gone low. It bothered her, the way she handled it. Any other time, she would have diffused it, diffused his anger. As much as he looked at us and summed up what we were, Sara had summed him up, too. For a reason I will never know, she reacted out of character and tried to hurt him. Maybe because he had tried to embarrass us, or humiliate me, or that she had wanted to call his bluff, or call out his bullshit. Or maybe she was just strung out. Whatever the reason, Sara wanted him to know she saw who he was, that his whole life was a lie and someone else knew it.

'What was it? What did she say?

'That she'd seen him and she knew his secret. That it was him who liked to bend over.'

Chapter Sixty Seven

The list (Part 2)

    1) Look into funding for building on the field.

    2) Clear an area for a basketball court.

    3) Look into cost of building a sports centre.

    4) Contact rehab programs about what training you need.

    5) Research trauma.

    6) Contact guards about ways I could help victims.

Chapter Sixty Eight

Ten people show up. Which is ten more than I thought would. Ryan is there, Tim too. The others are present in response to the poster I stuck on pillars and poles, walls and windows of shops.

Some, I hope not all, are here to gawp at Sara's mother, or the one from the telly.

'Right lads,' I say, clapping my hands to stop their talking and grab attention.

'Let's make Carrigshill pretty again.'

We scoop up rubbish, paint over the graffiti on the factory wall, line shabby abandoned buildings with potted plants, adding some much needed green back to the town.

It is while scrubbing at a window that I see him, his elbow stuck out at rigid angles. His eyes are bright in the grubby glass.

I drop the sponge.

My hands shake. I turn around, but no one stands behind.

When I look back at the glass, he is still there.

Troy.

No matter how much I scrub. No matter how clean I make this town, I cannot erase him.

Chapter Sixty Nine

After dinner, I break the silence.

'I can't stop thinking about what we might have done if we were offered help. It can't all be for nothing. Her death can't be the end of her story. Sara's life was... is significant, she shouldn't just fade away. She was meant to make a mark, I always felt that, that she was better than most of us. Her life meant something. Can my life mean something? Do I deserve for it to mean something? I don't think so.'

Ryan purses his lips.

'For her I'd make it mean something.'

'Same here.'

'I don't want any mother or loved one to feel as alone. You want to help teens. What if we tried to help both? Help prevent kids choosing the wrong choices. Help people whose choices were taken away.'

'I'm listening.'

'If another victim of a crime or parent of a victim approached me, I would have listened, I would have trusted what they said. Can't I tell people how it will feel to have a camera thrust in your face at the funeral better than anyone? I can prepare them and they won't turn me away Ryan, I know they won't, because everyone knows who I am, everyone knows what I went through. When they don't know who to turn to, when they need to get away from looking at the place their loved one once lived, they can come here.'

He looks around the room.

My smile nearly splits my face, I'm so excited. 'Get ready now, I've big plans. It was your talk about those basketball courts, it got me thinking about how much land is going to waste here, about the stream, the woods, about Barry selling the field next to us. We could make a sanctuary. A place for victims and their families to heal. A place for teens to relearn. We...'

A rap on the door makes me startle. We look at each other, both frozen to the spot.

'I don't want anyone knowing where I am. I'm not ready,' Ryan says.

'Go,' I say.

My palms are sweaty before I open the door. Unused to callers, even though I expect trouble, my legs still buckle when I see the shape of the man's shadow through the glass. He isn't wearing his uniform but I would recognise the shape of him anywhere. The door opens to Nick, shifting from foot to foot.

'Sorry to call at this late hour Lorna but I need to have a word.'

I stay at the door.

'Inside, if that's all right?'

'Course, sure.'

I open the door wide, letting him walk past me. He takes a good look around, doing a full turn before heading for the kitchen. He knows this house well.

'Tea?'

'Please.'

I cringe. This isn't going to be a quick visit.

'You've done the place up since I was here last.'

I look around as if noticing it for the first time, more to buy myself time than anything else. I fill the kettle and flick the switch. 'It keeps me busy. Busy I've found is good.'

'That's true Lorna.'

I hate the way he says my name. It makes me think of other times, happier times. Times that for a long while I needed to forget.

We fall into silence and I know there is no point making small talk, something has forced him to come here for he wouldn't just pop in for a chat after what went on between us. I flinch at the images coming to mind, of me hitting him in this very kitchen, screaming at him to get out. He was the only one I raged at. The only one I knew would take it. Until he didn't. Until he closed the door when I told him I hated him.

This I know about Nick: whatever he has come to say won't be attempted until I sit facing him. Nick likes eye contact, likes sizing you up every time he speaks. I used to love the way he looked at me, when it became less about his job and more about us. There was a time when I longed for his eyes to take in all of me.

Instead of talking, I busy, getting the milk, the sugar bowl, laying them on the table. Pulling some soda bread out, getting some cheese and butter. He doesn't refuse when I place them in front of him.

'Thanks.'

He scoops out a big lob of salty butter and smothers his bread with it. Yet he doesn't take a bite. I take my time making the tea, as if we are both prolonging what is about to be said. In my case, it is better to prolong than wait for him to speak. His delay is on purpose, probably to see if I am nervous, because he knows me well, knows all my bodily reactions and I can't risk him seeing me fidget or act too calm. I never knew what to do in front of him, always on edge, always interested in his interest. After delaying as much as I can, I take a deep breath and place his tea down, then sit with my hands cupping my own mug.

Only then does he take a bite. As anticipated, he eyes me as he chews, his mouth working the crumbs over and over, his jaw going from side to side reminding me of a steam roller, those brown eyes not leaving mine. I won't make small talk; I won't give him anything until he talks. I smile, sip at my tea, hold my cup tight so not to shake, waiting all the time, waiting for him to reveal what he is here for.

Finally, he finishes the last bite, he pushes his plate away, settling back on the chair. Now that he is ready, I realise I'm not, I will never be ready for this conversation. I brace myself.

'I heard he got out.'

I look him in the eye. 'Who?'

'Troy. They released him a month ago.'

Red cheeks flush, I don't even have to pretend.

'And you're only telling me now?'

'I wasn't told. We only round the bad guy's up, we aren't informed of what happens after we catch them.'

'What do you mean they released him? He got years. Are you here to tell me he could come looking for me?'

He tilts his head, his eyes never leaving mine.

'You know I'm not.'

I keep my features passive, begging them not to betray me. Then think, if I didn't know anything, his statement should confuse, so I furrow my forehead.

'I don't understand.'

'Troy O'Callahan has died.'

'What do you mean?'

'Let's not do this. Lorna, I'm not here to question you. His parents believe it's murder and you had something to do with it. On paper, as far as the coroner is concerned it looks like an overdose but they're insistent. They hired a private investigator. Paid for their own autopsy and have been gathering evidence. Christ, they didn't even inform us.'

He strokes his face, brushing the stubble on his chin. He looks tired all of a sudden. My heart pangs for him, because I have done this, I have made him tired. Those brown eyes search for something in mine and I can see he's sorry to pass this information on.

'They have something. Your car was in the area, something about phone location? Supposedly you bought some equipment off the internet too.'

My stomach churns. *The phone call from Patrick's son telling me of his death. The taser.*

'I bought a taser before the trial. After you told me I needed to be careful, that he was a dangerous man. It was in case he broke in, in case he sent someone over to do his dirty work.'

He flinches at this and I know the comment is unfair. I carry on.

'It wasn't like ye provided protection. I bought it to scare them off, but I've never used it.'

'I would've protected you if you let me.'

He tips his head, looks embarrassed.

'Look, I know I'm not your favourite person these days, that you didn't want to see me afterwards... but you should know I wouldn't blame you for wanting to do something drastic. What he did to Sara... it was inhumane. If she was my child... I could only imagine how much rage I'd feel.'

Nice try Nick, I want to say. Instead, I tell him the truth.

'There's nothing that could be done to him that would give me back my daughter.'

He stares, sizing me up, wanting more.

'It was the court's job to deal with him. Your job. I handed that responsibility over. I let you all take care of it.'

'That's just it though, isn't it? The very day it was in the paper that he was released, he died. They're saying it isn't a coincidence. What he took was laced, it was tainted on purpose. The spoon had no drugs on it. Someone else mixed it beforehand. They said you ordered rohypnol. Searched the dark web about how to kill someone. You think I didn't notice you driving around Carrigshill in your car spaced out half the time?'

He leans nearer.

'Lorna, I know you. I know it was you.'

What I see from him isn't judgement. I want to cry for what we lost.

'Why are you here Nick? Are you about to arrest me?'

He drops his shoulders.

'I'm here as a friend. At this stage I haven't any involvement. Since I'm not on the case, I can talk freely and I think you are owed a heads up.'

He sighs, leans back in the chair, lays his hands on his lap, palms up, as if confessing all.

'Look, I'm on your side, OK? I didn't like one bit the way all this was handled, the way the verdict went, it stank but I have no say, all I do is catch them and put them in the cell. You know me, better than anyone. You know I'm by the book but with Sara, with you, if I could have done more... I would have.'

We stare at each other for a long time. Is it Nick my ex or Nick the guard here with me?

'Thank you.'

He leans over the table. 'If you want, we can leave but we would have to go now, tonight.'

'You would do that?'

He leans closer.

'For you? Yes.'

His words take the breath from me. I take in this man sitting in my kitchen. He is not just Nick the guard. Before he was the man who informed me of my daughter's death he meant more than something. Once, I loved him. Once, he lifted my day, and softened my night. Once, I saw a future with him, looked forward to a life with him at its centre. After Sara's death, there was nothing but grief, nothing but pain, nothing I could give to another and it stripped me of being able to receive any love. Three words made it clear he still loved me. Made it clear what he would be prepared to do: he would give up his job, his reputation, his life for a new one with me. I allow in our memories. All the nights he sat on the porch with me when I didn't know where Sara was, how he traced his fingers over my lips when I cried, sopping up the tears, how he made me laugh, how he looked when he lay on top of me. I ache with the loss, for the closeness we once had. For all the time I wasted. And now it is too late.

'I won't run.'

He hangs his head, taps his fingers on the table. When he looks up his eyes have glistened over but are harder than before.

'If you stay, if you had anything to do with his death, I'm telling you now, you'd be better coming in of your own free will. Confessing. It will stand to you more if you do. They will be more lenient.'

I clench my teeth, despite trying not to show emotion.

'What? Would I get less than a year in a cushy expensive clinic like the man who murdered my daughter got?'

He shakes his head.

'Probably not.'

I fold my arms about to deny any involvement.

'There's something else. Ryan is missing. They are saying you had something to do with it, that they have proof you took him, that you were seen.'

My head runs a million miles. They know everything. It is only a matter of time. Will it be better to just admit it all? It would feel good to unburden, to unleash the truth I've locked away. But I am scared and I don't want to go to prison. I don't know what to say, what to admit to, what to offer as an explanation. But it is Nick in front of me, a man I loved once, a man who has just offered to run away with me.

'Nick, I...'

Ryan bursts in the back door, holding tomatoes, his head down, pretending not to see us, but from the shake in his hands he has been listening. He offers up the tomatoes as if in communion. 'Look how these beauties turned out.'

Nick stands.

'Sorry. I didn't know you had company. I can go, if you like?' Ryan says.

Nick arches his shoulders. 'Funny, we were just talking about you.'

'Oh yeah?'

Ryan with his back to us, pours a glass of water. Only after he downs it in one go, does he turn. He wipes his mouth with his forearm, calmer now.

'In what regard?'

'You were reported missing. According to my source, there is evidence Lorna took you against your will.'

Ryan laughs and not for the first time, I notice the progress he's made since he overdosed, the thickening of muscle, the colour back on his skin, the eyes shiny and something stirs inside me, something that resembles pride.

'Against my will, my arse. Didn't you see me six months ago?' Ryan asks.

Nick says nothing.

Ryan pulls out a chair and sits down.

'I was a complete mess. This woman should be commended. She saved my life. I am a very willing occupant of her household.' He grins at me. 'For however long she'll have me.'

'Right.'

Nick nods, when he turns his face to mine, there is more than confusion there.

Even though I have not been intimate with Nick for years, something in me wants to say it isn't romantic, that Ryan and I are like son and daughter but the words would be ridiculous, Nick is here to warn me, not get jealous.

Nick edges to the door. Ryan and I exchange glances, both standing to follow him out. As he reaches the doorway, he places his hand out to block the door frame, taking up the full space, only inches away.

'Tell me this so, Ryan. When did you come here?'

Ryan hesitates.

'You should tell me; I wasn't exactly at my best at the time. About the first week of April?'

Nick stares.

'Right. So where would you have been on the night of the 20th of that month?'

'Well, that's easy.'

'It's easy to remember that date? Why so?'

'Cos I've been in the same place every night since I got here. Me and Lorna stay up till about eleven and then go to bed.'

Nick rocks back on his heels.

'Together?'

'At the same time. Separate rooms,' Ryan says, pausing between each word.

'So, from eleven at night till the morning, no one can vouch for you or you can't vouch for Lorna?'

'Well, I would have heard the car leaving if that's what you mean. And every night I wake between four and five to go to the bathroom. I've never told Lorna this but I always peek in, just to make sure she is all right. She has nightmares, since Sara died. So, I can guarantee even before checking out what the date is, every night without fail, I've never heard any car drive off, and she was in her bed between four and five.'

'Every night you say?'

'Every night, that's right.'

'Funny, I've got a record of you having to be treated for concussion and you were kept in for a few nights at the CUH.'

'Ah well, in fairness, I wouldn't count that as I was unconscious, wasn't I?'

Nick massages his temples.

'Ryan, I'll say the same to you as I've just said to Lorna. If there is anything you're hiding, you're better off coming clean before they find evidence. It will turn out better.'

'Better than Sara dying?'

The two men stare at each other. Ryan leans his head closer to Nick's and for a minute I think he is about to attack.

'The worst has already been done.'

Nick rocks back again.

'That's what I'm worried about. That the two of ye had nothing to lose.'

Ryan flinches. Then he smiles.

'What can I tell you? It's not a crime to want to get clean, is it?'

'I think you already know.'

He stares at Ryan. I am afraid to look, afraid to face Ryan in case I betray him, in case my guilt shows all over my face. And then I see Nick's eyes go above Ryan's. Above to the wall in the kitchen.

The list.

But the list isn't there anymore. All that is left is a strip of paint missing from where I ripped the cellotape off.

'It's Troy.'

'Troy who?'

'Don't play dumb.'

'Oh, you mean Sara's murderer?'

'You know just as much as I do that he wasn't convicted of murder.'

'Like you know he should have been.'

Nick nods.

'I agree with that, yes. But now he's dead there's people trying to work out what happened to him.'

'What did happen to him?'

I hadn't even thought to ask that question. Nick would know a murderer didn't need to.

'Looks like an overdose but there are reasons to believe it wasn't. The investigators believe it was intentional.'

'Pity.'

Nick cocks his head, wanting more. Ryan leans closer.

'There would be a list as long as the river Lee of people who would want to hurt that fella. I just wish whoever did it made him suffer. An overdose sounds too lenient. If it was me I would have made him bleed. I would have made sure it was an awful death.'

'Be careful now Ryan.'

'There's no wrongdoing in wishing.'

Nick looks at me.

'Remember what I said. You know where I'll be if you decide. If you stay, it will look better if you approach them.'

I nod. Nick is saying: *Go now.*

Ryan's shoulders relax, for now he understands. He holds his hand out to Nick. They shake. 'I'll walk you out.'

I go to the chair and sit, holding on to the table. As soon as the door clicks shut, my hands start to shake.

Ryan returns with a finger to his mouth, in warning.

'Do you want a cup of tea?' he asks loudly.

As he passes, he whispers. 'Wait until his car leaves.'

He sets about gathering cups and pouring water and all it takes to make tea. All the while my hands shake. The sound of the engine fires up and then, after a minute, the car drives off. I wait until the sound of gravel fades to nothing.

'I have to confess.'

Ryan continues to pour. 'No, you don't.'

'Nick's right. They'll come after me, they'll figure it out and it will be worse.'

'What will they have?' He takes the cups and lays them down on the table then sits across from me. 'That a drug dealer, by his own admission in court, a recovering addict, overdosed? Yeah, strong case I'd say.'

'They have evidence.'

'Like what?'

'I bought some stuff on the internet. A taser.'

'So? Did you leave it there?'

I shake my head.

'So what? You bought it for your own protection in your home.'

'That's what I just said to Nick.'

'Good. Like you said before, people were calling to the house all the time, journalists and the like. Ringing you, leaving abuse on your phone. Any lawyer could argue you were at your wit's end with the door going at all hours in the night, and after the way he killed your daughter anyone would be frightened he could come for you too.'

'They know from my phone location I was in the area on the night he died Ryan.'

'So, we say we went for a drive together. I'll give you an alibi.'

'And have the two of us go down for it?'

'I'll make sure that doesn't happen Lorna. I'd do the time before I'll let you serve one day in prison.'

'I answered a call that night, right outside the house. They'll know it was me.'

'What time was that?'

'I can't remember, two in the morning, maybe?'

'And what time did you do it?'

'A few hours later.'

'So, you came home and told me about him being released. I went back later. I'm telling you Lorna, if they try to arrest you, I want you to say it was me.'

'I can't do that.'

'Yes, you can.'

'You don't understand Ryan. Even before this, before Nick turned up, I thought about confessing. Then I started to fool myself that maybe by doing good I could forget. Nick showing up... just proves what I tried to hide. If I don't tell the truth I'm always going to have to carry it. I can't do that anymore, I have to cleanse my conscious.'

'But Lorna if...'

'He haunts me, Ryan. I can't get over it.'

'You have to.'

'I can't. Why would you go to prison for me anyway? Your whole life is ahead, I've had my shot, I got to live. You're only starting.'

'Don't you understand I wouldn't even be alive if it wasn't for you?'

'Don't you understand I wasn't trying to save you, I was trying to kill you? I hated you.'

He doesn't even flinch.

'You didn't though. When you saw me on that couch you could have left me. If you had really wanted me to die, all you had to do was watch. What you wanted was to force a connection between us again. Maybe you believed you wanted to kill me. I never did. Even if I did, I would have welcomed you doing it. Death was all I wanted. You didn't watch me die, even when you hated me, your instincts kicked in and you came to my rescue.'

I snort.

'It wasn't like that at all. I wanted you to suffer and dying that way meant it would be over for you too easy.'

'You've saved me all my life. When I broke my leg, it was you that tried to piece me back together. It was you that checked on my mother until my father stopped you. How many times did you help us when we were on heroin? What we put you through. All that time on the gear.'

'You were addicts.'

'You knew there was no coming back with that overdose. You put me in your car and brought me home. You saved me.'

'Well, now it's time I save myself.'

Chapter Seventy

Ryan is waiting for me when I come home from the bank.

'All right?'

His brows knit in concern.

'It went well.'

'Well is good, yeah?'

I bite my lip, wanting to delay the words. Not wanting to break the moment, not wanting to change everything.

'What?'

I lay my keys on the table. Slide them towards him.

'I only came back to say goodbye.'

'What are you on about? This is your house... came here to say goodbye.'

He scoffs, turns serious when he sees I'm not joking.

'Are you kicking me out?'

I shake my head.

'No. It's me that isn't staying.'

The chair screeches as he pushes backwards and stands.

'Ryan, sit down.'

His chest heaves, his knuckles stay on his hips.

'Sit. Let me talk.'

He sits.

'When I told you my idea to help families of victims, I was telling the truth. If I met with them, the first thing I would promise is to be completely honest. How can I do that? If I hold on to the lie, I'll have to carry that untruth around for the rest of my life.'

'No, Lorna.'

I meet his eyes.

'Yes Ryan. I went to the solicitor last week and transferred the deeds of the house to your name. When I said I was going to the bank, I was telling the truth, just not about the reason. It wasn't to get a loan. I changed my account to a joint one, giving full permission for you to use it without my signature. With my savings, there shouldn't be an issue, even if you need a loan after.'

He looks like he is about to cry. 'Look at all the good you can do. We are only starting. Don't ruin it.'

'But I already did. I ruined it the day I injected him. Now I have to right my wrong.'

'How can you help anyone if you're in prison? You know that's where you'll end up if you go to spill your guts. You understand that, don't you? It's not like they'll go easy. Do you think it's going to erase anything? It won't take away what you did. It won't bring him back. You saw his family. You know they'll make sure you go down for it.'

I nod.

'I know all that.'

'Think Lorna. All you want to build here, how will you do it from inside? Think of all the people you won't be able to help, or how many people you will set back from recovery, or how many will hurt because of you confessing.'

'They won't because you're going to help them.'

'Don't put this all on me.' He spits his words.

'Ryan, I need to look in the mirror again. He follows me. Haunts me. Even if Nick didn't turn up, even if they didn't have a case, I can't pretend anymore, can't just plaster on a smile and get on with my day.

Doing good deeds, making amends, doesn't work. I need to tell the truth.'

Ryan groans.

'The grief for Sara I can carry. I've learned to live with it even, but I can't live with knowing I did that to a man while everyone thinks he did it to himself. What if he'd burned her body? Or hid her? What if we never found out what happened to Sara, or couldn't have a funeral? Nobody has the right to take a life. I didn't have the right, no matter how bad he was.'

Ryan puts his hands together. He closes his eyes, like he's praying to me.

'Please Lorna, you did what I couldn't. You shouldn't have to pay.'

At that moment, he resembles a child. I want to go to him; take him in my arms, reassure him I will always keep him safe. But I stay where I am.

'You are a good, kind man. The kindest soul I ever came across. It isn't in your nature to hurt another, even if you think you could. Maybe, if you found a chance to get near him, you would have hurt Troy but I know you Ryan, afterwards you wouldn't cope with what you done. You loved Sara. You loved me.'

'Still do,' he says.

I wish I could stay right here, in this exact moment. Where the love between us stays just like this. I'm afraid to speak in case I brush away its significance with my reply.

'You are the type of good man who will do anything for the ones you love, even if it means convincing them what they did wrong is justified. Deep down you know, deep down you already know what I need to do.'

He shakes his head. 'No.'

'No matter how much I do right, I can't undo my wrong. It doesn't take away the guilt. Every right thing I do is only a reminder I could have done the same for him.'

Ryan flashes teeth before he bites down on his bottom lip.

'He wasn't your problem. His mistakes were his own. You can't compare yourself to him. He wasn't a good person. Are you forgetting that? All the pain he caused her, caused your daughter, it was... what he did was unforgivable. He was scum.'

He bangs his fist on the table. My hand goes to my chest as if on instinct. I am not scared. His eyes, his mouth, slopes, as if caving inwards at my resolve.

'Why can't you see you're being too hard on yourself? Remember what he did to your daughter.'

'Don't Ryan. I should have asked him. I should have tried to talk to him.'

'For what? What could you have asked him that would have helped? What answer would have eased anything?'

My answer comes out without a pause or breath.

'Did she cry out? Did she want me at the end? Was she scared? Was he with her when she died or was she alone?'

Ryan closes his eyes as if in pain. When he opens them, he is serious.

'None of those answers would have helped. You know the answers already, Lorna.'

'I don't. I don't know how she coped. Or exactly how she died. At what point did she give up? Why did she give up?'

'You know her, Lorna. You know why.'

'I don't. That's the point, I don't.'

'You do. It's just too painful to admit.'

'How can you know?' I whisper.

He purses his lips. The tears well, but do not spill. 'Because your daughter would have only done it one way.'

'What? What would she have done?'

He rubs his face, blocking me.

'Tell me, right now. How do you know what she would have done?'

He drops his hands, resigns to telling.

'Do you remember the time she had to get stitches when she fell on the gravel?'

I nod.

'Do you remember that condescending nurse who told us we had to leave then stitched Sara without checking if they administered the anaesthetic?'

'Yeah, so?'

'Remember what Sara said after we asked her why she didn't scream to alert anyone?'

'Yes,' I say, a low, thudding ache forming in my stomach.

'She said, when someone wants control and you can't get out of the situation, if you don't react, they lose.'

I nod, remembering.

'Sara wouldn't have reacted, not crying out anyway. She would have tried to talk to him, get him on side. She would have fought him when he tried to touch her, until he immobilised her with the Rohypnol, until he took her fight taken away. Are you sure you want to do this?'

I nod, even though I'm not.

'You know your daughter. Even when he robbed her of movement, when he took the possibility of fighting back away from her body, Sara's mind would have been whirring with ways to get out. Sara would have thought of you, of me, of getting back to us every second. You want to know if she was alone or whether he was with her? Why she gave up? Lorna, I have no doubt the pain was so intolerable it was better to stop her heart than take another minute. Sara gave up because she couldn't live through it.'

'No.'

'Yes. You know it. You've known it since you heard.'

He is right. I have known Sara suffered. Now the words are out I know the truth can be nothing but. Sara would have done everything she could to return to us. He made it impossible.

'You did the right thing. He took away the most precious person for both of us. Sara should be alive. If you go, you'll kill me. Did you ever think about that? I'm still an addict. If you go, I'll give up, I'll go back on it.'

'You won't. And if you do, you can't put that on me. What you do with the rest of your life is your choice. How I deal with what I did is mine. For weeks now I've tried to make amends. It isn't working. I've been trying to fix what I did, with all these gestures, but no matter what I do, I'm lying, I'm hiding and I can't do it anymore. Every charity I set up, every cent of money I raise in her name, is tainted. I have to own up. It is not fair to Sara.'

'They'll lock you up.'

'I know.'

'For what? It won't bring him or Sara back. It won't change anything.'

'It will change something for me.'

Ryan slumps in the chair. He knows better than to argue.

'I have to live with myself, Ryan, and I can't like this. I won't live with the lies anymore and if it's meant to be, if we are meant to do this, we'll find a way. If I'm going to spend the rest of my life helping the loved ones of victims and I *do* want to, then I have to speak my truth. All of it. All my mistakes, the worst I have done. Killing him has to be included in my story or I can't help them. It's a part of it, part of helping them heal because I'm living proof revenge won't help. I can prove to them getting even doesn't make you feel any better.'

Ryan pushes past me and slams the door.

One day, I hope, one day, he will understand.

Chapter Seventy One

The courtroom waits for my answer. I consider what the judge has just asked.

'Would you have still done it, knowing you would stand in front of me now?'

I lift my head, look straight at him.

'Yes.'

There are shocked gasps from the crowd.

'Yes I would, but not for the reason you think. Killing Troy didn't make it better. It didn't make it any easier to cope, or make getting over Sara's death any quicker. Nothing would have. I get that now.'

Troy's mother dabs at her eye with a monogrammed handkerchief. My barrister has warned me not to smile. Even if I wasn't, I wouldn't.

'Causing pain to someone doesn't take away your own. When you kill someone, they never leave. You carry a part of them around always. Troy is with me, even though I don't want him, even though I want rid of him, I can't, for he is part of my history. What he did linked him to Sara, to me. What I did entwined us. He is part of my story now.'

The judge eyes me.

'Do I wish I'd known that before I did what I did? Yes. It would have helped to know he would carry that; no matter how you act on the outside, there's no escape. If you murder someone, they follow you. They are with you when you try to sleep at night. You see them when you close your eyes, you dream about their death as they haunt you. After, there is never another minute where you are alone. When I murdered Troy, I forced the two of them to stand beside me. Sara I could carry, but Troy, he is harder to lift.'

There is a woman my age in the courtroom. She puckers her lip in a half smile, aware she shouldn't show me emotion, but I see it, the empathy, I see she understands my pain. If she was a juror, she would be on my side, but I do not need to win anyone over. Only the judge will decide my fate.

'Taking someone's life made me want to help others, to change the way the country handles murder. It has pushed me on every day. Maybe if I'd received help or advice, I would have done things differently. As it was, as the system is, nothing could have swayed me. Troy had to die. I wouldn't have rested until I'd erased him, and I don't think any conversation or action would have altered that. Do I wish I hadn't killed him?'

His parents startle.

'Yes,' I say to them.

'What I wish I'd did instead was confront him. I wish I'd listened to what he had to say, because maybe then I could have forgiven, help him even. Nobody knows what another is dealing with, nobody can see what's led another to the decisions they made. Then again, maybe I can only say this because he is dead. I'm not sure if he stood here, I wouldn't do the same.'

There is a sharp intake of breath. I don't look to see who it's from.

'If Sara survived, she wouldn't have cared about hurting the man who had done it; she wouldn't have looked for her own retribution. Sara would have handed the responsibility over to the police, to the people in charge of justice. She would have said, "hurting people only hurts you." Sara believed in karma, in reaping what you sow. She believed any wrong doing would ultimately come back to the person and she wouldn't need to play a part in his reckoning. Sara believed in kindness, in showing love, in caring for others. This is the Sara you should know, the one never wrote about in the papers, the one that the news left out, filling the headlines with the shock element rather than who she was, or what she sounded like, or the words she left us thinking about, or the kindness in her heart. I let her down…'

My throat goes dry. I sip some water.

'…when I took the course of nature in my own hands and changed it. I should never have killed him, even though he deserved to die, even though the world is a better place without him in it. Sara had no say in her death. But I should have respected her wishes. I should have remembered what she wanted from life.'

Chapter Seventy Two

At the sentencing, the Judge speaks.

'Taking into account your confession, and the way you tried to make amends. Your effort has resulted in a much different, much better town of Carraigshill. However, I cannot overlook the actions you took that night or the fact you committed murder. You premeditated taking another person's life, you injected a man with a drug you knew would kill him, then left him to die for his distraught father to discover. For that I cannot make a judgement any other way.'

He clears his throat in warning to silence the murmurs from the courtroom.

'Confessing before any arrest, at least spared the family further anguish. By pleading guilty, you also took the burden from them of gathering evidence to rule out doubt. All of this, I have considered. The minimum sentence for murder is twelve years and this time frame will be implemented.'

Groans go up around the room. The judge raises his tone.

'Murder is murder no matter what the circumstances or excuses and the sentence has to reflect the crime, but there are many layers to this case and I have to acknowledge that if Mr O'Callahan's sentence was twelve years for your daughter's murder, he wouldn't have been in a position to be accosted by you. Maybe then you would have felt retribution from the judicial decision. Regarding this, I have taken into account the time you have already spent in custody. In this regard, I am suspending four years, starting from the date your daughter was murdered, as I believe this is the actual day your sentence started.'

IV

Part Four

Chapter Seventy Three

Dear Ryan,

Thank you for allowing this letter to be sent. I know you weren't happy with me with my decisions but I have to say, seeing you in the courtroom meant more than I can describe.

The prison noises are loud, something I'll never get used to. When I entered that first day, holding my blanket and gear, I thought I'd die of fright, my chest fit to burst with fear. As I walked past the cells, I could see the women, standing there, getting a good look. Some of them, most of them, appeared terrifying. Noises erupted straight away. Clunking, rattling, as if they were trying to pull the metal from their doorways. The noises got louder until my eardrums hurt. At first, I didn't understand, I thought maybe they were rioting or something. But then one of them spoke, shouted at me, 'Well done girl.' And next there was hundreds of them, all shouting, 'Go on girl,' 'You showed him.' 'You got justice for your daughter.'

Ryan, I think I'm going to be all right here. There are some women not to be messed with, but most have shown respect, a respect I don't deserve. Most of them are addicts. Most of them understand Sara could have been one of them. Some of them crossed paths with Troy or heard of him. Even if it isn't all right, there is nothing they can do to me in here that is worse than what's already happened.

If you don't mind, can I write to you? In here, the words don't stop.

You started this in me, with your writing. It helped, to read your words.

Back home I couldn't share, couldn't write or read back what I held inside about Sara, scared that if I prised, it would crack me wide open and there would be no way of putting me back together. Time is one thing there's plenty of in here, with little else to distract, so I'm putting down my memories too, recording what I remember before Sara disappears from me. Now that I've started, I can't stop and I find I'm writing enough to fill a book, at least four thousand words a day.

I understand if you just want to move on. If you have already made your peace with her death and don't want reminders, I get that.

God, I hope you have. Ryan, I hope there are days when you wake up and she is not the first person you think about. Or at night you don't still cry yourself to sleep thinking of her.

Lorna.

* * *

Dear Lorna,

Write the book and I will find a way to get it published. What you said in the courtroom was spot on, everyone should know what Sara was really like. Everyone should know what she meant to us. I will be the first to read anything you write.

Ryan.

* * *

Dear Ryan,

When Sara was a child, I used to get up early to do the school lunches and if I was quiet, if there was enough time, I wouldn't call her straight away but sit and listen to the almost silence. To the sleeping sounds of her and Tim.

My heart would leap at her content breathing as I slipped into her bedroom. Watching the rise of her chest, marvelling at how unaware she was of my being near. She was completely lost to her dreams, her mouth open, her body still, vulnerable and innocent, trusting of everything around her being safe. I would lay beside her and breathe in her used breath, wanting to take every part of her that I could claw back. Wanting to keep her with me forever. That was when I was at my happiest, I think; knowing she was safe and happy and next to me. It was at those times my love would threaten to overwhelm.

I was so hung up on silence back then, when you're a mother you do, you crave it, but it's more than that, you think its silence you need, but it isn't. Silence I've found, is hollow, silence is empty and devoid of love. What I really wanted is peace and that doesn't hide in silence. Peace hides in you and unless you find it, no noise or lack of, can make it appear.

Lorna.

* * *

Dear Ryan,

I worried about Sara's hair more than I should have when she was a child. It had been a source of pain when I was younger. Growing up, I had loved the colour, but school showed me a child shouldn't stand out, shouldn't ever be different. Carrot top, ginger nut, foxy, all names given to me the day I entered. I didn't mind the kids that said it as an observation, it was the ones who spat the words that hurt. What had I ever done to them? What had my hair ever done? In the delivery room when Sara was handed to me, I didn't know how my heart could feel two opposites at the same time. It soared and sunk.

What they tell you is true; being handed your baby is the happiest moment. But seeing that dark red hair, I felt guilty for inflicting my child with the worst part of me, of the part guaranteed to cause her pain. The only way I could help was to teach her, prepare her for what they would say. Growing up, I taught her comebacks for when someone called her carrot top, giving her permission to invent better one's. She was so used to our game that by the time anyone ever said it, her responses were automatic, bored even, but never, ever hurt. That one gift I gave to my daughter, at least. In her acceptance of her hair, I learnt to love my own. Seeing someone else with the same colour helped me appreciate the way the strands caught the light, like lines of gold thread sparkling in the sun. When she ran with her hair loose, a million different reds swayed. It was truly beautiful. After that, I stopped running hair dye through my own, covering the vibrance of it, letting it loose, letting my hair be seen. When she saw the real colour she pointed at me and called me Ginger. Sara took the insult and turned it. After that, I embraced the name. Children teach adults more than we teach them.

When I get out, if I ever get out, I want to take a trip, take you to the same cabin on Inishmore that first Tim and I, then the three of us, then two stayed in. Those were Tim and I's happiest times. My favourite memories were when Sara was at that perfect age for parenting, being able to look after herself but still not brave enough to do anything too wild, happy to just dig in the muck or play with sea shells. After Tim left, we still went every Summer, Sara and I. There was something magical about the island, bringing a peace between us that we were never able to replicate once home, where we would sit on the bench in front of the house and just take in the view from sunrise to sunset, watching swallows as they swooped down almost touching our heads to say hello, doing nothing but exploring the crevices and hiding spots and private beaches.

And then she met you and never wanted to leave your side. I always meant to bring you too, with teenagers both your lives were busy. When you both became adults, you'd left.

After Sara got clean, we swore to go back there the following Summer. When I take you there, if I can, we will hike to the top of Dún Aonghasa, where you can see all of the island, where a lighthouse stands with nothing else around, a place Sara still talked about years later. She said, at the top, if you stayed very still, you could hear heaven talking back to you. I want to go there Ryan, I want to hear what Sara has to say, I want to go there with you if it's something you still want to do. This keeps me going. The promise of reliving the old memories mixes with the hope of creating new ones, carrying Sara with me as I go on.

All I could think about when she died was how she was gone and how I wanted to join her, taking with me everyone who made her suffer. Now, with nothing to do all day but think, but remember, I've discovered I don't need to go anywhere; I never needed to go anywhere or do anything. For when I close my eyes she is still here, as here with me now as when she was alive. Nothing has changed in that blackness, in that present state when I lie still in my bed. She is still here right beside me. Sara never left. It was me that went away.

And I've realised I want to live Ryan. I want to see the places Sara wanted to get to. In a place like prison, when opportunity is taken away, when you cannot experience any spontaneous activity, life feels more precious. These days I dream of simple things: a walk with nature, listening to the sway of trees, planting seeds, hearing bird song, drinking coffee on the porch. I miss our chats, Ryan. I miss you.

Love, Lorna.

* * *

Lorna,

When I bring up memories, I like to think of Sara before or after drugs. Not so much during, when we were at our worst. Mostly, I want to remember when she was vibrant, most alive; I don't want to just remember her, I want to pretend she's still living. It's easier to imagine that happening before drugs. After, when we walked the tightrope of death many times, it became comprehensible. I look back at that time and wonder who we were, or how we got that low, that quick, so quick we couldn't pull each other up. I'm sorry I didn't say no, that I didn't stop her taking anything. Back then, I told myself she would dismiss what I said because it suited me to go down the road of using. Sara would have listened. If I gave her an ultimatum that time, or one of the times at the start, if I'd put my foot down and said choose, she would have chosen me. Instead, I joined her, deciding to wallow, but if you wallow in the sea of pity, you either drown in the water or need a life buoy to get out. For too long we chose to tread water next to each other. Getting better for her was my life buoy. We should have come to you sooner but the shame kept us away. Back in the house, I couldn't talk to you about how we survived. What we had between us was fragile and I couldn't ruin it with horror stories. If you want, I can tell you now. If you want, I can write to you and say it all, good and bad. Just say the word.

Ryan

* * *

Ryan,

I want every memory you have because each one brings her back. I want good and bad because that is how I remember her. Each fight, each low point was a hurdle we got over, brought us closer. We are human, we have flaws. I don't want an icon for a daughter, I don't want a perfect version. Like you, I just want her back. If I can't have that, I'll take the memories. Giving me an insight that is not mine heals the surface of deep scars. It will take all my lifetime and more to heal fully but your memories make the day liveable. I spent years thinking Sara shattered the trust we'd built and chose drugs. Your stories revealed the truth. Each day I hold onto the tales you tell me, I read the pages over and cling to them like a blanket. Nothing during, done in the thick of addiction will change my opinion, we are all *human, we all do wrong on this earth.*

Lorna.

* * *

Lorna,

Sara bites her lip when she dances, not down on, not cutting, only catching the flesh between the teeth, resting it there, in concentration, listening to the music and shutting everything else out. When she dances, she turns fluid, her body working with the beat, even if she's never heard the song before, she keeps in time. It is innate, natural, aligned. I tap my feet or shuffle facing her, always facing her, because I can't tear my eyes away from the freedom she has in movement, while my body feels clumsy and unsure and I wish her arms would drape around me, become a safety net but I can't do it, I can't rip her away from her inward ecstasy, it is a bliss I cannot penetrate, cannot give. So, I just stare, at the beauty of her, as one arm reaches for the air and her hips sway and ribs stretch and her hair flops over her face and then she looks straight at me and she smiles, a smile that runs across her whole face, and as she dances towards me the rest of the room fades away.

Ryan.

Chapter Seventy Four

I don't tell Ryan on his visits that his letters give me strength. There is no need. By this stage, he knows me more than I know myself. He knows my thoughts, my fears, my wishes. He has become a landmark, a desire to reach, a goal to get to, a home. Ryan doesn't write to me about his daily occurrences, he leaves those pieces of information for when he sees me, until he has me face to face. He likes to gauge my reactions, something he says a letter can't convey. We keep the letters for the memories. Exactly what I need to survive the place. I sleep with his words close to my chest. They become a pillow of comfort, replacing a person to hold. Sara forms in those words. Some days, her face becomes a blur. On those days, when the panic comes, I still it by reading his letters and she comes back. She is there with me again.

When she visits me in a dream now, she smiles.

Sara is with me always, in every breath, in every word. I carry her with me in my heart and in my pocket. And then I start to write, about how all this has helped me, adding Ryan's words to mine until there is enough material for a book. Until it becomes a survival manual and a memory box entwined. As I get lost in written lines, the prison walls evaporate and even though I am completely enclosed, trapped more than ever before, as my brain goes somewhere else, I am free.

Chapter Seventy Five

Dear Lorna,

When we were at our worst, Sara would whisper to me about the phoenix. Legend said the bird could combust and die, only to rise again. Sara would say we were like that bird, me and her, that we needed to go to our lowest ebb, only to rise from the ashes of our life. She would talk about living two lives, two alternative lives. For each choice we made, the other choice carried on in the alternative, alongside the other. When someone died, the other alternative carried on beside all their loved ones. In this way, they still had an outlet, could still connect. I asked her once if she would prefer the alternative life. She didn't hesitate with her no, saying when you looked at that life, it was empty of all that made it worthwhile. I asked her what was the point of the alternative then. She took a moment and smiled. Then she said, 'Because if you make a choice you can't come back from, if you die, there is still a way to return to the people you love.' I laughed at that, told her she was crazy. It gives me comfort now, that somehow, she may be beside us, laughing when we hear a joke, smiling as we remember her, loving us still.

The other day as I passed a jewellers, a brooch caught my eye. It was a two headed phoenix. Which made me think of those alternate lives. Made me feel Sara was right there with me again, whispering in my ear.

I feel her now, something I couldn't do when I went back on the gear, and what I feel isn't haunted or angry. I feel her on a sunny day, when I have a good idea, or when I pass the café that serves the milkshakes we used to buy. The smell of ice cream wafts over and for a moment, she is as here as she can be. When you feel someone beside you, you can't miss them.

Yet I do. All the time.

And I miss you Lorna, and the strength you gave me. I never could put it into words how you helped, so I tried to show it in my actions by doing up the house. I wait for the day you are back home too. When we can sit together on the porch and drink some coffee and you can see all that has been done. I think you will be proud. I think Sara would be proud, too.

Ryan.

Chapter Seventy Six

Five years later.

The checks are complete. They have wiped the cell out, cleared it of all my possessions, of any sign that I ever lived inside. My goodbyes are already said, so I leave the words and just nod and salute at the other inmates as I pass. A few stimulate tears I fight back; seeing me cry as I leave will not help the ones I leave behind. Elsie, the oldest prison guard, a year away from retirement, strolls beside me. Most of our walk happens in silence, except when I tell her as she opens my cell door that I'm glad it is her sending me home.

Being released takes time. Even though you've counted down the days since you arrived to leave, there is a process. Even when you have a date, there is always paperwork, always lines to sign and legalities to smooth. As I said before, I've always been good at waiting, and patience has stood to me all these years in this place. I've seen people tear their hair out before they learned the lesson, before they ever found out about patience. This is one wait I don't mind. The door is in sight. I close my eyes.

Nearly there.

Nearly home.

Chapter Seventy Seven

Ryan stands at the entrance, waiting.

When he walks towards me, a pressure in my chest makes me gasp. He is not my son, but I love him as much as one. The words are too much today to tell him how I feel, how his letters saved me, how his plans for the land got me through the dark times, how his talk of a future gave me a future too.

I walk to him and our bodies fold in, lean until we are touching and our arms are around the other and I feel it then, in our embrace, as I look up at the sky, blue and full of white cotton candy clouds, at a bird that flies past going about its business. In every bit of sensation, Sara is there with us. And only at that moment I understand those arms are the only homecoming I need.

We don't talk straightaway. We have time now, so much time. Time is all you have in a place like prison, so over the years, I learned to use it wisely. I took online counselling courses starting with the basics, then moving on to family therapy, addiction and cpd therapies. Ryan can tell me on the journey, and he will, about how he finished his sports degree, and I'll listen, all the while taking in the sights denied to me for years. I will smile as we discuss the microscopic, everyday details of the retreat Ryan set up for teens in trouble, how he gets them out in nature, hiking and learning to survive, showing them a strength they didn't know they owned. As I listen, I will say a silent thank you as children skip down the street, as I see cars and traffic and rubbish and shopping centres, as I see libraries and clothes shops and runners and people on their phones.

And they will all be glorious.

Ryan will tell me of the book signing he has set up, and we'll talk about the book I wrote in prison about learning to forgive. He has worked hard, securing interviews and funding from that. He will show me a poster with my face blown up, with the book's title: *Revenge Is Best Warmed Up.* And when we have caught up, he will pull up outside my drive, where I will see the gate with a huge engraved phoenix. As we embark on the long drive, now lined with orchids I planted years before, it is only then the tears will flow.

For years, I believed revenge needed to be planned. That revenge was a dish best served cold. Now I see. In order to heal, my mind needed revenge. It wasn't my mind that mattered, but my heart. The heart doesn't ask for retribution. The heart takes no joy from watching another suffer. The heart is a vessel. Life runs through and out of it. In order for the heart to work, there has to be a constant flow. In and out. If one side gets blocked, the other side will carry on but will get tired, until the flow cannot continue. When that happens, the heart will come to a halt. Left untreated, the body will die quickly, the heart will cease to pump. When you remove the blockage, it can prosper. It never asks for much. Good food, exercise, love. There is a reason people die from a broken heart. Forgiveness, understanding, opening yourself up, all mend a person battered by life. What the heart craves is to heal. What the heart wants is to love. What the heart needs is to allow love in.

Vengeance could never heal me. The best revenge is warmed up with love.

I've done my time. I paid the price for my mistakes. I asked for forgiveness. And now I'll live.

Chapter Seventy Eight

It is nine in the morning as I sit in my car. My hand grips the steering wheel, waiting. A child crosses, darting between the cars and only when she hops onto the kerb, her braid swinging from side to side, I relax. Once I am sure she is safe, I turn on the radio and tap my fingers to the beat of the music. It is apt that it is Sara's song. I sing along to the tune. One...

At Ryan's place, I beep the horn and within seconds he runs out from his drive, fit and tanned from working outside most of the day. All suggestions of the addict he used to be is gone. His muscles show through his top as he pulls open the boot and drops his gear bag inside. After closing it, he opens the car door and grins, then dives into the front seat.

'You ready?'

'I'm ready.'

'You sure you don't want to bring Alison?'

He reddens, still not okay talking to me about his girlfriend, even though Sara passed away nearly ten years ago. Even though he has been with Alison for over six months, and as a counsellor on the ranch, we have both seen her every day for a year.

'Nah. It wouldn't feel right.'

'I wouldn't have minded.'

He looks out the window. 'I would have, though.'

'Sara would have liked her.'

'Thank you,' Ryan says, still looking out the window, his voice wavers as he does.

'It's the truth.'

And it is. If there is anyone Sara would pick for Ryan, it is Alison. Fun, sincere, kind, always kind, she has become a staple in our lives. Often working twelve hours a day, Ryan and Alison spend more time with me than at their own homes. We are a family.

I drive on and we fall into silence, both thinking of what will happen on this trip, I'm sure. It doesn't take long to pull up outside the next house. We only just park up when Tim runs out. He has no qualms about bringing a new girlfriend. I wave at them both. Libbie is her name, and actually I can see how good she is for him. Whether it was her, or grief, maturity or sobriety, Tim is steadier these days, more tolerable, and is the best person in the world to talk to about Sara when she was young. Together, we have pieced back many memories.

After depositing their bags, Tim and Libbie climb into the back and snuggle in to each other.

He claps his hands, rubs them with glee.

'It's gonna be a great day for a walk.'

'The weather looks good. Perfect for a hike. Clear skies and low winds.'

'Inishmore here we come!'

'Where's Nick?' Libbie asks, probably hoping not to be the only outsider in the group.

I smile at the mention of his name.

'He's following behind. He has an early start tomorrow so thought it better not to wake lazy bones.'

'Hey, I'm a changed man,' Tim says, pretending to be offended.

The nearer I get to Inishmore, the bigger my smile grows. The passing flowers remind me of back home. Once I saw how the orchids bloomed, I haven't been able to stop sowing. Planting foxgloves and bluebells along the edges of where the garden meets forest. More birds visit now, more butterflies to watch. Sometimes, on a windy day, the waft meets me on the porch, while I watch teenagers getting ready for a walk or listen to the sound of balls bouncing on the court or hear sweet ballads from women unafraid now to use their voices, in the refuge that was once Barry's field.

I plant the flowers elsewhere sometimes, in a nod to the path me and Ryan took to do good things in secret. There's no need to hide anything anymore, our good deeds out for all the world to see, but this I like to keep for myself. I pick a spot, usually derelict, starting with the soil. I tend to a patch, then come back, cultivating, adding the fungi needed, finally, eventually, planting the seeds. Then someday, when I'm not expecting it, when I'm driving past, a shock of colour will hit me, and I smile and think, I did that.

Here you go Sara, I left my mark on the world like you wanted.

That is all I can do. That is all she ever wanted to do. To leave her mark and I will spend my life making sure her name is never forgotten.

There are many memories to still remember, there are many ways to bring my girl back. Sara. Each day I try to honour her. Each day I try to make her proud and I think she would be, knowing what her legacy has turned into. How in death, she brought together her mother, the first man, and the last man she loved. And because of that, we fix each other, paper the hole her death left inside. Never fully, there are many parts of us still broken, for no amount of glue can cover those cracks. There are days when the loss of her still hits me with such force my legs buckle, like hearing of her friend's pregnancy or marriage, when I'm reminded of all the lost opportunities that should have been available to her.

I've learnt if you don't try to hide or cover them, it's in those cracks that the love gets through. The cracks enforce the surrounding edges, strengthen them. We all have cracks. We just need to catch and hold on to the love leaking out instead of gluing them shut tight.

I am doing that now. That is Sara's legacy.

When I reach Inishmore, I will stand on the top of *Dún Aonghasa*. There, I will call her name and I will listen to what Sara thinks Heaven has to say. Most of all, I will listen, hoping she has something to tell me. If I'm lucky, I will hear.

An Exclusive Gift For You

Wish the story didn't end?

As a thank you for taking the time to read this book, I want to give you a gift. If you subscribe to the Natasha Karis newsletter, you will get an **exclusive follow on story** you will not find for sale anywhere:

The Phoenix Will Rise

This is a quick read giving a sneak peek into what happened *after* **What The Heart Needs,** so no reading beforehand! Told from the perspective of three people, it highlights the impact of Lorna's actions.

Get it here: https://www.subscribepage.com/whattheheartneeds

Coming Soon...

Disorientated and naked, an old man stands in the middle of the street.

Just what Garda Vicki Fitzgerald needs right before the Samhain festival.

As she tries to make sense of the man's sudden appearance, the weather takes a turn.

Acting confused, the man will not tell her who he is, yet he knows her name.

Vicki has never seen him before.

The old man is adamant he has a story to tell,

and it is in Vicki's best interest to listen.

But a storm is brewing.

And by the end of the night,

Vicki's life will change forever.

An emotional tale of secrets, buried pasts and friendship.

Release date September 2024

Enjoy this book? You can make a difference

Honest reviews of my books help bring them to the attention of other readers. If you enjoyed *What The Heart Needs*, I would appreciate if you could spend a few minutes leaving your feedback. Reviews help the buyer understand the 'feel' of the book so your review could be the difference in whether someone picks it up. It doesn't have to be long - even one sentence helps.

My deepest thanks,
  Natasha Karis.

About the Author

Natasha Karis lives in Cork, Ireland, and spends her days navigating between writing and raising her three children. She writes contemporary, emotional, uplifting stories. Natasha carries a book with her everywhere she goes, so the invention of eBooks have made her bag lighter at least.

She is the author of The Sisters You Choose, The Breaking of Dawn, The Truth Between Us, The Initiates, The Initiation of Alayne Adams and Send Me Home For Christmas.

Also by Natasha Karis

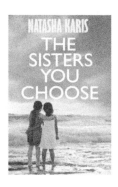

The Sisters You Choose

A daughter desperate to discover what happened to her parents. A stranger claiming she has the answer. A secret book that holds the truth.

It is near dark and pouring rain when Abbie Ellis visits her mother's grave for the first time.

Not to mourn or cry.

For the last thing she wants is to forgive.

That night is the tenth anniversary of when her mother, the famous writer Gabrielle Ellis, took the lives of both Abbie's father and herself.

Finally ready to confront her past, Abbie hopes visiting the grave will unleash the anger she has held on to for too long.

But she is not alone.

A woman appears out of the shadows.

The stranger claims she knows Abbie and has a message from her mother.

Gabrielle wrote a secret book, only for her.

If she reads it, will Abbie get the answers she's hoped for all her life?

Will she finally learn what happened that fateful day?

A sweeping, emotional tale of wrong choices, of the power of friendship and enduring love that outlasts even death.

The Breaking Of Dawn
An emotional novel about finding your voice.

Taken for granted by her boss and friends, Dawn Moloney can never find the right way to stand up to them.

Forced to move back to her childhood home after an attack leaves her bruised and broken, Dawn struggles to adjust.

When her mother suggests she try classes at a local centre for the unemployed, she reluctantly agrees. There, she meets Alayne Adams, who prefers to focus more on Dawn rather than what classes she is taking. Talking about herself is Dawn's worst nightmare, but if she wants to get better, she will have to learn.

Can Dawn finally find the right words?

The Truth Between Us

A make or break holiday. A love that should last a lifetime. A truth that threatens to rip them apart.

When Adaline decides to book a trip away to contemplate her failing marriage, her husband Andrew suggests he join her. As they embark on a last chance holiday to Cyprus, Adaline looks back over her life in the hope to fix what went wrong. But the past contains much pain, and a secret threatens to ruin everything.

Can they confront the truth and still salvage the relationship?

The Truth Between Us is an emotional and uplifting tale about love, loss and hope.

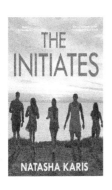

The Initiates

A suicide note. Five lost students. One teacher who will stop at nothing to help them.

When the Principal of Knockfarraig school suggests a series of detentions for some wayward sixth year students, teacher Alayne Adams volunteers. But the discovery of a note reveals one student intends to end their life.

Taking inspiration from a book based on ancient teachings, Alayne embarks on a series of life lessons that encourages each of them to discover ways to heal their pain.

Can she steer them onto a path that will change all their lives?

With characters that will have you rooting and crying for them, this contemporary, emotional novel set in Ireland, will leave you inspired.

Send Me Home For Christmas
An emotional, heartfelt novella about finding your way home.

Four strangers stuck in an airport at Christmas. One snowstorm. Only two tickets home.

Peggy believes in good deeds. In the past, whenever she's felt low, helping people has always turned her good fortune. Lately though, no matter how kind she is to others, she still has no luck.

Desperate to get home to her daughter for Christmas, a huge snow-storm threatens to keep them apart. In the airport, her path crosses with three other strangers who are just as eager to get home. Going nowhere and all longing to get on the last flight, they all stake their claim for one of only two tickets left to Cork.

Each will tell their story.

Each one wishing for a Christmas miracle and hoping that maybe, this Christmas, they may get one.

If you like uplifting women's fiction, this heartwarming short read will leave you inspired.

The Initiation Of Alayne Adams
What breaks you, can also make you.

Torn between partying with her friends and doing the right thing, Alayne's life lacks any direction. Until an incident leaves her spiralling. Left with nowhere to turn, Alayne struggles to find her way. But an encounter in a library opens up new possibilities and a chance to learn.

Can Alayne change or will old habits prove too hard to resist?

Printed in Great Britain
by Amazon

42205871R00182